Please return/renew this item by the
last date shown to avoid a charge.
Books may also be renewed by phone
and Internet. May not be renewed if
required by another reader.

www.libraries.barnet.gov.uk

BARNET
LONDON BOROUGH

Ambitious Love

Also by Rosie Harris

Turn of the Tide
Troubled Waters
Patsy of Paradise Place
One Step Forward
Looking for Love
Pins & Needles
Winnie of the Waterfront
At Sixes & Sevens
The Cobbler's Kids
Sunshine and Showers
Megan of Merseyside
The Power of Dreams
A Mother's Love
Sing for Your Supper
Waiting for Love
Love Against All Odds
A Dream of Love
A Love Like Ours
Love Changes Everything
The Quality of Love
Whispers of Love

Rosie
HARRIS
Ambitious Love

arrow books

Published by Arrow Books 2010

2 4 6 8 10 9 7 5 3 1

First published in Great Britain in 2010 by
Arrow Books
Random House, 20 Vauxhall Bridge Road,
London, SW1V 2SA

www.rbooks.co.uk

Addresses for companies within The Random House Group Limited can
be found at: www.randomhouse.co.uk/offices.htm

The Random House Group Limited Reg. No. 954009

A CIP catalogue record for this book
is available from the British Library

ISBN 9780099527435

The Random House Group Limited supports The Forest Stewardship
Council (FSC), the leading international forest certification organisation.
All our titles that are printed on Greenpeace approved FSC certified paper
carry the FSC logo. Our paper procurement policy can be found at
www.rbooks.co.uk/environment

Mixed Sources
Product group from well-managed
forests and other controlled sources
www.fsc.org Cert no. TT-COC-2139
© 1996 Forest Stewardship Council
FSC

Typeset in Palatino by Palimpsest Book Production Limited
Falkirk, Stirlingshire
Printed and bound in Great Britain by
CPI Mackays, Chatham ME5 8TD

For Nicola Sak and John Ockerby

Acknowledgements

A huge thank you to my wonderful editor Georgina Hawtrey-Woore and also to Caroline Sheldon my excellent agent.

Chapter One

Fern Jenkins knew that 1918 was a year she would remember for ever even if she lived to be a hundred. At the moment, she was only a plump schoolgirl with a thick mop of brown hair, a round face and dark eyes.

The year was starting on a high note; it was the second week in January and today was her thirteenth birthday and, although her brother Barri had been called up and was serving in the Army over in France, her mother, Wynne, and her father, Cradock, were doing their best to make it a very special day for her.

The first thing Cradock, a dark-haired, dark-eyed wiry man of medium height, did that morning when he arrived home at the end of his night shift at Big Pit was to rake out the ashes and light the living-room fire so that their small terraced house would be warm and cosy before Fern and her mother were up.

That done and with the fire drawing well, he filled the iron kettle and wedged it on top of the glowing coals so that he could make a cup of tea and take it upstairs for Wynne before she got dressed and came down to prepare breakfast.

While he waited for it to boil he had a quick wash at the kitchen sink to remove some of the grime from his face and arms. He'd already taken off his working jacket and heavy boots which were coated in coal dust and had left them outside the back door.

It was a routine he always followed because he knew how much Wynne hated dirt and disorder. Everything in their home was neat and tidy and in its allotted place; floors and surfaces were scrubbed to within an inch of their life and gleamed from zealous polishing.

They lived at the end of a long terrace of identical houses which were tucked into the mountainside and had been built by the pit owners and then rented out to the miners. Wynne always made sure that the knocker on their front door shone brighter than any of their neighbours' and their windows were always sparkling clean.

No matter what the weather was, Cradock always enjoyed the walk home, anticipating the warm welcome which he knew he would receive when he arrived there.

Coming up to the surface after having spent hours in the black, fetid mine was like being born anew. As he strode out he would breathe in deeply, hoping the fresh air would help clear his lungs of the choking dust; perhaps even ward off the dreaded disease of silicosis that seemed to affect most miners before they were fifty.

Wynne was so house-proud that she always

laid down old newspapers on the kitchen floor inside the back door so that he didn't leave dirty footprints, even though she knew he would have removed his boots already and would be in his stockinged feet.

At one time, the first thing Cradock did was to bring in the big zinc bath that hung on the wall outside and half fill it with hot water so that he could scrub away every vestige of coal dust from his body. Now that Fern was older and her sharp, inquisitive eyes missed nothing, he waited until she had gone off to school before stripping off to do this.

Wynne was up long before the kettle boiled. A short woman with boundless energy and a ready smile, she was very thrifty and practical and put her home and family's well-being above everything else.

Usually in winter their breakfast consisted of a big bowl of porridge, sprinkled with brown sugar and the top off the milk, because Wynne maintained it stayed with you all morning and kept out the cold. Today, though, because it was Fern's birthday, they sat down to a special feast of bacon, eggs, sausages and fried bread for the three of them to enjoy before Fern went off to school.

'Only another year, my lovely, and then you'll be leaving school and starting work.' Her mother smiled as she handed Fern a bulky parcel wrapped in shiny green paper. 'It seems like only yesterday that you were a bonny baby in

3

your pram and Barri was just starting at infant school. When you're that age every small achievement is a milestone,' she added as she dabbed at her eyes. 'In next to no time, though, it seems that both of you are grown-up and starting to lead lives of your own.' She sighed. 'Think how wonderful it would be if we could call a stop when we reach our happiest moment and simply stay there for the rest of time.'

'So that would be with me still in my pram and Barri on his first day at school, would it?' Fern smiled as she unwrapped her parcel and gave an exclamation of delight when she found the red woollen scarf and matching woollen gloves inside it.

'Oh, I don't know about that, cariad. You were both a lot of hard work in those days. Perhaps a few years later on . . .' Wynne's voice drifted off as she dabbed at her eyes again. 'I can see you now when you were just a toddler dressed in a little white dress with your frilly knickers showing underneath it and Barri in his grey flannel shorts and grey shirt holding your hand to steady you.'

'There's sentimental you are, girl,' Cradock admonished as he leaned forward and cupped her hand tenderly between both his own. 'Birthdays always seem to have this daft effect on you.'

'Perhaps it's because I am so happy and know how lucky I am having such a wonderful husband and beautiful daughter,' Wynne said in a choked voice. 'I wish our boy was here as well; I won't rest easy until he is home again.'

'That won't be for a while yet.' Cradock sighed. 'This damned old war is dragging on and I can't see any end in sight.'

'They should never have sent boyos as young as our Barri to the Front, it's a positive disgrace,' Wynne said fervently as she put the frying pan over the glowing coals and dropped a lump of lard into it. 'Barely out of short trousers and they put a gun in his hand and send him out to kill.' She shuddered. 'It's not right, I don't hold with it for one moment,' she added as she popped some rashers of bacon into the frying pan and shook it gently to make sure they were lying flat.

'None of us do, my lovely, but what choice do any of us working-class people have? If it wasn't for the fact that I work at the coal face I'd be out there as well.'

'Then you'd be able to keep an eye on him,' she pointed out, straightening up and smoothing a tendril of dark hair out of her eyes with the back on her hand.

'That's highly unlikely, cariad. I'd probably be fighting on one front with him miles away on another. We'd be such a long way apart that you'd get letters from both of us before we ever met up or even had news of each other.'

'Let's not talk about it today,' Fern pleaded as she spread a white cloth on the table and began laying out knives and forks in readiness for their meal. 'Let's pretend that Barri will be coming home later on,' she added as her mother placed a plate of sizzling bacon, fried bread and fried egg in front of her.

They ate their meal with quiet enjoyment, commenting on how good it tasted. Birthdays were always special occasions in the Jenkins family and this was the first time that they'd not all been together and each of them was conscious that their minds were occupied with thoughts of Barri and wishing he could have been there with them.

Fern pondered on her father's words as she set off for school. She could understand that as a schoolgirl she had very little choice about what she could and could not do, but surely grown-ups could decide for themselves what they wanted from life?

Her train of thought was broken as soon as she met up with her friend Sybel Roberts from the next street who was waiting to walk to school with her as usual.

Sybel admired Fern's new scarf and matching gloves enviously. 'Red's your favourite colour, isn't it?' She smiled. 'I wish I could wear such bright colours but because my hair is so fair they don't really suit me.'

'I wish I was tall and skinny and had blonde curls like you,' Fern told her enviously. 'Barri thinks you're the prettiest girl in Blaenafon.'

Sybel blushed at the mention of Barri's name. 'Have you heard from him today?'

Fern shook her head. 'No, I was hoping I would and that he'd send me one of those lovely embroidered cards that they seem to be able to buy over there. He sent you one for your birthday, didn't he!'

'Yes, it's ever so pretty, pansies and—'

'I know what it's like, you've showed it to me enough times,' Fern reminded her.

'Well, now I've framed it and put it on my bedroom wall right next to his photograph, the one he had taken the day he was called up,' Sybel told her.

'That's almost six months ago; I bet he looks a lot older now. Mam and Dad were only saying this morning that they shouldn't send boys as young as Barri off to fight in a war.'

'Most parents probably say the same thing,' Sybel agreed. 'I'm glad I haven't any brothers and that my dad works down the pit the same as yours. Because they're so much older they won't be called up to go in the army.'

'Well, let's hope not, although my dad says this war is likely to go on for ages and ages and once all the men who are at the Front have been killed or injured, they'll be looking for older men to train as soldiers to send out there.'

'They won't call up the miners, though, because they need them down the pits to cut the coal. If they haven't any coal, then they can't sail the ships or keep the factories going or anything else.'

The two girls looked at each other. 'Come on,'

Sybel grabbed hold of Fern's arm, 'we've dawdled so much that we are going to be late if we don't hurry and you know what that means.'

'Yes,' Fern pulled a face, 'we'll be late for assembly and then I won't have to stand out in front after prayers when Mr Peterson announces that it's my birthday and tells you all how old I am and everybody sings "Happy Birthday".'

'And you'll be blushing because you know that then you have to make a speech.' Sybel laughed, squeezing Fern's arm affectionately as they broke into a run.

'Yes, I'll be as red as a beetroot because I know you will all be laughing at me,' Fern admitted.

'No we won't. Why should we? We all have to go through it when it's our birthday. Mr Peterson says it is good for us and helps us to speak out for ourselves.'

'He doesn't say that if he catches us talking in class, though, does he?' Fern laughed as they entered the school gates and crossed the yard.

'No, then it's a rap over the knuckles with a ruler and a hundred lines of "I must not talk because it distracts other people",' Sybel agreed as they made their way to the cloakroom.

'So what are you going to talk about in your birthday speech? Have you been rehearsing it?' Sybel asked as they took off their outdoor clothes and hung them up on their respective pegs.

'No, I haven't, because I was hoping that perhaps I would wake up with a sore throat or a cold and not be able to go to school and then

I wouldn't have to do it,' Fern admitted as they made their way to their classroom.

'There's daft! Now you really will make a fool of yourself because you'll be all tongue-tied and stuttering when you get up on the platform and you won't be able to think of a thing to say.'

'I will. I know exactly what I am going to say,' Fern said determinedly. 'I'm going to say that there shouldn't be any wars and that it is all wrong sending boys of eighteen, the same as my brother's age to fight in France. I'll be looking straight at you when I say it and I bet you will be the one blushing, not me,' she added triumphantly.

'I don't think that will go down too well; it won't be considered very patriotic. You'll sound like one of those suffragettes who chained themselves to the railings in London or lay down on the roadway in front of the horses to draw attention to themselves.'

'If anything happened to our Barri, I think I would do just that,' Fern said heatedly. 'Seeing you're so sweet on him I would expect you to come with me, mind,' she added with a grin.

Sybel gave an affected shiver. 'You shouldn't talk like that because it's tempting fate. Of course he's going to be all right, I pray for his safe return every night.'

'So do I, but I'm not sure that the Germans know that or that they even care.'

Their conversation was cut short with the arrival of their teacher and as they lined up in an orderly fashion to walk through to the assembly hall, Fern's mind was a jumble of all the things she wanted to say in her speech.

As she entered the hall with the others, Fern stood together with Sybel and the rest of her classmates, wondering if she dared say what she wanted to or whether Sybel was right and they would all think she was being unpatriotic.

As Sybel had warned, Fern's speech had a mixed reception. Mr Peterson cleared his throat in a disgruntled manner, some of the other teachers frowned and the rest looked impassive, almost as if they couldn't believe what she was saying or didn't want to hear it.

Several of the children who had brothers or fathers already fighting cheered her but one or two of the older boys who longed to be at the Front doing their bit actually booed her.

Fern held her head high but her cheeks were burning by the time she finished speaking. She stepped down from the platform and made her way back to take her place alongside Sybel.

She was so blinded with tears of frustration and embarrassment that she stumbled awkwardly as she joined her classmates. Shaking like a leaf she took a deep breath and managed to regain her composure when she felt Sybel grab hold of her hand and squeeze it.

The rest of the day passed in something of a haze. One minute she felt proud of what she'd done, the next embarrassed at making such a spectacle of herself.

*   *   *

'You won't forget your thirteenth birthday in a hurry,' Sybel commented as they set off for home at the end of the day. 'None of us will, if it comes to that. I never thought you'd have the nerve to go through with it,' she added admiringly.

'Let's forget about it, shall we; don't go saying anything in front of Mam and Dad, I don't want to spoil my birthday tea. You are still coming, aren't you?' Fern asked.

'Of course I am, as soon as I've nipped home to put on my best dress and picked up the present I've got for you.'

'You needn't bother to get changed, there's no one else coming,' Fern told her. 'Barri won't be there this year, remember,' she added with a teasing smile.

'We can always pretend that he is, or that he will be joining us before it all ends.'

'I'll see you in ten minutes, then.' Fern laughed as they reached her house. 'That will give me time to put my best dress on as well, if you insist that we must dress up.'

When she answered the door to Sybel fifteen minutes later, Fern was still wearing the same clothes she'd had on when they'd come home from school.

'I thought you were going to put your best dress on.' Sybel pouted. 'I wouldn't have bothered, if I'd known you were going to stay in your school stuff.'

She stopped as she saw that Fern's cheeks were streaked with tears. 'What's the matter, are you in trouble over something? It's not that speech you made?'

Fern shook her head and waited for Sybel to come inside so that she could close the front door. 'There's been a telegram,' she explained in a whisper.

'You mean . . . you mean about Barri?' Sybel's grey eyes widened in alarm. 'Do you mean bad news?' she questioned.

Fern nodded.

'Has he been injured? Is it very bad? Are they sending him home? When did it happen?' Sybel gabbled.

Fern shook her head from side to side. 'No, he's not been injured; it's far worse than that.' She gulped as more tears streamed down her plump cheeks.

'You mean . . . ?' Sybel's eyes widened even more. 'Oh no, it can't be true, Fern. There must be some mistake.'

'No, there's not. The telegram came early this afternoon. Mam's taken to her bed and won't talk to anyone. Dad should have gone on night shift but he's getting someone to stand in for him because he's so upset and feels he ought to be here with us.'

'That's terrible, Fern. Look, cariad, I think I'd better go, don't you? Here,' she thrust the parcel she'd brought into Fern's hands. 'I'll tell my mam what's happened,' Sybel promised as her own eyes filled with tears. 'I'm sure that if you want her to do so, she'll come and sit with your mam.'

12

Fern nodded, sniffing back her tears and rubbing her eyes with the back of her hand.

'Will you be coming to school tomorrow?'

'I don't think so, it depends how my mam is. If I don't turn up, can you tell Mr Peterson why I'm not there before he calls the register at assembly?'

'Of course I will. Shall I pop round after school and see how you are or would you rather I didn't?'

'Come round, I'd like to see you. Perhaps we can have our special tea then, that's if Mam is feeling better.'

'Don't worry about that and . . . and try not to be too upset, though I don't suppose you can help it. I shall probably cry my eyes out when I go to bed because he was special to me too.'

'Sybel,' Fern called after her as she started to walk away, 'do you think it's my fault? A sort of punishment for all the things I've been saying today?'

'Don't be so twp!' Sybel exclaimed crossly. 'Of course it isn't your fault, however could it be?'

Fern pushed her hair back from her tear-stained face. 'Yes, I suppose I am being daft but you did warn me not to say all those things this morning and I took no notice of you,' she said ruefully.

Chapter Two

As she closed the door behind Sybel and went back into the living room, Fern could hear her mother sobbing, so she went upstairs to see if there was anything she could do to comfort her.

The speech she'd made at school that morning kept echoing in her head and she was more convinced than ever that what she'd said was right. Nevertheless, the realisation that Mr Peterson and perhaps many of the other teachers and even some of her classmates had thought she was being foolish and unpatriotic made her feel uneasy and even a trifle guilty but she knew there was nothing she could do about it now.

Perhaps they would understand when they heard how distressed her mother was about Barri being killed, she thought miserably as she went upstairs. Not that it mattered what anyone thought, nothing was going to bring him back.

In the days that followed she still couldn't believe it was true that happy, smiling Barri was gone from their lives for ever. The thought that they would never see him with his cheeky grin again, or hear his cheerful whistle as he came down the road, filled her with despondency.

Her mother was absolutely distraught; Fern felt sure that if his body had been brought back to England and they'd been able to bury him in the traditional way, then it would help to lessen her mother's heart-rending grief. As it was, there would be no funeral, so they would not have a chance to say goodbye; there'd been no proper ending. Thinking about him and knowing that he would never come home again after the war ended was going to be agonising; it would be like waiting for something you looked forward to but which never happened.

Fern stayed home from school for the rest of the week because her dad felt that her mother shouldn't be left on her own. She did what she could to help by doing the shopping and having a hot meal ready for her dad when he came home but the house was like a mausoleum without her mother bustling around putting everything to rights. Wynne hovered around like a ghost, pale and listless, clutching a photograph of Barri and studying it from time to time as if to remind herself what he looked like.

She had no interest in what was going on around her and barely touched the food that Fern put in front of her. She'd always been plump and cheerful but almost overnight she had not only lost weight but also looked so haggard and drawn that both Fern and Cradock were very worried about her.

Fern struggled to keep things going but although she did her best she didn't have her mother's knack of running things or her skills when it came to preparing meals.

'Things can't go on like this any longer,' Cradock stated at the end of the week. 'I think it would be best if you went back to school next Monday, Fern.'

'If you say so, Dad, but what about leaving Mam on her own – are you sure she will be all right?'

'I'm hoping that when she finds you're not here she'll pull herself together and start taking care of things around the place once again so that everything will soon get back to normal.' He sighed. 'We'll give it a try, anyway, cariad,' he added, patting Fern's shoulder.

Wynne was in a tearful mood on Monday morning and, knowing that her dad's shift started at two o'clock that day, Fern suggested that perhaps he should give her a note to take to school asking if she could come home at midday so that her mam wouldn't be left on her own.

'No, cariad, your education is too important and you've already missed out all last week.' Cradock frowned worriedly. Then his face brightened, 'I'll tell you what I'll do, I'll nip along and ask Bryn Evans if he will do my shift for me and then I'll do his, which doesn't start until ten o'clock tonight. That way, my lovely,' he told Fern, pulling her close and planting a kiss on her brow, 'you'll be home long before I have to go out and I'll be back here again to be with

16

your mam before you go off to school in the morning.'

It proved to be the perfect solution. Bryn agreed to change shifts with Cradock for the whole of the following week so that he could be at home while Fern was at school.

As the days passed, much to Fern's and Cradock's relief, Wynne seemed to be considerably better. Although rather quiet and withdrawn, she appeared to be more resigned about what had happened and to have accepted the situation. Bit by bit she resumed her household duties and towards the end of the week it appeared that things were more or less back to normal.

As Cradock was about to leave for the night shift on Friday, she surprised both him and Fern by saying, 'Look, you can tell Bryn Evans that there's no need for him to change shifts with you any more because I'm perfectly all right now. Thank him for his help and understanding and tell him I am very grateful to him.'

'That's wonderful news, cariad.' Cradock beamed as he kissed her goodbye. 'You mean things are back to normal from now on, then, my lovely?'

'That's right. Tomorrow I'm going to get Fern to help me pack up all our Barri's belongings. I've already started sorting out his clothes and folding them up. I thought I'd pack everything that was his away in big boxes and when you come home tomorrow night you can put the whole lot of them up in the loft out of the way.

They can stay there until I decide what I'm going to do with them. Once everything is out of sight and I don't see them then I'm sure I'll feel even better.'

Fern looked shocked and was about to protest but a warning look from her father silenced her.

'If that's how your mam wants to handle things then go along with her,' he said quietly as she followed him to the front door. 'We all have to deal with this terrible loss in our own way, remember.'

Although Fern knew he was probably right and that he, too, must be grieving in his own way, she still felt resentful that her mam intended to hide all Barri's belongings. Seeing his coat hanging in the hallway, his long striped muffler still draped lopsidedly on its peg, was somehow comforting. It made her feel that perhaps the terrible news they'd received from the War Office might be a mistake after all and that any time now he would walk through the door, home on leave.

She could picture him in her mind's eye, head and shoulders taller than their dad with his dark hair brushed back from his forehead, a wide grin on his face, bursting into the kitchen, dumping his kitbag on the floor before giving them all a big hug.

Fern wondered how her father felt about getting rid of all Barri's things. She knew her mam was being practical and since she'd decided that it was the best way to deal with the situation they'd all have to go along with it.

Nevertheless, she hoped she would have the chance to retrieve something or other as a memento, either with her mam's permission or secretly, if she was against the idea.

Probably she ought to keep something back as a keepsake for Sybel since she'd been so fond of Barri. Every day when they met up to walk to school the first thing she did was ask Fern if there had been any news from Barri, even though he sometimes sent a letter direct to her. When she did receive one she would carry it around for days, reading out odd bits, savouring each scrap, almost as if she was opening a box of chocolates and enjoying each one separately.

Fern was quite sure that Sybel would love to have a keepsake, something that she could treasure for ever. Deciding what it was to be was the problem. If she asked her what she'd like to have and it was something her mam had already squirrelled away and refused to be parted with, then Sybel would be very disappointed. Perhaps it might be better if she said nothing but picked out something she thought would be suitable, Fern mused.

She puzzled over what this should be. It had to be something very personal and the only things she could think of were his collection of cigarette cards or his stamp album.

She took them out of the drawer in his room and spread them out on the counterpane on her bed. The stamp album still had a great many gaps but now she intended to go on filling them as her own personal tribute to Barri. She wouldn't be able to do that, though, if she handed the album over to Sybel.

The cigarette cards were also precious because there were several full sets, ranging from motor cars to flowers and even film stars. It had taken a lot of hard work to collect them – their dad usually rolled his own cigarettes because it was cheaper to do that than to buy them in a packet. Anyway, it was only the more expensive packets that contained cards and other children were avid collectors too. There was always a mad scramble if anyone spotted a discarded cigarette packet lying in the roadway, each child hoping that the card might still be inside the packet. If it was one they already had, then they would try and swap it for one they still needed to complete their own set.

Fern was so intent on what she was doing that her mother's sudden scream startled her so much that she felt goose bumps running along her arms. As she hurried into the next room where her mother was engrossed in sorting and folding Barri's clothes, she heard the booming noise rolling down the valley. At the same moment she realised that the house was shaking as if a giant hand was rocking it.

Her heart lurched with fear as she put her arms round her mother and held her close. They both knew only too well that the noise and shuddering meant that there had been an explosion at Big Pit.

The rest of the night plunged them into even deeper heartache than they were already experiencing. Without a word, Wynne freed herself from Fern's embrace and ran down the stairs and out into the street, heedless of the cold, damp night air.

Fern stopped to grab her own coat and pick up her mother's shawl before following her out into the roadway. Men and women were streaming out of their front doors and, along with Wynne, they were hot-footing it towards the pit.

'Here, put this on, Mam, or you'll be catching a chill,' Fern panted, as she caught up with her mother and wrapped the shawl round her mother's shoulders. 'Is there any news?'

'Word so far is that there've been two explosions up at Big Pit,' Wynne told her worriedly as she straightened the shawl Fern had put round her and pulled it up over her head.

By the time they reached Big Pit the rescue operation was already under way. The pit manager himself was there, waving his arms importantly and shouting out instructions as he endeavoured to clear a path for the rescue vehicles.

He refused to give a statement about what had happened. As the crowd grew larger there were countless rumours not only about what had caused the explosion but also concerning the extent of the damage and the number of men trapped underground.

Bryn Evans elbowed his way through the crowd in order to speak to Fern and her mother.

'There's sorry I am that your Cradock is one of those trapped underground,' he told Wynne, 'especially as I'm the one who should be down there by rights. If we hadn't changed shifts again he'd be safe and sound at home with you.'

'Nonsense; the arrangement was our doing, not yours, Bryn Evans,' Wynne told him quickly. 'Very grateful we were, see, that you agreed to change shifts with Cradock. You were doing us a good turn so there's no call to start blaming yourself.'

'Fair-dos, cariad, but remember, if there's anything at all that I can do to help, then you've only got to ask,' he told her sombrely.

The hours dragged by and it was dark, cold and damp. The waiting seemed endless and was made worse by lack of information. Rescuers came and went but it was the early hours of Saturday morning and the bright early morning winter sun was creeping up over the top of the mountain before they started to bring the injured men out.

Each time the cage came to the surface a hush fell over the scene as the waiting crowd strained their ears to catch the names of those who'd been brought up.

The moment a name was called out family and friends would rush forward to help move him. Those who were severely injured were loaded into waiting ambulances and taken to hospital. The less seriously hurt were sent home with the promise that the doctor would be calling on them as soon as he possibly could

22

and that he'd check them over and tend to their cuts and grazes. Meanwhile, the families were advised to keep the injured men warm and as comfortable as they could.

As friends or relatives accompanied the injured away the crowd gradually dwindled into a mere huddle of a dozen or more people, Wynne and Fern amongst them.

As they continued waiting no one spoke; their hearts were too heavy because by now, for most of them, all hope had drained away.

They knew the policy was to bring up the seriously injured first so that they could be taken to hospital. Next they brought out those who'd suffered only bruises and lacerations. The dead were left until last and now those who were still waiting were fearful that the next time the cage came to the surface the dead would be in it, their own loved ones among them. Then, although they could take them home, there would be no doctor calling the next day; his verdict would have been given already.

There were only three men still missing and as their bodies were brought to the surface and their names called out, Cradock was one of them.

Fern was shaking as though all her bones were about to disintegrate. She took her mother's arm and accompanied her over the uneven ground to where Cradock's body lay on a stretcher.

Wynne was so numb with grief that she didn't even utter a sound as she stood staring down at the inert figure, his features almost indistinguishable under the heavy coating of coal dust. When she was asked by one of the officials if she would confirm that it was the body of her husband, she merely nodded her head.

It was Fern who spoke up and in a trembling voice stated, 'Yes, that's my dad; that's Cradock Jenkins.'

Bryn Evans, who had been hovering in the background, came forward and insisted on joining the small group of volunteers who'd offered to carry Cradock's body back to his home.

Wynne, her arm tucked through Fern's for support, led the way in dignified silence.

'Would you like me to wash him and tidy him up for you, cariad?' Bryn Evans asked Wynne gruffly after they'd carried Cradock's body indoors and laid it on the big table in the living room.

'No.' Wynne shook her head very firmly. Her round face was impassive but she looked composed and her voice was quite calm. 'Thank you very much for your kind offer, Bryn Evans. I do appreciate it, but since it's the last thing I'll ever be able to do for him, I'd like you to leave me to do it on my own, if you please, boyo.'

Bryn Evans nodded, brushing away his own tears with the back of his hand as he shuffled backwards towards the door. 'I understand; that's as it should be. Call on me, then, if there is anything else I can do to help you,' he mumbled, looking at Fern.

Chapter Three

Many times in the days that followed Fern marvelled over the change in her mother and wondered where she found her energy and spirit.

Wynne's listless, ghost-like apparition of a week ago was all in the past. Even though she smiled very little she seemed to be her old, bustling self again. She handled the arrangements for Cradock's funeral so efficiently and with such composure that no one would ever have known that she'd lost both her only son and her husband within days of each other.

When the funerals of the other men who had died in the explosion took place, Wynne attended them all so that she could pay her last respects to her husband's workmates. Those of Cradock's colleagues who were not in hospital attended his funeral along with a great many neighbours and friends.

Fern felt subdued and weepy as she stood beside her mother, shaking hands with all those who were there and thanking them for coming. Wynne was dry-eyed and quite calm and composed throughout.

Fern expected her mother to collapse into a sobbing heap when they returned home afterwards, but not a bit of it. Instead, Wynne carried on as though everything was normal, even to the point of scolding Fern because she didn't hang her coat up neatly.

'Come along,' Wynne insisted firmly as she began preparing food for them both, 'you must eat a proper meal or else you'll be catching a chill and won't be able to go to school tomorrow.'

'I don't want to go to school, Mam,' Fern protested. 'I can't bear the thought of having to face people again for a few days. I thought you'd want me at home with you to keep you company.'

'Rubbish. Off to school with you in the morning and no argument. Keeping your mind occupied is the best medicine there is,' her mother told her brusquely.

'That means leaving you on your own, Mam.'

'I shall have plenty to do. This house needs cleaning from top to bottom. There are your dad's clothes and stuff to be packed away and a hundred and one other jobs I need to do. I shall be so busy that the time will fly by,' her mother told her forcefully.

Fern wanted to argue but she was hesitant about doing so for fear of upsetting her mother. It was far better to have her in this brisk, bustling mood than weeping and listless.

Before she could formulate what she wanted to say there was a loud knocking on the front door. They looked at each other in surprise, wondering who it could be. When they'd spoken to all the mourners at the funeral, Wynne had made it quite clear that she didn't want visitors because she needed a few days to herself to get to grips with the situation and she knew they would all respect this.

'Shall I go and see who it is?' Fern asked.

Wynne hesitated. 'No, cariad, you stay here.' Tightening her mouth as the loud rapping was repeated Wynne patted her hair into place and hurried to answer the door.

Fern heard her exclamation of surprise as she opened the door and when she heard a man's voice greeting her mother as if he knew her well, she was so curious that she went out into the hallway to see who it was.

Her own gasp was equally spontaneous when she saw her mother talking to a dark, wiry man who looked so like her father when he was all spruced up in his best clothes that it could have been him.

'So this is Fern, is it?' The man smiled, his dark eyes crinkling up at the corners in exactly the same way as her father's had. 'Well, well. You were a babe in arms the last time I met you, Fern. I saw you at the funeral, of course, but even though you were standing by your mam's side I wasn't sure that you were her daughter. You don't know who I am, do you?' he said with a smile.

'No, not really,' Fern admitted in a puzzled voice. 'You look so very much like my dad, though, that I'm sure you must be a relation,' she added.

'This is your Uncle Bryson, your father's younger brother. He left the Valleys so long ago that none of us remember him these days,' Wynne said pointedly.

'Is that why you ignored me in the cemetery?' Bryson asked, raising his dark eyebrows enquiringly. 'You saw me even though I kept to the back.'

Wynne didn't answer but Fern was quick to notice that she looked uncomfortable and that her cheeks had reddened as though with embarrassment.

'Aren't you going to ask me in, then?' Bryson asked. He shrugged when Wynne said nothing. 'I understand . . . I came to have a word with you because I thought I might be able to give you a helping hand in some way now that you are on your own.'

'A helping hand from you!' Her voice was so derisory that Fern felt shocked by her mother's rudeness and even more astounded when she began to close the door in his face.

'Hold on, Wynne.' Bryson Jenkins quickly put his foot over the threshold to stop her from shutting the door. 'Here's my address in Cardiff. If you do need any help, then you know where to find me,' he said, holding out a piece of paper.

When Wynne ignored it he tried to push it into her hand but she stepped back and let it fall on to the floor. With a final shrug of his shoulders Bryson withdrew his foot and without a word turned and walked away.

'Whatever was that all about, Mam?' Fern asked in bewilderment.

'Nothing you need worry your head over,' her mother told her sharply. 'What about making us a cup of tea, I could certainly do with one,' she added as she sank down on to a chair.

As Fern was about to do as she'd been asked there was a sharp rap on the front door and, before Wynne could protest, Fern hurried to answer it.

'If that's your uncle back again, then make sure you don't let him in,' her mother warned as she stood by the living-room door waiting to see who it was.

It wasn't her uncle. The man who stood on their doorstep was a smartly dressed portly man wearing a black bowler hat and an expensive-looking black overcoat over a dark pinstriped suit. He was carrying a clipboard and looking very officious.

He ignored Fern and, looking over the top of her head at Wynne, he enquired, 'Mrs Jenkins?'

'That's right.'

'Good!' He stepped into the hallway, pushing past Fern and moving towards the living room.

'I'm Mr Tyrell, the pit owner's representative,' he informed her. 'I'm here to remind you that this property belongs to the pit owners and since you no longer have a member of your family

29

working in the pit then you must vacate these premises immediately as they will be needed for other workers.'

'You mean you're turning me out?' Wynne gasped.

'You have until Saturday to vacate but we will extend that deadline for one week if necessary. I must also inform you that you must pay your rent of six shillings the day before you leave or your possessions will be confiscated in lieu of this sum. A further six shillings will be due, of course, if you stay until Saturday week.'

'Where can we go? I have no family who can take us in,' Wynne asked in bewilderment as she sank back down on to the chair.

'I'm afraid that is not my concern. The terms I've read out to you are all on here,' he told her, handing her a sheet of paper as he prepared to leave.

Wynne bit down on her lower lip as she took it from him but she said nothing. As soon as the door closed behind him, however, she gave vent to her feelings.

'The hard-hearted swine,' she muttered angrily. 'Cradock worked down that pit for over thirty years; from the time he was twelve. A mere slip of a lad, he sat there in the dark for hours at a stretch, opening the doors for the wagons to come through.'

'Don't take on so, Mam,' Fern begged, putting her arm round her mother's bowed shoulders.

'Over thirty years of slavery in the dank

darkness of the pit. He started as a boy at Milfraen Pit, a mile or so from Blaenafon, but once he started earning a man's wages he had the chance to transfer to Big Pit and that's where he's been ever since, working his way up to become one of their most skilled cutters. You could say he devoted his entire life to King Coal and this is the reward: his family kicked out of house and home at almost a moment's notice before he's cold in the ground.'

'Dad wouldn't want you to get yourself all upset like this, Mam,' Fern said awkwardly, choking back her own tears. 'We'll survive somehow, we'll manage; we always do.'

The words were meant to console her mother but they only seemed to irritate Wynne even more. Shaking Fern's hand away she stood up and went upstairs.

Fern went into the kitchen and made a cup of tea and took it up to her. She expected to find her lying down but to her surprise her mother was busy piling things up on the bed.

'Whatever are you doing, Mam?' she asked as she handed her the cup of tea.

'Sorting out what we must try and sell before we have to leave, of course,' Wynne said sharply. 'No point in delaying things now, is there? If we can be ready to leave before Saturday, then we won't have to pay any rent.'

'We'll have to pay for this week,' Fern reminded her.

'Don't be so twp! I'm not giving them another

31

brass farthing,' her mother told her scornfully. 'We'll be out of here before the rent man calls; packed up and vanished,' she went on forcefully. 'Not a word about this to anyone else, mind, or it will get back to that man Tyrell and he'll send the bailiffs in before we can skedaddle.'

'You mean that I can't even say goodbye to Sybel?'

'Not a word to her; promise me now! One whisper in her ear and it will be all over Blaenafon and our plan will be scuttled.'

'How are we going to do it, Mam? We can't do a midnight flit; you know what people are like. Someone going on night shift, or coming home from a night out is bound to spot us moving all our stuff.'

'We won't be moving any of it, though, will we?' her mother declared triumphantly. 'No, we'll sell off what we can before we leave. There will be enough furniture and such like left behind here that will more than cover the rent so there's no need for you to have a conscience about us walking off without paying our dues.'

'So where are you planning on us going, then?' Fern asked in bewilderment.

'We'll go to Cardiff, of course. They'll never even bother to start looking for us in a city that big.'

'We don't know anyone there,' Fern argued.

'Yes we do; it's where your uncle Bryson is

living and there's always his promise of help, now, isn't there?'

'Oh Mam! You didn't even take the piece of paper with his address on it when he tried to offer it to you,' Fern reminded her.

Her mother laughed cynically. 'That's true enough, but I know you did because I saw you pick it up and put it in your pocket, my lovely, and I'm quite sure you still have it.'

Fern and her mother spent the next couple of hours sorting out what they could hope to sell. Cradock's best Sunday suit and his second-best jacket and trousers, Barri's suit and his working clothes – all of which Wynne had washed and ironed when he'd been called up in readiness for the day when he would be demobbed. To the ever-growing pile Wynne added one or two things of her own and several frocks that Fern had outgrown.

'You may as well put in any toys or dolls you have because we won't be able to take them with us and, anyway, you've outgrown such things now. It's time for you to grow up and face life,' Wynne commented grimly.

'Where are we going to try and sell all this stuff, Mam? If we go to the pawnbroker's here in Blaenafon, there's a chance he might suspect what we're planning to do.'

'We're not going to the local pawnbroker's. They hold a mid-week market in Pontypool and that's where we're taking everything. With any luck there won't be anyone there who knows us because the men will all be working and the womenfolk think it's too far to walk.'

'In that case, then, isn't it too far for us?' Fern questioned.

'Well, it's a tidy walk but we've got reason to do it, they haven't,' her mother answered.

'So what time are we setting out, then, Mam?' Fern asked as she added some of her own belongings to the pile.

'Quite early. Somewhere between the time the men set off for the day shift at the pit and the time most people are up and about getting their kiddies off to school.' Wynne sighed as she looked at the bundles they'd made ready. 'Since we've done all we can we may as well have an early night.'

It was still dark next morning when Wynne shook Fern awake. 'Come on. I've made the porridge, so get a good basinful of that down you before we leave because there's no knowing when we'll get anything else,' she told her.

They set off with their bundles the minute they'd finished their breakfast, trying hard not to let then appear too heavy or obvious in case they met anyone.

When they were well clear of Blaenafon they sat down on a fallen tree by the roadside to have a rest. Wynne pulled a small package from her coat pocket and unwrapped the jam sandwiches inside it.

'I should have brought along a bottle of cold tea but I didn't think about it,' she said as they munched away.

'I'm happy enough with these; I didn't think you'd packed anything, Mam,' Fern said, smiling.

'If you've finished, then we'd better start walking again. There are still a few miles to go.'

'What will we do if none of the stallholders will take them?' Fern asked as they picked up their bundles and set off again.

'Don't say that; we don't want to have to carry this lot back home again and we can't afford to simply dump it all. I'm counting on what we get for this lot to pay our fares to Cardiff.'

It was almost ten o'clock when they reached Pontypool. The stalls were already set up in the market place; those selling food were busy but on both the clothes stalls they approached the traders looked glum as they waited for customers.

One of the stallholders wouldn't even look at what they had in their bundles. 'No call for men's clothing, see,' he told Wynne disparagingly. 'Half the men are in the army and those that are still working down the pit are making do with what they've got.'

The second trader agreed to take Cradock's best suit and the boots they'd brought along but said he didn't want any of the other stuff. 'There's a rag-and-bone place on the edge of town, they might take the rest of the stuff off you,' he told them.

35

Footsore and disappointed, they sat down on a low wall and wondered what to do for the best.

'I'm not going to give up just yet,' Wynne said defensively as she eased her aching feet out of her boots and flexed her toes. 'I don't intend taking it all back home and I don't want to take it to the rag-and-bone yard either. All we'll get for it there is a few coppers.'

'So what else can we do?' Fern pondered. 'We could take it along to the pawnbroker's here and see if he would give us a few shillings on it,' she added hopefully.

Wynne shook her head. 'We'd have to give our name and address and the moment he knew we weren't local, he'd probably refuse it; he might even think we'd stolen it and tell the police.'

'Don't tell him we're from Blaenafon, then,' Fern persisted. 'Give him the name of a street in Pontypool; it's not as though we are ever going to redeem any of the stuff is it?'

'You're so damn sharp you'll cut yourself one of these days,' her mother told her tartly. 'Nevertheless, it's not such a bad idea. Come on, let's try it and see what we can do.'

Their ruse worked. Half an hour later they were heading back home and Wynne had twelve shillings and sixpence safely tied up in a handkerchief and secreted away in the pocket of her skirt.

Without their heavy bundles and satisfied

with their day's work, they both found the long journey home much less tiring. As they walked along Wynne revealed some of the plans she was hoping to put into practice in the days to come.

'Tomorrow perhaps we'll chance it and take along as many bits and pieces as we can to the pawnbroker in Blaenafon,' she told Fern.

'I thought you said you didn't want to do that because it was taking too much of a risk?'

'Don't worry, I'll tell him I need the money to pay off the funeral debts. I'll keep back your dad's watch and any other small items like that and we'll take those to Cardiff with us. We can pawn them when we get there if we need to raise some money to see us through the first few weeks. We'll both have to look for work, of course, the minute we arrive there.'

'Mam, I'm not fourteen yet,' Fern interrupted. 'I can't leave school until next Christmas at the earliest.'

'Rubbish, you're a big girl for your age, so who's to know that you're not already fourteen? No one will, unless you're twp enough to tell them.'

'Stop saying that I'm daft, Mam. Someone is bound to find out. Mr Paterson will report it to the school board man when I don't turn up next week and then they'll come looking for us.'

'By then we'll be in Cardiff and it's a big city; far too big for them to ever find us,' her mother told her confidently.

37

Chapter Four

Worn out by their expedition Fern and Wynne
had an early night, but they were up at daybreak
the next morning making preparations for their
departure.

'Do we have to leave all our furniture behind?'
Fern asked sadly as they filled two battered fibre
suitcases with their personal belongings and any
knick-knacks that Wynne thought they might be
able to sell in order to raise a few shillings later
on when they were in Cardiff.

'I don't see what else we can do. We need to
be out of here tonight because the rent man will
call first thing tomorrow morning and we
certainly don't want to waste what little money
we have paying him, now do we?'

'Can't we sell the furniture before we go? Dai
Roberts buys and sells second-hand furniture.'

'Not much chance of that. I had considered it
but I was afraid to do anything about it in case
anyone got wind of our plans. Even now it's
risky because someone might spot what was
happening and we don't want anyone knowing
we are leaving Blaenafon.'

'What about if we could persuade Dai Roberts
to agree to buy it and we asked him to come

and collect it tomorrow and we make sure that it is not until after we've gone?'

'How on earth is he going to get in if we've already left?'

'We could tell him we had to be at work early tomorrow morning and that since we couldn't hang about waiting for him to come, we'd leave the door unlocked so that he could come in and collect the furniture whenever he's ready to do so.'

Wynne shook her head. 'I doubt if Dai Roberts would swallow a tale like that, my lovely. He knows I haven't got a job and that you are still at school.'

'Well, then why not give him the door key and ask him not to disturb you?'

'What about payment? Knowing him, he won't want to part with any money until he's got the goods.'

'He might do, if you say that you've come to do the deal tonight because you need to have the money ready for the rent man. Everyone knows that he calls first thing in the morning on anyone who is behind with their payments so he'll understand.'

'Well, I suppose it might be worth a try,' Wynne admitted. She looked at the clock and shook her head. 'He probably won't want to do business at this time of night.'

'All we want him to do is to come round and see what there is here and tell us how much he'll give us for it. Everybody says that Dai

Roberts can't bear to miss a bargain. If he thinks there's any money to be made, he's always ready to do business.'

Giggling nervously like a pair of school children they put on their outdoor clothes and went to see Dai Roberts.

Although he pretended it was far too late to discuss the matter when Wynne explained the situation and how she desperately needed the money for the rent man by first thing the next morning or else he would be sending the bailiffs in, Dai eventually agreed to come and see what was on offer.

He drove a hard bargain, haggling over the price even though he agreed that there were some good, solid pieces of furniture and that it would be a shame to let the bailiffs get their hands on them.

He was reluctant to part with money in advance but when Wynne offered to hand over the door key his eyes narrowed and he pursed his mouth, pulling on the long droopy ends of his moustache thoughtfully.

'That's a cock and bull story about you being in bed and not wanting to be disturbed, isn't it?' he said with a sly smile. 'You're going to skedaddle, right? You don't intend leaving any money for the rent man, now do you? Well, fair-dos, that's your business, but what happens if I don't get all the stuff I've bought out of the place before the rent man calls?'

'Then it's up to you to make sure you get here

bright and early, before he does,' Wynne told
him.

'Yes, but there's a big risk in all of this for
me,' he pursued, tugging away at his moustache.

Wynne and Fern waited anxiously for his
decision.

'Tell you what,' he said at length, 'I'll do the
deal with you but not at the price I agreed to
pay; I'll give you half of what I offered you.'

'That would be daylight robbery,' Wynne
protested. 'I might as well leave it for the
bailiffs.'

'If that's your decision, then there's nothing
more to say.' He turned and made for the door.
'Damno! I ought to be charging you for wasting
my time,' he said in an angry voice.

'Hold on, Mr Roberts, we'll be gone before
you come tomorrow morning so you can take
anything else you want, everything that we leave
behind,' Fern burst out.

He paused and stared at her. 'Everything?'

'That's right,' Wynne agreed. 'We've already
packed what we are taking,' she pointed to the
two suitcases and the large bundle in one corner
of the room. 'There'll be the beds, the bedding,
the pots and pans, everything that you can see
around you.'

Dai Roberts pushed his cap back and
scratched his head. 'Big risk you're asking me
to take.' He held out his hand for the door key.
'I'll be round long before first light so make sure
you're gone by then, understand?'

'The money first,' Wynne demanded, holding on to the key.

'I think you should give us the amount you first offered because now you are getting so much more; even the zinc bathtub and the big wooden mangle, if you want them,' Fern chipped in.

'You've got a lot of lip for one so young,' he told her sourly.

He delved in his pocket and brought out a handful of silver and carefully counted it out on the table. Fern watched, counting every coin with him.

When he began to put some that was still in his hand back in his pocket, she stopped him. 'You said more than that, a lot more. Don't forget you are getting everything,' she reminded him.

Dai Roberts hesitated, shaking his head. Then with a chortle he put the money that was still in his hand down on the table. 'You deserve it, my lovely,' he told Fern. 'I like your spirit and the way you've stuck up for your mam. Good luck to the pair of you, wherever you're going.'

Before either of them could say anything he had taken the key and was gone. Fern and her mother stared at the pile of silver on the table and then Fern began putting it into piles, counting it out loud as she did so.

'There's nine pounds and threepence here,' she exclaimed, her eyes round with wonder. She counted it carefully again. 'It's a small fortune, Mam.'

'Well, it will certainly help us out over the next week or so,' her mother agreed. She handed Fern a big black leather purse. 'Put it all in here and I'll hide it away safely. I've got the money for our train fare and a few shillings more in another purse and I'll put that one in my pocket. And we'll pack some of the smaller bits that I intended to take to the pawnbrokers. We don't want anyone seeing us with that lot; not a word to your uncle about it, mind.'

'So do you mean we are still going to try and find Uncle Bryson when we get to Cardiff and ask him if we can stay with him?' Fern asked in surprise. 'I thought that now we had some money you wouldn't want to do that.'

'I've given it a lot of thought and I think it would be the best thing to do – for a little while, anyway. We've never been to Cardiff before so we know nothing about the place and it will give us a chance to get our bearings,' her mother explained.

'You mean that you think he might be able to help us to find somewhere to live?' Fern asked hopefully.

'Possibly, but we'll worry about that when we get there. Come on, get your coat on and we'll be off.'

'Now? Tonight! I thought we weren't going until first thing in the morning?'

'I want to be out of this place before that Dai Roberts comes back to take the furniture,' her mother told her sharply. 'Knowing him, he'll be here so damn early tomorrow morning that if we go to bed, he'll be in the house before we have a chance to be up and dressed, let alone have any breakfast.'

'If we leave now, it will be almost midnight by the time we get to Cardiff,' Fern protested.

'It certainly will be the way you are dawdling,' her mother scolded. 'Now come on, Fern, pull yourself together and let's get going. It's as good a time as any, if we don't want folks knowing what we're up to. At this time in the evening most of the women will be indoors putting the kiddies to bed.'

'I suppose so, and the men won't yet be setting out for their night shift,' Fern agreed.

'Right. Now you carry one of the suitcases and I'll carry the other one as well as the bundle and let's get going,' Wynne said briskly as she took a last look around.

There wasn't time for recriminations or sadness as they left their home. As Wynne pulled the front door closed for the last time she pulled back her shoulders, picked up the case and bundle, and set off so briskly that Fern had a job to keep up with her.

They reached the railway station with only minutes to spare before the last train left for Cardiff. As they settled into their seats on opposite sides of an almost empty carriage they were both too breathless to even talk to each other.

Going on the train was such a momentous adventure that at any other time Fern was sure

44

she would have enjoyed it. Now, though, she felt far too unhappy about leaving the home where she'd grown up and the friends she'd known all her life. Instead of sitting back and relaxing she sat bolt upright, staring out apprehensively at the dark world outside the carriage window.

As the train pulled out of the station Fern saw her mother surreptitiously wipe away a tear from the corner of her eye but she thought it was better to say nothing.

Fern suspected that having to leave their home in Blaenafon was an even greater wrench for her mother than it was for her but the die had been cast and there was no turning back. They no longer had a home there and her mother was far too proud to ask any of the neighbours to take them in even for a few days.

Fern felt confused about what lay ahead and their new life in Cardiff. It was such a big city and completely unknown to them both and although she was excited she was also fearful about what they might encounter.

It was very late when they arrived at Cardiff General and the few people who'd been on the train handed in their tickets and hurried through the barrier, obviously anxious to get home or wherever it was they were going.

As they handed in their tickets, Wynne hesitated as if she didn't know what to do next.

'Do you know where Angelina Street is? I believe it's somewhere off Bute Street, can you tell me how to get there? Is it too far for us to walk?'

'Bute Street!' The ticket collector's voice rose in surprise. 'That's Tiger Bay, I wouldn't want to walk down there in broad daylight, let alone at this time of night,' he said, shaking his head.

Wynne frowned. 'Why ever not?'

'It has a terrible reputation, missus; surely you know that? What d'yer want to go there for?'

'Is it very far?' Wynne persisted, ignoring his question even though his warning struck a chord of fear in her.

'If you hurry you might catch a tram, some of them run as far as the Pier Head right up until midnight,' he said dourly. 'The tram stop is just outside the station, you'll find it easily enough.'

'Let's hope that somebody will be able to tell us where we have to get off,' Wynne said worriedly as they boarded the tram and it clanged its way down Bute Street.

'Going visiting at this time of night!' the conductor commented in surprise as he took the money for their fares from Wynne. 'Come far, have you?' he went on, indicating their luggage as he punched two tickets and handed them to her.

'We're going to visit my family in Angelina Street so will you let us know where to get off?' Wynne said stiffly.

'Oh, I see! First visit, is it, and that's why you don't know where to get off. What a pity they

46

couldn't get along to the station to meet you. I wouldn't fancy having to walk down any of the side streets off Bute Street, not this time of night.'

'If you would be kind enough to let us know when we reach our stop then I'd be very grateful,' Wynne told him primly as she took the tickets from him.

'Oh, don't worry, I'll sing out. You know which way to go when you get off, do you?'

'No, but I expect we'll find it,' Fern piped up, noticing that her mother was getting more and more tight-lipped as the questioning went on. 'If not, we can always ask someone.'

The conductor shook his head and made a long face. 'I wouldn't do that, cariad, not if I was you,' he said in a warning voice. 'It's easy to see that neither of you know anything about the sort of place Tiger Bay is. It's not so bad in daylight, but after dark, once you leave the main road, it's very different, my lovely.'

'Thank you for your concern, but I'm sure we will be quite all right,' Wynne said stiffly.

Fern felt relieved when he shrugged and moved away to collect the fares from other people on the tram, but as he walked back to take up his position by the door he renewed his promise to let them know in good time when they were to get off.

When he did alert them that they were at the nearest stop he took so long explaining which way they should go that the other passengers began complaining loudly about the delay.

As the tram pulled away he was still on the step waving his arms and shouting out instructions. They waited until the tram had disappeared before they picked up their luggage and set off in the direction he'd indicated.

It was a cold night and as they crossed the road towards the side street he'd indicated, they were suddenly plunged into darkness.

'What on earth has happened?' Fern exclaimed in alarm, dropping her suitcase on to the pavement.

'Didn't you see the lamplighter going down the road in front of us?' Wynne asked.

'I didn't think they put them out until midnight.'

'They don't, so it probably is midnight. It was late in the evening when we left Blaenafon and I've no idea how long the journey took, but it seemed endless.'

'Come on, pick up the case, there's no point in hanging about grumbling. Bryson will probably do enough of that when we knock on his door. I don't imagine he'll be any too pleased at having to take us in, especially at this time of night.'

'He's probably in bed and asleep by now,' Fern said worriedly. 'Anyway,' she went on, 'we still don't know where Angelina Street is; we're not there yet, are we, Mam?'

'No, I think we're still in Maria Street,' Wynne agreed, 'because, according to what the tram conductor told us, we have to go right to the

48

very bottom of this road and then turn left and then we'll be in Angelina Street. After that it will be easy; the house we want will be only a few doors along.'

'How are we ever going to find the right one now the street lights are out?' Fern asked worriedly as they neared the end of the road. 'It's much too dark to see the numbers on any of the doors.'

'Then we'll have to count them as we go along,' Wynne told her. 'If the first house is number one, then his house will be the ninth one along the street.'

'Uncle Bryson lives at number seventeen Angelina Street, not number nine, Mam!'

'I know that but the odd numbers will be down one side of the road and the even numbers down the other side,' her mother pointed out.

'It wasn't like that at home; the numbers went one, two, three and so on,' Fern argued.

'That's because we lived in a terrace and there were no houses opposite,' Wynne reminded her. 'We're in a big city now, Fern. You're going to find a lot of things different here from what you were used to in Blaenafon.'

'I suppose so, and I expect that having to live with Uncle Bryson will be one of them,' Fern agreed apprehensively as they found the house and banged on the door.

Chapter Five

They waited on the pavement for such a long time that they were on the point of walking away when Fern looked up and saw that there was a dim light shining from the front bedroom window. As she stared up at it she was sure she saw the curtains twitch.

They banged on the door again to make sure that whoever was awake didn't simply go back to sleep but knew that there was someone outside. A minute or so later the door opened and a dark-haired, wiry man stood there holding a lighted candle in one hand and glaring at them as though angry at being disturbed. Fern's heart thundered. It was her uncle Bryson.

For a moment she thought he hadn't recognised them but when she said, 'Hello, Uncle Bryson', the look of triumph on his face hit her like a hammer blow.

'So you've turned up after all, just as I expected,' he said in a derisory tone, ignoring Fern and addressing his remark to Wynne. 'The pit owner turned you out into the street, did he?'

'Are you going to ask us in or are we going to stand out here all night?' Wynne countered.

'Since you obviously have nowhere else to go you'd best come in,' he told her as he opened the door wider and stood to one side to let them pass into the hallway.

Fern wrinkled her nose at the dank, musty smell as they edged past him with their bag and suitcases. As Bryson slammed the front door shut a voice from upstairs called down asking who the hell was banging on the door and what did he think he was doing letting them in at this time of night.

'Take no notice,' he muttered as he led the way along the passage towards the back of the house.

As they made to follow him a figure appeared on the landing above and both Wynne and Fern gasped in disbelief as a huge coloured woman wrapped in a bright multi-patterned cotton dressing gown lumbered down the stairs towards them.

'This is Bertha,' Bryson told them as they all went into the back room. He placed the candle he was still carrying down on a saucer in the centre of the wooden table. Turning away and picking up the poker that was lying on the brass fender, he began to stir the glowing embers in the kitchen range back to life before ramming the iron kettle down on to the middle of them.

'Get moving and put some cups on the table, then, Bertha, and make us all a hot drink,' he ordered.

The woman was still standing in the doorway,

arms akimbo, surveying Fern and Wynne as though they were from another world.

'Who the hell are these people?' she asked, frowning. 'I've never seen them in my life before.'

'Well, you'll be seeing plenty of them from now on; they're my brother's family; his widow Wynne and his daughter Fern. They'll be staying here with us for a while.'

'Your brother's family!' She breathed in deeply, seeming to grow larger by the minute. 'Huh! You never told me you had a brother,' she said suspiciously.

'Well, I have – leastways, I did have. He was killed in a pit explosion a couple of weeks back.'

Bertha shrugged, staring at them, shaking her head from side to side in bewilderment.

While the argument between Bryson and Bertha continued Wynne and Fern hunched together by the range, holding out their hands to the glowing coals as they tried to get warm. They both felt tired and cold and Fern was already wishing they hadn't come. She sensed that Bertha had taken a dislike to them and didn't want them there and it seemed that in some strange way Bryson was revelling in their situation although she couldn't understand why.

'They can't stay here,' Bertha protested loudly, her huge bosom heaving in protest. 'We haven't any room for them.'

'Then we'll have to make room. After they've

had a hot drink and something to eat they can sleep in our bed for tonight,' Bryson told her. 'Tomorrow we'll sort things out. Now fetch out some bread and cheese or whatever there is in the pantry.'

'Now? You expect me to put out food and make hot drinks at this time of night!'

Bryson ignored her protests and, after lighting another candle, began taking cups off the nearby shelf and putting them down on the table in a higgledy-piggledy pile.

'Move, woman, you heard what I said, so find them something to eat and be quick about it,' he ordered as Bertha remained standing there with her hands on her hips, looking aggressive.

'Look, you don't have to bother with any food, we're really far too tired to eat,' Wynne protested. 'A hot drink would be nice, though,' she added.

Bryson ignored her remark. 'Food!' he demanded, banging his fist on the table.

Bertha shrugged her massive shoulders and, after glaring at Wynne and Fern, lumbered over to a cupboard at the far end of the room and brought out half a loaf, a covered cheese dish and a jar of pickle. Making as much noise as possible she put these on the table alongside the assortment of chipped cups and saucers that Bryson had already placed there.

'Is that all you can find for them to eat?' Bryson frowned as he surveyed the table.

Out of politeness Fern did her best to eat the

slice of bread that Bertha hacked off the loaf and covered with a scraping of margarine. There was no cheese; when Bryson lifted off the top of the cheese dish there were only a scattering of mouldy crumbs underneath it.

The tea was strong and the milk that Bertha had splashed into it floated on the top and was a rancid yellow colour.

In an attempt to distract her mind from what she was trying to eat and drink Fern stared round the gloomy, untidy kitchen. She found it hard to believe that her uncle lived in such squalor. When he'd called at their home in Blaenafon after the funeral he had appeared to be so well dressed that she thought he had made a success of his life in Cardiff, but now she was not so sure.

They were still sitting in flickering candlelight that cast ugly shadows on the drab walls and she wished he would light the gas mantle so that they could see each other better. When neither he nor Bertha made any attempt to do so she wondered if it was because they had no money for the meter.

Bryson looked so like her father that it made her heart ache. There the resemblance seemed to stop. Her father had been kind and courteous, but the way Bryson had spoken to Bertha had been harsh, almost contemptuous. It was almost as if he regarded her as his slave. Fern didn't like the way he looked at her mother, either, or his tone when he'd greeted them.

Her head ached and she longed for sleep and as she swallowed down the last of the bread and scrape and took a mouthful of the strong tea she felt her stomach churning.

'I need to go to the lavvy,' she whispered to her mother.

'Is the lavatory in the yard outside?' Wynne asked looking across at Bertha.

'There's a pot upstairs under the bed, can't she use that?' Bertha asked.

Fern shuddered at the thought and shook her head.

'Tell me where it is and I'll take her,' Wynne said quietly.

'It's out in the yard and you'll have to take a candle with you,' Bryson told them as he led them from the kitchen down a couple of stone steps into the scullery and unlocked the back door. 'Mind the rats,' he added as they went past him, 'and you'd better shield the candle with one hand or it might blow out.'

Fern was shaking with fright and gave a small shriek when she heard a rustling as they pushed open the rickety door of the wooden building adjacent to the house.

The stench from the latrine was so over-powering that neither of them dared breath and it took all of their willpower not to rush back inside the house. When they did go back into the kitchen, they found Bertha had already gone back upstairs to bed and had taken the candle with her and Bryson was sitting in the dark. He had dragged the battered leather sofa as close to the fire as he could and was hunched on it with an old blanket round his shoulders and a couple of cushions behind him.

'I'll doss down here tonight and you two can share the bed with Bertha,' he told them. 'We'll have to make some other arrangements tomorrow.'

'We'll sleep down here, Bryson, you go back up to your bed,' Wynne told him. 'Leave us the blanket.'

For a moment Fern was afraid he was going to argue and she silently prayed that he wouldn't refuse to do as her mother suggested. The thought of sharing a bed with the huge black woman terrified her even though her mother would be there as well.

'Probably suit Bertha better if we do that,' Bryson admitted with a wry grin as he handed the blanket to Wynne. 'Will you be warm enough with just that?'

'We'll manage,' Wynne told him. 'You get off to bed; you probably need your night's sleep so that you are ready for work in the morning.'

Bryson seemed to be about to say something then changed his mind and left them to their own devices.

With only the light from the dying embers of the fire to see by they cuddled up to each other on the sofa and made themselves as comfortable as they could. They were both too tired to talk and so exhausted that in no time they were asleep and all the many questions that Fern wanted to ask her mother remained unasked.

When Fern woke, a grey light filled the room and for a moment she had a feeling of panic. She wondered where she was and why she was lying on an uncomfortable lumpy sofa with her mother's arms round her instead of being stretched out in her own single bed.

'Are you awake at last, cariad?' her mother whispered. 'Can you sit up for a minute? You've been lying on my arm all night and it's cramped; it's full of pins and needles.'

Fern struggled into an upright position, gazing at their squalid surroundings with growing distaste while her mother rubbed and flexed her arm to restore the circulation.

'Do we have to stay here, Mam?' she questioned in a tight voice. 'It's really horrible, isn't it?' She shuddered. 'I do wish Dad hadn't died and we could go back home.'

'It's not very nice, I agree with you there, cariad, but perhaps the rest of the place is better,' Wynne said brightly. 'This room certainly looks as though it could do with a good cleaning. Still, cariad, we haven't much choice, now have we? We've only a few pounds left. I'm hoping that Bryson will let us stay here for a couple of weeks until I can manage to find a job, then as soon as I've saved a few bob, we'll look for a nice tidy place somewhere else and move on.'

'Do you think he will let us stay? I don't think

Bertha likes us; come to that, I don't like her very much either.'

'Her ways are probably different to ours but then, if she can adapt to living with Bryson, I'm sure we can fit in and live with her,' Wynne said primly. 'Remember that now and keep your thoughts to yourself and be as cooperative as you can, cariad,' she cautioned.

'I'm not sure Uncle Bryson wants us here either. Did you two have a row at some time?'

'No, not exactly,' Wynne said evasively. 'There's no call to start dragging the past up. Let sleeping dogs lie, I always say.'

'I know that, Mam, but, the way he speaks to you and looks at you, I think it would be better if you told me about it.'

'What's been and gone is best left alone,' Wynne told her and from her decisive tone Fern knew better than to pursue the matter.

'Perhaps we should get up now, have a wash and tidy ourselves before Bryson and Bertha come down,' her mother said briskly. 'I'll have a look in the scullery and see if there is any soap and a towel out there that we can use.'

The scullery was cold and even danker than the kitchen. The towel hanging there was thin and grubby. Fern washed her hands and face in a bowl of cold water and used a corner of the towel to dry herself, and Wynne did the same.

They had just opened one of their suitcases to find some clean underclothes when Bryson appeared and Wynne hastily closed the lid again.

'Did you sleep well?' he asked, yawning and scratching his chest as if he was only half awake.

'We managed,' Wynne told him stiffly.

'You'd have been a lot more comfortable if you'd gone up and slept in my bed,' he smirked.

When Wynne didn't answer he went over and stirred the fire to life and pushed the kettle into place. 'You'll probably feel better after a cuppa,' he commented.

'Are you off to work now, Uncle Bryson?' Fern asked, giving him a bright smile.

'Fern, that's enough! What have I told you about asking questions?' Wynne said reprovingly. 'Why don't you take the cups we used last night through to the scullery and wash them up, cariad, while I have a quiet word with your uncle?'

As she did as she'd been told, Fern could hear them talking but they kept their voices so low that, even though she strained her ears to find out what was being said, she was unable to do so.

When she came back into the kitchen with the clean cups she noticed that Bryson was looking rather smug and her mother was tight-lipped. Bertha had joined them and instead of the jazzy dressing gown she'd been wearing the night before she was in a bright orange dress and was wearing a band of the same colour round her head like a small turban.

There was no milk for their tea and Bertha hacked some slices off the loaf they'd had the night before and scraped the remains of the margarine on it.

59

'Bryson picks up his dole money tomorrow but this is all we have until then,' Bertha commented as she began to clear away. 'That's unless you can let us have some money to help out until then,' she said looking meaningfully at Wynne.

'I have every intention of paying my way,' Wynne told her forcibly. In fact, that's something I want to discuss with Bryson. I'm hoping he will say we can stay here for a short while until I find work and that he can tell me the best way to go about finding a job.'

'Ha, ha, ha!' Bertha's huge bosom shook like a giant blancmange as she rocked with laughter. 'You want him tell you how to find work; he doesn't know the meaning of the word. Lives on his wits, does Bryson,' she added spitefully. 'He's even managed to dodge being called up for the army by claiming that he has a dodgy back because he has flat feet.'

'That's enough from you. I keep you in food and clothes and I've been doing so for years now,' Bryson scowled, 'so keep your opinions to yourself.'

'As for staying here,' Bertha went on in a loud voice, drowning out his words, 'heaven help you. We have only this room and our bedroom; the rest of the house is let out. He might be able to persuade the landlord to rent us an extra room, and then you could have a bedroom. The back attic has just come empty but the landlord will want to see the colour of your money up front, especially if he knows you are anything to do with us.'

Wynne looked questioningly at Bryson. 'Could you look into it?' she asked when he remained silent. 'That's, of course, if you don't mind us living here for the time being and sharing your living quarters with you.'

Chapter Six

Settling into Bryson's place was not easy for Fern and Wynne but the squalor of where they were being forced to live faded into insignificance when set against the many other obstacles they had to overcome during their first weeks in Angelina Street.

It was almost Easter and Fern dreaded the fact that in a few more weeks, once the holiday was over, she would have to go to school. So far she hadn't got to know anyone who would be attending the nearby school in Eleanor Street and Bertha seemed to take a special delight in telling her what little ruffians her schoolmates would be, especially the boys.

Wynne tried to console her and make the best of the situation by telling her that there were bound to be some nice girls there as well, and they'd befriend her.

Wynne had her own battles to fight. Although the war wasn't yet over and women were still being employed by many of the factories, they all knew that their jobs wouldn't last once the men started coming home from the Front. Even though it cost less to employ a woman than a man, most companies still felt obliged to honour their promises to the men that their jobs would be there waiting for them when they did come home.

Wynne had found work at Currans' – a factory where they had been working flat out all through the war years producing ammunitions. Now there were lots of rumours going around that very soon they would be reverting to their normal production lines which consisted mainly of tin ware; pots and pans for domestic use and metal utensils for business outlets.

Wynne hated it there. The noise, the smell and the heat made her head ache and her stomach churn. Added to which she disliked the raucous laughter and rough talk that went on all around her. The working day was long and arduous and when she returned home to Angelina Street at the end of her shift she felt almost too tired to eat.

All she really wanted to do was to take refuge in the small top-floor bedroom she'd been able to rent for herself and Fern. It took a tremendous effort to force herself to go down into the room they shared with Bertha and Bryson and to sit down to the meal that Bertha had prepared.

Throughout her working day Wynne worried about Fern. The women she worked with were very rough and so different from those they'd known when they'd lived in Blaenafon that she found it difficult to talk to them.

Wynne knew that Fern disliked Bertha and that as soon as she'd finished the tasks that

Bertha had set her she was off out, roaming the dockside streets of Tiger Bay on her own. Wynne was always anxious about who Fern was with and what she was doing.

When they returned to their room at night and Fern talked about what she'd been doing during the day, Wynne often felt so alarmed by what Fern told her about some of the people she met and talked to that she would have given anything to pack up their few belongings and return home to the quiet respectability of the Valleys.

The biggest worry of all was the thought of Fern starting school. There were times when Wynne was tempted to say there was no need for her to do so. She would be fourteen next January and that meant she would be able to leave school and go to work. It seemed senseless to start at a new school for the matter of a few months.

Yet, if she kept her at home and the school board man managed to track them down, they'd probably both find themselves in trouble. She knew so little about the ramifications of such matters and how they got to know if a child was playing truant from school that she was afraid to take the risk.

Fern tried to reassure her mother, but on the first day of the new term she was feeling so nervous that she could hardly stop herself shaking as she walked in through the gates at Eleanor Street School and made her way to her appointed classroom.

Although she had met the headmaster and been told that her teacher was called Miss Woodman, she had no idea what to expect.

Miss Woodman was a small, thin woman about the same age as her mother who wore her hair screwed in a topknot and had a pair of pince-nez perched on her rather bony nose. She didn't seem to be at all the sort of person to teach a class of thirteen-year-olds, especially some of the boys who appeared to be twice her size and towered over her.

After waiting by Miss Woodman's desk for what seemed an eternity, Fern was told to go and sit at the end of the front row. As she took her place she was conscious of the many eyes fixed on her and the tittering and whispers that were going on behind her back. These stopped when Miss Woodman rapped on her desk with a ruler and called the class to order, but the chatter started up again every time her back was turned while she wrote something on the blackboard. This was when Fern found herself bombarded with small hard wads of screwed-up paper that hit the back of her neck with a sharp sting. Or when a hand would reach out and tug at her hair or give her a nasty pinch to the top of her arms.

She tried to ignore these taunts and was surprised that it was happening in the top class at school. She'd expected curious questions about where she'd been living and what school she'd attended before coming to Cardiff, but not childish pranks of this sort.

When they went out into the playground at break time, most of the girls ignored her but one or two started jibing at her, calling her Fatty Fern, laughing about her clothes and commenting on her hair. Then some of them started sneering about how hard she'd been working in class that morning in order to get into Miss Woodman's good books.

When she ignored them and went to walk away, Fern found her way barred by a group of boys. Egged on by the girls they started to jostle her and push her around.

Determined not to show how scared she was, she backed away only to trip over an outstretched boot and end up sprawled on the ground while they cheered and laughed.

When a tall, broad-shouldered boy with a mop of floppy dark hair elbowed the others aside and stretched out a hand to help her to her feet, she hesitated to take it, wondering if this was also some sick joke. Before she could decide whether or not to risk it he'd taken hold of her arms and pulled her to her feet. Keeping an arm round her shoulders, he steered her clear of the crowd.

'That's enough,' he told the others. 'Now back off, all of you! Understand?'

There were some angry mutterings but the crowd broke up and dispersed in small knots, the children looking back over their shoulders at Fern and pulling faces. A couple of girls came over and began talking to Fern in a fairly friendly way and before she had time to thank him the boy who'd helped her had disappeared.

'That's Glanmor Williams, but don't go thinking that he's fallen for you,' one of the girls tittered when she asked them who he was. 'He's supposed to keep order when we're out in the yard, that's why he came to your rescue.'

For the rest of the day Fern was left alone and when school ended she found Glanmor was by the school gate, waiting to walk along the road with her.

'How did you like your first day here?' he asked.

'This morning, first thing, it was awful.' Fern shivered. 'No one has bothered me since, though, not since you stepped in and helped me up off the ground.'

'If you have any more trouble, let me know,' he told her with a smile.

'Thank you, I will. This school is so much bigger than the one I used to go to in Blaenafon, before my mam and I came to Cardiff, that I feel a bit lost.'

'Where are you living?'

'In Angelina Street. We're staying there with my uncle for the moment.'

'I'm going that way, so we might as well walk together then,' he said.

She nodded gratefully. She'd been worried that some of the boys who'd been taunting her that morning might either follow her home or be waiting to waylay her but she knew that with Glanmor at her side she'd be quite safe.

'See you tomorrow, then,' he said and smiled as they parted on the corner of Angelina Street.

Fern thought about him for the rest of the way home. He was so tall and broad-shouldered that he seemed older than the other boys in her class and the boys of her own age she'd known in Blaenafon.

After that, they often walked home together. She would have liked to know more about him but he didn't seem prepared to talk about his family or what he did after school and, because she had so few friends herself in Tiger Bay, they generally talked about what had happened in school that day, the lessons they'd been doing, or what they hoped to do once they left school.

Simply being in his company gave Fern a feeling of happiness.

When she asked him what sort of job he'd be looking for once he'd left school in July, his face clouded.

'I'm not sure. I would like to go to sea but that would mean leaving my mam on her own and I don't want to have to do that.'

She waited for him to say why his mother would be on her own but when he didn't, she thought it was better not to ask. Instead she told him how her own dad had been killed in an explosion at Big Pit in Blaenafon.

'Is that why you came to live in Cardiff?'

Fern nodded. 'The pit owners turned us out because there was no one else in the family working down the pit. My brother would have been, but was called up and was killed in France a week before my dad died.'

'You've had it pretty tough,' he commiserated sympathetically.

'Was your dad killed in the war, Glanmor?' she asked tentatively.

'No!'

His tone was so abrupt and his mouth tightened into such a hard line that although she was curious to know more Fern sensed it was not the time to ask questions. Instead, she turned the conversation back to herself by saying, 'I'll have to look for a job soon because I can leave soon after Christmas.'

'If your birthday isn't until January then you'll have to stay on until Easter,' Glanmor told her.

'I hope not because I want to earn some money to help my mam. She's working at Curran's but she says that once the men start coming home from the war she will probably lose her job.'

'So what sort of work are you thinking of doing?' Glanmor asked.

'That's the trouble, I don't know. At one time, before my dad died and we moved here to Cardiff, I had hoped I could train to be a teacher. That's out of the question now because when I do leave school I'll need a job right away in order to earn some money.'

'Have you thought about getting a Saturday job? It's one of the best ways of proving that you are a good worker when you go after a full-time job,' he explained.

'I know, and I've tried at most of the shops around here but none of them seems to want to employ me because I'm considered to be a stranger. Most of them make the excuse that they have someone in the family who helps them out.'

'I'll ask around,' Glanmor promised. 'You don't mind what sort of shop you work in, do you?'

'Not really.' Fern shrugged. 'I can't afford to be choosy now, can I?' she said with a forced smile.

It was a Friday in the middle of December and Fern still hadn't found any work when Glanmor came up with an answer. They were walking home along the banks of the canal, staring down into the dark waters, when he suddenly said, 'Would you consider selling flowers?'

Fern turned to look at him; her dark eyes alight with hope. 'Do you mean work in a florist's?' she asked excitedly.

'No! Well, no, not exactly.' He hesitated, as if wondering whether to say any more or not.

'Come on, Glanmor, tell me what you have in mind,' she urged.

'It would mean working out of doors and at this time of the year . . .' His voice trailed away and he dug his hands deeper into his pockets as if he was cold.

'Stop teasing me with hints and tell me what sort of job you are talking about,' Fern insisted.

'Have you seen the woman who stands

outside Cardiff General selling flowers?' he asked. He was speaking so quickly that she had a job to catch up with what he was saying.

Fern frowned and shook her head. 'No, not really. I'm not even sure where the station is. I haven't been near it since we arrived here and that was ages ago and in the dark.'

'Then meet me tomorrow morning at about ten o'clock and I'll take you along there and you can see if you are interested in helping her,' he gabbled. 'I shouldn't say anything to your mam or anyone else until after tomorrow in case you don't want to do it.'

Fern longed to share the idea with her mother but she wasn't too sure that she would get the job, even if she wanted it. The woman mightn't like her, or think she was suitable, she told herself, and it would only be raising her mother's hopes for nothing.

She brushed her shabby coat, polished her lace-up shoes and put fresh, folded-up newspaper inside them to cover up the holes in the soles to make sure that her feet would stay warm. Finally, she pulled on her cloche hat, found a clean handkerchief, then took a deep breath and set off to meet Glanmor, hoping he wouldn't notice how nervous she was.

Glanmor was waiting for her as he'd promised but he seemed to be every bit as on edge as she was. As they walked up Bute Street she tried to thank him for coming with her and for arranging for her to meet the flower seller.

'I think I ought to explain she's a relation of some sort; she's my mam's cousin or something and that's the reason she's agreed to meet you,' he mumbled.

Far from feeling relieved Fern felt all the more worried. If the woman didn't like her and she didn't get the job, then she would feel that she was letting Glanmor down.

At Glanmor's suggestion they stood in Wood Street for a few minutes so that they could watch what was going on. The woman standing there was in her late fifties, red-cheeked and buxom with a heavy black shawl over her shoulders and mittens on her hands. She wore a stout black apron which had copious pockets and as they watched Fern noticed that she used them rather like a cash box, sorting silver into one and coppers into the other. On the rare occasion when she was handed a note, she carefully smoothed it out and tucked it away into a special pocket in the waistband of her apron.

At her feet were two huge wicker baskets filled with carnations, roses, chrysanthemums and bunches of holly and other greenery already made up into large bunches and tied with fancy string. On one arm she carried a small, shallow trug containing a dozen or more neat little posies of violets. As people came hurrying out of the station she would take one of these and hold it out to them in the hope that they would buy it.

Mostly it seemed to be men who stopped to buy from her. Some merely took one of the small posies but others seemed intent on buying a larger bunch of flowers from one of the wicker baskets.

'Her name is Maria Roberts,' Glanmor told Fern. 'Now that you've seen her in action and know what the job is all about, are you still interested?'

'Of course I am,' Fern breathed excitedly. 'I love flowers and it would be wonderful to sell them to people and make them happy.'

'She only wants someone to help out over Christmas when she is usually quite busy and then perhaps at the weekends,' Glanmor cautioned. 'Now, do you still want to meet her?'

'Yes, of course I do,' Fern nodded.

She straightened the collar on her coat and pulled her hat straight in an attempt to hide her nervousness.

'Come along, then.' He took her arm and propelled her over to the other side of the road. They waited until Maria had dealt with a customer and then Glanmor, still holding Fern by the arm, approached the flower seller.

'Glanmor, what are you doing here at this time of the morning?' the woman questioned sharply as they reached her side. 'They won't keep you on at the ironmonger's if you keep skedaddling off on Saturdays when you should be in the shop helping out,' she scolded.

'I've only taken an hour off because I wanted to bring Fern along to meet you,' he told her.

'A good excuse!' She turned her attention to

Fern. 'Glanmor has told me all about you and I expect he's told you plenty about me, so we won't waste time on any palaver. All I want to know is are you interested in selling flowers or not?'

'Yes, I am, if you will give me a chance. You'll have to tell me what to do, of course.'

'Oh, I'll do that all right. I like things done my way but I like the look of you and with your pretty face you should make a capital little assistant. When do you leave school?'

'At Christmas. I'm not fourteen until the second week in January but my mam says that I should be able to leave school at Christmas and that's what I hope to do.'

Maria Roberts studied Fern for a moment in silence. 'And do you think she will let you come and work here during the Christmas holiday after you break up from school?'

'I'm sure she will,' Fern said eagerly. 'She'll be ever so pleased that I've found a job.'

Maria Roberts frowned. 'Does that mean you haven't told her you will be standing outside the railway station selling flowers?'

'Well, no, not yet. Glanmor only told me about it a couple of days ago and I wouldn't want to raise Mam's hopes. She knows I've been trying very hard to find a Saturday job. So far, though, all the shops I've been to have turned me down and she's as disappointed about that as I am.'

'You'd better talk to her about it, then, and see if she has any objections. It's not the same as working behind a counter and she mightn't like the idea.'

'I really do want this job and the chance to earn some money, Mrs Roberts,' Fern told her earnestly.

'If your mam says you can do it, then it's yours, cariad. You'd better bring her along to meet me, though.'

'I don't think that's necessary, Mrs Roberts.'

'Oh yes it is, my lovely. I'd like to set her mind at rest in case she has any worries about what you will be doing. If she's in agreement about you working for me, then you can start as soon as you like. I could do with some help in the weeks up to Christmas and it will be a good way for you to learn the ropes.'

'Thank you, Mrs Roberts, that's really wonderful,' Fern said excitedly.

'Right, well, you go home and find out what she thinks and you, Glanmor, get back to work before they sack you.'

Chapter Seven

Working for Maria Roberts opened up a whole new world for Fern. Her Saturday started very early; she had to be on the platform at the railway station at six-thirty in the morning in time to meet the early morning train that brought the daily supply of flowers.

Maria Roberts had a small wooden shed behind the goods depot where she opened up the crates and sorted out the flowers. She made them up into various bunches depending on the flowers she received at different times of the year. She seemed to know instinctively what size the bunches should be as well as which flowers would mix well together and how much to charge for each bunch.

Fern watched the older woman's nimble fingers in awe. When she tried to create attractive bunches she found that either she had difficulty in keeping the stems together, or, if the stems were neatly aligned, that the flowers themselves didn't look right.

Maria Roberts was very patient and in next to no time Fern found that she was equally adept at making up bunches. Because it was almost Christmas, Fern was handling a great deal of holly as well as winter greenery. The prickles of the holly leaves were almost as sharp as the rose thorns and drew blood if she wasn't careful.

After a few fumbled attempts Fern became even better at selling than Maria and she enjoyed what she was doing. Except for first thing in the morning when there was a frosty nip in the air and her hands felt so numb with the cold that she thought her fingers would drop off.

Maria was quick to notice this and gave her a pair of mittens to wear. She also insisted that Fern must wrap a large black woollen shawl round her shoulders as protection against the cold.

'Folks won't buy flowers from you if they see you standing there shivering,' she told Fern sharply when she tried to protest about wearing the shawl. 'Customers want to see a happy, smiling face, not one that's all screwed up like a prune because you're cold.'

Although she had only expected to be working on Saturdays, to her delight, the week before Christmas, Maria asked her if she could work every day right up until Christmas Eve.

Most of their customers were men and many of them either gave her a small tip or said 'keep the change' so that by the time they packed up on Christmas Eve Fern found that in addition to her wages from Maria she had over three pounds to take home.

'Shouldn't I be sharing the money I've been given in tips with you, Mrs Roberts?' she asked rather self-consciously.

'Goodness gracious me no, my lovely!' The older woman smiled. 'Your bright smile and helpful manner earned you that and you should spend it on a Christmas treat for yourself.'

In the next half an hour as they cleared everything away Fern mentally spent her money several times over. There were so many things she wanted to do with it.

The money she'd earned was already earmarked as savings towards herself and her mother moving out of Angelina Street but now, with so much extra, she felt her spirits soar. It meant that she could buy a present for her mother to bring back a smile to her face. There would also be something to pay for extra food for them all at Christmas so that Bertha wouldn't be so crabby about having to share the Christmas dinner she'd cooked for herself and Bryson with them.

Fern hoped she would see Glanmor sometime over Christmas so that she could thank him for introducing her to Maria Roberts, since that had been the start of her good fortune. If he hadn't introduced her to Maria Roberts, then she would never have been selling flowers and would never have earned all the tips she'd been given. It also made her wonder if it would be all right to give him a Christmas present by way of saying thank you. She wanted to, only she couldn't think what would make a suitable present.

All the way home, while also juggling in her

mind how she would divide up her extra money, she pondered on what to buy Glanmor. In the end, she decided she'd ask her mam what she thought about it all.

Somehow, she reflected as she reached Angelina Street, it didn't seem right to be getting excited about Christmas or even looking forward to enjoying the day itself when only a few months earlier her dad had died and, just before that, her brother had been killed in action.

She shuddered as she thought of how many other families would be feeling sad because, although the war was now over and most of the soldiers had returned home, so many sons and husbands were missing, having lost their lives in the trenches over in France.

A year ago they had all been so safe in their little house in Blaenafon, celebrating Christmas and looking forward to the year ahead. Who would have thought that in such a short space of time she and her mother would find themselves sharing a sleazy living room and kitchen with almost complete strangers in Cardiff's notorious Tiger Bay?

All she could hope was that things would improve in 1919 and that very soon she and her mother would be able to find somewhere better to live.

Fern's dream of a happy Christmas was short-lived. The minute she stepped inside the house she could hear voices raised in anger. Bertha was complaining bitterly about having to share their Christmas dinner and her mother was pointing out that she had given her extra money towards buying the food and that she was willing to do her share of preparing it and clearing up afterwards.

'Well, there's no need for you to do either of those things, Mam, and we certainly won't be asking you to share your meal with us, Bertha, because I've decided to take my mam out tomorrow for her Christmas dinner,' Fern interrupted.

'Take her out!' Bertha jeered. 'Where do you think you will find anywhere open on Christmas Day? A workman's café is about all you can afford and even those down on the dockside will be closed tomorrow.'

'Take no notice of Bertha, she's just letting off steam,' Bryson said quickly. 'If you've managed to earn a few bob, you'd be better off letting us use it to buy some extras,' he added in a cajoling voice.

'I suppose by that you mean you'll buy some extra booze and more ciggies,' Fern commented.

'Extra drink, extra food, and anything else you fancy, my lovely.' He grinned, puffing a cloud of smoke in her direction.

'Not for us, thank you very much,' she retorted primly. 'Mam doesn't like drink, anyway.'

'So what sort of Christmas are you planning on having? Going along to the Sally Army canteen for a bowl of vegetable soup and a crust of stale bread? If you're lucky, you might even get a chicken drumstick as well.'

Fern didn't bother to answer. Out of the corner of her eye she could see her mother frowning and knew she was worried about how she was going to answer Bertha. She knew her mother didn't like it when she was rude or cheeky so she merely smiled and said nothing.

'You want to remember that if you start upsetting them, and your uncle Bryson throws us out, we have nowhere else to go,' Wynne warned her the minute they were on their own. 'All this grand talk about us going out for our Christmas dinner, how can we do that without spending the wages you've earned? We've already agreed that money is going to be put away towards getting a place of our own.'

'Here're my wages and you can put every penny of it away, Mam,' Fern announced as she handed over the envelope Maria had given her. 'I don't intend spending a single penny of them. I don't need to, because I've earned enough in tips to pay for us to go out for our meal tomorrow and that's what we'll do.'

'You'd be better off buying yourself a warm coat or something you need rather than spending it like that,' her mother scolded, but the frown had gone from her face and Fern could tell that she wasn't really cross. The thought of eating a meal in pleasant surroundings, away from Bertha and Bryson, had brought a smile to her lips.

* * *

The next morning they took their time getting up and getting ready to go out. They both put on their best clothes and made sure that they looked as smart as they possibly could.

The night before they'd talked endlessly about where they would go and Fern was afraid that, as it was Christmas Day, everywhere might be so busy that they wouldn't be able to find anywhere suitable.

Bertha spotted them when they came downstairs shortly before midday and reminded them that she was cooking a Christmas dinner if they wanted to change their minds and share it with her and Bryson.

'I didn't think you wanted us to do that,' Wynne said quietly. 'Only last night you were complaining that having us here over Christmas was creating far too much work for you.'

'No more than usual,' Bertha responded quickly, shrugging her broad shoulders dismissively. 'So are you staying or not?'

'We wouldn't dream of imposing on you and Bryson.' Wynne smiled. 'Another time, perhaps.'

'Now where on earth are we going to find somewhere serving food today?' Wynne asked as they walked briskly along Angelina Street.

There was a light drizzle falling and though it was not very cold for the time of year, they couldn't help recalling how warm and cheerful it had been back home in their cosy little house in Blaenafon this time last year. Their living room had been festooned with colourful home-made paper chains and around the overmantle there had been sprigs of holly, its bright, red berries gleaming in the firelight.

'I don't know,' Fern admitted, 'but I suppose there might be a restaurant open in the centre of the city. Shall we walk to the Pier Head and catch a tram from there and see what we can find?'

'Probably everything will be more expensive than usual because it's Christmas Day,' her mother said worriedly. 'How much did you say you have to spend?'

'Three pounds and two shillings. I had planned to buy you a present and also to buy one for Glanmor,' Fern explained.

'Treating me to a meal will be a wonderful present, cariad,' Wynne told her, squeezing her arm. 'Who's this Glanmor, though, and why were you going to buy him a present?' She frowned.

'I told you all about him, Mam. Glanmor's mother is a relation of Maria Roberts and Glanmor took me along to meet Mrs Roberts and that's how I got the job.'

'Oh, of course. I do remember you telling me now,' Wynne said quickly. 'Wasn't he the boy who stuck up for you when you first went to Eleanor Street and stopped the others teasing you?'

'That's right. I wanted to get him a present but I was going to ask you what sort of thing I should buy him. I thought perhaps a nice tie, but I've never seen him wearing one.'

'Wouldn't a scarf be better, something to keep him warm?' Wynne suggested.

'Well, it's too late now.' Fern sighed. 'Anyway,' she went on philosophically, 'it will probably take all my money to pay for our meal.'

There was no tram in sight when they reached the Pier Head and they both wondered if perhaps there wouldn't be any running because it was Christmas Day.

'There's a young chap over there leaning on the railings, so let's go and ask him. Mind you, from the way he's staring out to sea, it's a boat, not a tram, he's waiting for,' Wynne added with a laugh.

Fern thought that from the broad shoulders and thick head of dark hair the boy looked vaguely familiar. When he turned round, she gave a gasp of pleasure. 'It's Glanmor, Mam, the boy we were talking about.'

Glanmor seemed to be equally surprised to see them as he ran his fingers through his hair, pushing it back from his eyes, and gave Fern a lopsided smile of recognition.

'Glanmor, this is my mam,' Fern told him. 'Do you know if there are any trams today?'

'Yes, but they don't start running until midday.' He looked up at the Pier Head clock. 'That means you have about a quarter of an hour to wait,' he told her.

'Well, that's not too bad.' She smiled. 'Are you waiting for one as well?'

'No, I'm just killing time. My mam's working

so I'm hanging around until she comes home and we can have something to eat. She works as a cleaner at the Seaman's Mission in Bute Street and they've asked her to go in today and give a hand. They are putting on a special Christmas dinner and they wanted her to help with the washing-up afterwards. I'm hoping that there will be some leftovers and that they'll let her bring them home for my meal tonight,' he added with a broad grin.

Fern looked enquiringly at her mother and when Wynne gave a tiny nod of agreement she said quickly, 'Look, Glanmor, me and Mam are going into town to see if we can find anywhere open where we can get a nice meal. Would you like to come with us?'

His mouth shaped into a silent whistle of surprise as he looked from one to the other. 'Do you really mean that?' he asked, the colour rushing to his face.

'Of course we do,' Wynne affirmed. 'You can probably tell us where to find somewhere open today.'

'I can do that without coming with you,' he said bluntly. 'You two are all dressed up as if going somewhere important, so you won't want to be seen with me.' Rather self-consciously he started to button up his coat to hide the much-darned dark blue jumper he was wearing underneath.

'We really would like you to come with us, Glanmor,' Fern insisted, her eyes shining. 'I've told my mam all about you and what a good friend you've been to me so it would be a nice way of saying thank you if you'd let us treat you to a meal.'

Although at first Glanmor seemed slightly embarrassed and awkward in their company, by the time they boarded the tram they were all at ease with each other. He even confided in them that the reason he'd been at the Pier Head was because he loved watching all the ships.

'I often try and work out what cargo they're carrying and where they've come from or, if they're leaving, where they're going to.'

'I like seeing the ships but I don't like the scream of the gulls as they circle overhead,' Fern told him.

'Some people say that the gulls are the souls of sailors drowned at sea,' he said.

'Oh, that makes me more scared of them than ever,' Fern said with a shiver.

Glanmor knew of a restaurant in Westgate Street where they were able to enjoy an exceptionally good meal at a reasonable price, complete with a helping of Christmas pudding as well as mince pies and coffee afterwards.

'That was a real feast,' he told Fern, 'I enjoyed every mouthful. What about walking up to Cathays Park before we go home?'

'Is that near here? I'm afraid we haven't found time to explore very much since we arrived,' Wynne explained.

'You mean you haven't seen Cardiff Castle or

the city hall or the national museum and the law courts?' he asked in surprise.

'We don't even know where to look for them,' Wynne admitted as they both shook their heads.

'I can see you need a guided tour of Cardiff.' Glanmor grinned. 'You'll only be able to see the castle from the outside today, of course, but even that is well worth a visit. Come on, it's not very far and then I'll show you the civic centre. It's not far to walk and it will give us all a spot of exercise after that big meal.'

Glanmor was right. As he took them from Westgate Street into Castle Street, Wynne and Fern were dazzled by their first glimpse of the magnificent walls and towers of Cardiff Castle.

'If you look through this archway, you can see on that little hill in the distance the original old castle built by the Normans on the site where there was once a motte that was topped by a wooden fort. Robert, the eldest son of William the Conqueror, was kept prisoner there and died in 1134. Since then there have been all sorts of additions made to it each time it changed hands. Most of the new castle was built by the Earls of Bute who still own it.'

'Goodness, you are well informed,' Wynne gasped.

'That's probably because I've always enjoyed history lessons,' he said laconically as they walked away and turned the corner into Kingsway and towards the civic centre which was just a short distance away.

Wynne and Fern were very impressed by the grandeur of the city hall and the rest of the grand buildings which were all built of gleaming white Portland stone and sparkled in the weak winter sunshine.

'It really is a wonderful setting,' Wynne exclaimed as Glanmor pointed out the national museum which stood at one side of the city hall and the law courts which faced it across the wide, tree-lined road.

'You should come back again when they're open and you can go inside,' he told them. 'There are some wonderful statues and pictures in the city hall and there are rooms and rooms of things on display in the national museum. You could spend a whole day in there looking around.'

'We will keep that in mind, Glanmor.'

'Once the cold weather is over,' he went on exuberantly as he led the way past the city hall to Cathays Park, 'this place is full of flowers, all through the summer and, on Sundays, when there is a band playing here it's lovely to sit and listen to it.'

'It sounds an ideal place for a weekend outing.' Wynne smiled. 'Thank you for telling us about it, Glanmor.'

By the time they'd returned home Bertha and Bryson had finished their meal and had drunk a great many cans of beer as well as a bottle of gin. Both of them were in a raucous mood and as Wynne and Fern walked in they bombarded them with questions about where they had been.

Bertha also regaled them with details of what a wonderful meal they'd both missed.

'There may be some bits left on the chicken carcass,' she told them. 'You're welcome to have them if you do the washing-up,' she chortled.

'Thank you all the same, but we are going up to our room,' Wynne told her. 'We've had a very enjoyable day and now we both feel we need a rest and some peace and quiet.'

Chapter Eight

Fern felt so pleased that her mother and Glanmor had met at last; now there would be no need to be secretive when she occasionally walked home from school with him or stopped to chat if she met him when she was out. Then she remembered that the possibilities of this happening in the future were becoming pretty remote because he had now left school and was working full-time.

She wasn't sure if Maria was going to keep her on. She'd employed her to help with the Christmas rush but would she be busy enough now to want her to help on a Saturday morning? she wondered.

There were still several days of the Christmas holiday left so she would have to go and find out. Perhaps the best thing to do was turn up on Saturday morning as if she was expecting Maria to need her.

On Boxing Day, because the factory was closed and Wynne wasn't working, Fern and her mother went for a walk.

It was a cold, wintry day but, as Wynne said, it was much better to be out walking around than staying indoors and having to put up with

Bertha carping on about how she disliked other people being in her kitchen or having to feed them.

To Fern's delight, when she turned up on the following Saturday, Maria Roberts greeted her as though she'd been expecting her to be there. They didn't have a very busy morning so they had time to talk about how they'd spent Christmas.

Maria looked surprised when Fern told her that Glanmor had been with them on Christmas Day and that he'd had Christmas dinner with her and her mother.

'What did his mam have to say to that?' she asked in surprise.

'I don't know. She was working, he said, and he was just mooching around the Pier Head, so we asked him if he would like to join us. He showed us the castle and the City Hall and all sorts of other places and then we went to Cathays Park. It was really lovely, they were all so impressive.'

'Yes, Glanmor is a great one for sightseeing. He's always exploring the back streets of Tiger Bay and spends half his life down at the Pier Head watching the ships coming and going. I'm never too sure in my own mind whether it's because he wants to go to sea or because he's just fed up and a bit lonely because he's on his own so much.'

'Do you know where he's gone to work now that he's left school?' Fern asked.

'The same place as he has been working on Saturdays, of course.'

'Where's that, then?'

'You mean he hasn't told you?' Maria Robert's eyes twinkled. 'Keeping secrets from you already, is he?'

'I've never thought to ask him,' Fern told her, feeling the colour rushing to her face.

'Oh, you have too many other things to talk about, is that it? You watch your step with young Glanmor,' Maria Roberts warned. 'He's young and good-looking, but don't let that bowl you over, cariad. One mistake at your age and you spend the rest of your life regretting it.'

Fern thought about Maria's words as she was walking home that night. There had been no reason for her to have been so critical, she thought crossly. Glanmor was too nice to take advantage of her and, anyway, they were merely friends, nothing more. He'd stuck up for her at school and he'd helped her find this Saturday job, nothing more. Why did grown-ups always have to think the worst of young people?

She didn't see anything of Glanmor until the following Tuesday – New Year's Eve – although he was often in her thoughts and she wondered how he was getting on in his new job. Working full-time was very different from being a Saturday boy, she imagined.

Bertha and Bryson announced that they were going out for the evening that night and ordered

Wynne not to lock the door as they had no idea what time they would be coming home.

'That probably means they will be roaring drunk when they do come home,' her mother told Fern glumly. 'Well, by that time we'll both be safely tucked up in bed and, with any luck, we'll be asleep and won't hear anything of their noisy carryings on.'

'I don't think we will be able to get off to sleep if we know the front door is unlocked,' Fern told her. 'We'll both be lying there waiting to hear them come home, won't we?'

'Yes, you're probably right,' her mother sighed.

'I tell you what,' Fern suggested hopefully, 'why don't we do what everybody else will be doing and go out? We could walk down to the Pier Head; there's bound to be a lot of celebrating going on.'

'Some of the women I work with were telling me all about that,' her mother told her. 'It seems that all the ships blow their hooters at midnight to celebrate the end of the old year and welcome in the new year, and people sing and dance in the streets.'

'There you are, then. It might be good fun,' Fern persisted.

'Would it be safe, though?' Wynne protested. 'All those strange people . . . we might get caught up in the middle of a fight or something.'

'We'll be careful,' Fern assured her. 'The first sign of any trouble and we'll hot-foot it back home.'

They waited until about nine o'clock before they went out. It was a cold night, but clear, and there was a touch of frost in the air.

'We look as if we are going on a polar expedition not out for a night of fun,' Fern laughed as they put on warm hats as well as gloves and scarves to keep out the cold.

The streets were busy; people were laughing and singing and calling out greetings to each other as they made their way to the Pier Head.

When someone tapped Fern lightly on the shoulder she let out a little scream of fright. Then as she turned to see who it was, her heart stopped racing from fear and began racing for a completely different reason.

'Glanmor! What are you doing here?'

'I could ask you the very same thing.' He smiled. 'Good evening, Mrs Jenkins, are you two hoping to take part in the festivities?'

'I don't know about taking part, it's more a case of watching what is going on,' Wynne told him.

'Then I'd better show you the best place to be when midnight chimes. What about having a hot drink first, though, to keep out the cold?'

He took them a little further along the street to where a vendor had set up a stall and was serving cups of hot Bovril, cocoa or tea at a penny a cup.

Fern and her mother decided to have cocoa but Glanmor had Bovril and he insisted on paying for all the drinks.

'I'm a working man now,' he said, grinning when they protested.

'Are you enjoying your job?' Fern asked. 'Maria Roberts told me it was at the same place as where you've been working on Saturdays.'

'That's right, only now that I'm working there full-time it's quite a bit different. Far more responsibility. Fortunately, I know a lot about the business and what is expected of me because I've watched how things are done ever since I started working there.'

By the time they'd finished their cocoa the streets were so packed that they were being jostled on all sides. Glanmor insisted on walking between them so that they could each take his arm if they felt they needed to do.

'Where's your mam then, Glanmor, is she working tonight or doesn't she like crowds like this?' Wynne asked.

'She's working but she'll be coming to the Pier Head so I'll be looking out for her.'

'You'll never spot her in this crowd,' Fern gasped.

'I will, she knows exactly where I'll be and I know precisely what time she'll be turning up.'

Skilfully he guided them through the throng, edging them ever closer to the railings at the Pier Head.

'This is one of the best places to be tonight,' he assured them, looking up at the Pier Head clock tower. 'My mam will be here in five minutes.'

'Well, thank you for bringing us here, Glanmor. We'll be all right now if you want to go,' Wynne told him.

'Go?' He looked at her questioningly. 'Don't you want to meet my mam, then?'

'We'd love to, but I thought you mightn't want that,' Wynne said quickly. 'We're strangers, after all.'

'I've told her so much about you that you won't be like strangers,' he assured them. 'Probably more like old friends.'

Alwyn Williams was a tall, well-built woman in her mid-thirties with fair hair and very clear blue eyes. She arrived at the Pier Head a few minutes before midnight and seemed to have no difficulty at all in finding Glanmor even though by now the crowd was quite dense.

Although her clothes were shabby she walked proudly and the hard, direct stare she gave them both when Glanmor introduced them left Fern feeling uneasy.

'It's nice to meet you, Mrs Williams, Glanmor has been so kind to my daughter,' Wynne told her.

'It's Miss Williams, but do call me Alwyn,' Glanmor's mother told her crisply.

'Oh, I'm sorry,' Wynne said in confusion. 'Very well, then, if I call you Alwyn, perhaps you'd better call me Wynne.'

'Wynne. Wynne Jenkins, isn't it? Will that be Mrs Wynne Jenkins?'

'Yes, that's right.'

96

Alwyn laid such emphasis on the name Jenkins that Wynne felt bemused and wondered why. It was almost as if she hated the name.

'We've only recently moved to Cardiff from Blaenafon,' Wynne explained. 'My husband Cradock was killed in a pit explosion and right away the pit owners turned us out of our home. We had nowhere to go so we decided to come to Cardiff and stay with my husband's brother, Bryson Jenkins. He lives in Angelina Street. Perhaps you know him?' she asked tentatively.

'Oh yes, I know Bryson Jenkins. Indeed I do,' Alwyn said curtly. 'I never knew that he had a brother or a niece either, for that matter,' she added, nodding in Fern's direction.

'I think they fell out or something. I hadn't seen sight or sound of Bryson for years and then he turned up at Cradock's funeral. Surprise, it was, I can tell you. In fact, when he offered to help, I sent him packing. In the end, though, I had to swallow my pride and ask him if I could move in with him. It's only temporary, mind you. Fern will be leaving school soon and once she starts earning regular money, we hope to move into a place of our own. I like to be independent, if you know what I mean.'

'Oh, I know what you mean all right. I'm sorry to hear about your husband, cariad. Sad old world, isn't it?'

'I lost my son as well. Just a few months before the war ended. He wasn't much older than your Glanmor.'

'A pit explosion?'

'No, he was in the army, killed in action over there in France. A sad day for us, I can tell you.'

'So coming down here to Cardiff is a new start for the two of you,' Alwyn said and her tone was far friendlier than it had been before.

'Yes, that's true and no mistake,' Wynne agreed. 'All these crowds and so much noise are all new to us,' she went on. 'I don't think I've ever seen so many people gathered in one place before to celebrate the new year,' she added with a nervous laugh.

'Wait until midnight and then you'll hear some real noise,' Glanmor told them. 'Come on; let's make sure we are standing in a good spot while we can. There are only a few seconds to go now until midnight.'

As Glanmor had warned, on the stroke of twelve the noise became absolutely deafening as the ships' hooters and foghorns all sounded to mark the start of the new year.

Fern found herself covering her ears with her hands, especially when the trams waiting at the pier head also clanged their bells and motor cars in the area sounded their horns.

To add to the general cacophony the crowd began singing at the tops of their voices; some sang in Welsh and others in English and the outpourings clashed and blended on the night air like some gigantic choir.

Strangers of all nationalities were shaking hands and uttering fervent wishes for a 'Happy

New Year' while close friends and neighbours were kissing and slapping each other on the back.

Although there were a number of men who were disabled by war injuries amongst the crowd, as well as many with sad memories, they all seemed to be optimistic about the future now that the war was finally over.

Fern felt bewildered by it all and very thankful indeed that Glanmor was there with them. She knew it would be a night she would remember for ever and she wished her brother Barri could have been there at their side as well. He'd only been a few years older than Glanmor and it saddened her to think that she would never see him again.

She saw her mother surreptitiously wipe away her tears and knew she was probably thinking the same thing. The events of 1918 had changed their lives so much, and not for the better; 1919 must surely mark an improvement, Fern thought hopefully.

Suddenly the excitement was gone from the evening. She wanted to go home and curl up snug and warm in bed where she'd feel safe, and before she drifted off to sleep she would think about all the good things that she hoped the new year would bring.

The new year did bring changes and also a great many surprises. Frequently, when Fern finished working for Maria on a Saturday, she found

Glanmor was waiting to walk her home and usually he suggested that they should meet up somewhere and go for a walk the next day because although he was now working full-time he didn't work on Sundays.

Towards the end of January, because it was so cold and wet, he suggested that perhaps Fern would like to bring her mother round to their house for a cup of tea on Sunday afternoon.

'Does your mam know you are going to ask us?' Fern asked hesitantly.

'Of course she does. It was her idea. If it's a nice day, then we can go off on our own for a walk and leave them together; otherwise we can stay in and have tea with them.'

The arrangement worked so well that it became a regular outing on Sundays and one they all looked forward to.

Alwyn Williams admitted that she didn't make friends easily and added, almost as a warning, that it was because she wasn't prepared to talk about her private life.

Glanmor had already told Fern that his mother enjoyed Wynne's company because she didn't try and pry into her background but accepted her for who she was.

Nevertheless, sometimes when they were making their way home after visiting Glanmor and Alwyn, Wynne would wonder if Alwyn had ever been married.

'She never mentions her husband and it's so strange that she still uses her maiden name.'

'She doesn't wear a wedding ring either, so perhaps he's dead,' Fern said dismissively.

'You may be right but I'm puzzled as to why Glanmor is called Williams which is her maiden name.'

'Perhaps she has never been married,' Fern pointed out. 'That might be the reason she doesn't want to talk about her past.'

'You could be right,' Wynne agreed. 'Anyway, she's a very nice woman and I enjoy her company. She certainly likes to keep herself to herself. She won't even come round to our place for a cup of tea but insists that we go there.'

'Does she know Uncle Bryson?'

'Well, she appears to. Perhaps it is Bertha she doesn't like, although she never mentions her name.'

'I think it is probably better to say nothing but simply accept her hospitality,' Fern said, squeezing her mother's arm affectionately. 'You enjoy going there and I certainly like the opportunity of seeing Glanmor every Sunday. I think he's one of the nicest chaps I've ever met.'

'Oh he's that all right and he's good-looking and well mannered. You couldn't have made a better friend,' her mother agreed.

Chapter Nine

Fern found that it was very difficult to settle to lessons during her last term at school. Learning pieces of poetry, writing essays and even doing sums seemed to be pointless when she was about to leave school and would have to start work.

Sometimes it seemed to her that Easter would never arrive. Then, the next minute, she was worrying that it was only a few weeks away and that she had no idea about what she was going to do when she did leave.

She would have to find a job and she knew that her mother didn't want her to go into a factory. Although Wynne was still working at Curran's, she didn't like it there. The hours were long and she hated not only what she was doing but also the noise and the people she worked with.

Fern was still helping Maria with selling flowers at the railway station but she didn't think that there was enough trade to enable Maria to employ her full-time. Weekends were different; Maria was always quite busy on Friday nights because many of the men had just received their weekly pay packet and liked to take a bunch of flowers home to their wives. It was much the same on Saturday; young boyos going off to meet their girlfriends would buy a posy of violets or a bunch of flowers to give them.

Finally, because she was so worried about her future, Fern mentioned the matter to Glanmor when they were out for a walk one Sunday afternoon.

'Have you told Maria yet that you are leaving school at Easter?' he probed.

'I think I've mentioned it once or twice when we've been talking,' Fern admitted.

'So did you tell her that you'd like to work for her full-time?'

Fern shook her head. 'I didn't see any point in doing that because she's always saying that she doesn't do all that much trade during the week.'

'Not at the railway station pitch, perhaps, but she might have other ideas,' he said laconically, kicking a discarded cigarette pack off the pavement into the gutter.

Fern looked startled. 'Do you know something that I don't?' she asked, looking at him sideways.

'No, not really; just some gossip I overheard.'

'Go on, then, tell me what it is.'

Glanmor shrugged his shoulders dismissively. 'I think you should mention to Maria that you'll be finishing school in a couple of weeks and that you would like to work on a flower stall.'

'I don't like to do that,' Fern said reluctantly.

'Why ever not?' Glanmor looked at her in astonishment.

'I don't know, really,' Fern admitted. 'She's always so busy,' she added lamely.

'You should do; speak to her about it this weekend,' Glanmor insisted firmly.

When he came to meet her the following Saturday, the first thing he did was ask her if she'd told Maria that she would be leaving school in a couple of weeks' time.

'Yes,' Fern told him, smiling broadly, 'and guess what? She's said I can work for her full-time. It won't be outside the railway station but on a stall in the Hayes,' she added excitedly.

'There you are, then, think of all the worry you would have saved yourself if you'd asked her ages ago if there was any possibility of her employing you full-time.'

'Maria said that she will still keep her pitch at the station so that means I will be on my own at the Hayes most of the time. She'll come to the stall on and off during the day to make sure I am all right.'

'That sounds like a first-class arrangement,' Glanmor agreed.

'Maria said that the stallholders there are all very friendly so if I do have any trouble with an awkward customer, I've only got to call one of them over and they'll sort things out.'

'Yes, I'm sure they'll watch out for you.'

'It seems that she's already made all the arrangements to open the stall on Easter

Saturday. I hope I'm going to be able to do it and not let her down,' she added anxiously.

'You'll be the perfect businesswoman,' Glanmor said teasingly. He took her hand and squeezed it affectionately. 'I'm proud of you. Maria must think you are capable of running it or she wouldn't have planned it all.'

'I can't wait to get home and tell my mam,' Fern exclaimed. 'She's going to be so pleased. I'll be earning a proper wage so it means we can really start planning to move away from Angelina Street.'

Wynne was highly delighted by the news when Fern told her. 'Tell Maria that as soon as we move into a place of our own we'll invite her round,' she said, beaming.

'Oh, I'm not too sure if I should do that,' Fern said hesitantly. 'She is my boss, you know. I'll ask Glanmor what he thinks. Perhaps we could have a real celebration,' she added quickly as she saw the look of disappointment on her mother's face, 'and invite him and his mother to come as well,' she added optimistically.

'I'm renting the stall in the Hayes from the Quarter Day,' Maria told her, 'so that means there will be less than a month to have it up and running if it is to be ready for trading on Easter Saturday.'

Fern started working at the Hayes the same day as she left school. Maria introduced her to some of the other stallholders and told her which ones she could call on for help if she needed it.

'They'll also keep an eye on the stall for you if you need to leave it unattended for a few minutes,' Maria told her.

As well as selling cut flowers Maria wanted to extend the range to include ferns, aspidistras and flowering plants that were already growing in pots.

'We won't have too many to start off with until we see if there is any call for them,' she told Fern. 'You must remember to water them two or three times a week, the moment the soil starts to look dry, otherwise they will droop and no one will want to buy them.'

Fern felt that her head was bursting with all the instructions Maria had given her but it was all so exciting that she was determined to remember everything.

She felt very nervous when they opened on Easter Saturday and after making sure she knew what to do, Maria left her to get on with things on her own. Fern kept telling herself that it was really no different from selling outside the station, only this time, instead of a tray of posies, she had a whole stall full of plants and flowers.

To her delight business was brisk. Because it was Easter a lot of people were buying flowers for their own homes, others wanted them to take to friends and several people wanted flowers to take to the cemetery to put on the graves of their departed loved ones.

Since most of her regular customers were on holiday Maria spent much of the day with her and, to Fern's relief, took charge of the money. When they finally closed, Maria was more than pleased with the way things had gone. Tired though she was Fern felt as though she was walking on air by the time Glanmor came to see how she'd got on and to walk her home.

'Don't expect to be as busy as that all the time,' he warned. 'It's a special weekend for one thing, and for another, a flower stall at the Hayes is a bit of a novelty.'

'I hope I won't be,' Fern sighed. 'I've never felt so tired in my life as I do at this moment.'

'Never mind, you've got all day tomorrow to rest and again on Monday because Maria won't open the stall on a bank holiday. I was thinking that perhaps we go out somewhere special but of course if you're too tired to do so I quite understand,' he added.

'I'll probably feel as right as rain after a good night's sleep,' she told him with a smile.

'I thought that if we arranged to meet at about half past ten, then we could go out somewhere on our own. Tell your mother to go round to my mam's in the afternoon and then we'll go back there for tea. How does that sound to you?'

'Well,' Fern said hesitantly. 'I'm pretty sure that my mam was looking forward to us spending the day together, so what about if we all go out somewhere?'

Glanmor gave a silent whistle. 'Do you think that's a good idea?' He frowned.

'Yes, I really do,' Fern insisted. 'I'm sure your mam would love it. All she ever does is work at the Seaman's Mission and then come home and wait on you,' she added giving him a cheeky glance.

'If that's what you want to do, then it's fine by me. Perhaps we could take the train to Penarth or something. I'll ask my mam to make up some sandwiches and we can sit by the seafront and eat them.'

'Great; we'll bring some cakes or something and we can all share them and have a lovely picnic,' Fern enthused.

'Yes, and then we can leave the two of them to sit and talk to each other while we go for a walk on our own.'

'That sounds perfect.'

'Right, that's the plan, then. You both come round about half past ten, and I'll make sure we're ready.'

When Fern appeared next morning she was on her own and she explained that she wasn't going to be able to go out for the day because her mother wasn't at all well.

'I heard what you said, cariad, but what's the matter with her?' Alwyn asked as she followed Glanmor to the door.

'I don't know, she says she aches all over and she's so cold that she can't stop shivering, yet her forehead is burning hot. She insisted I come and let you know how sorry she is that we can't come. I've left her huddled under the bedclothes trying to get warm.'

'Well, you hurry back home, cariad, and make her a hot drink.' Alwyn advised.

'I asked Bertha to listen for her in case she called out and Bertha said she thought it might be the three-day flu that Mam's got,' Fern went on worriedly.

'Oh, don't say that,' Alwyn gasped. 'I thought the epidemic was supposed to be over.'

'Bryson said there's a second wave of it. This time it only lasts three days, but it is even worse.'

'It sounds to me, from the state your mother's in, as though Bertha might be right.' Alwyn agreed, 'so I certainly think you should call a doctor.'

'Would you like me to go for the doctor so that you can get back home?' Glanmor suggested.

The doctor confirmed their worst fears; it was the flu and there was very little he could do for Wynne. Fern sat up with her all night, repeatedly bathing her face and forehead and spooning tepid water on to her parched lips.

By next morning Wynne was delirious and Fern was so frightened that she even asked her uncle to come and see if there was anything he could do to help.

'You stay well away from that room,' Bertha told him, wagging her forefinger at him in warning. 'The last thing we want is for one of us catching the flu, and if you go anywhere near either of them then the chances are we will.'

Bryson nodded in agreement. 'It seems to be very easy to catch and there's no cure, so there's no point in taking silly risks,' he agreed.

'I don't want you coming down here into my kitchen either,' Bertha told Fern. 'I'll put some food and stuff out on the stairs for you and you can take it back upstairs to your own room and eat it. Like I've said, if you get too near to one of us, then we might end up with the flu so make sure you stay well away from us.'

Fern felt too worried about leaving her mother alone to stand there and argue with them or even to tell them how heartless she thought they both were.

When she went back into the bedroom her mother didn't seem to be aware of anything and she didn't respond at all when she spoke to her or touched her. She didn't even appear to be breathing.

In desperation, Fern called down to Bryson and asked him if he would go and fetch the doctor again.

'Duw anwyl, girl, there's no point in wasting money doing that again. We've already told you there's no cure for this flu.'

'Perhaps it isn't flu,' Fern screamed back at him. 'She's not moving at all and she is having difficulty in breathing. She needs a doctor,' she sobbed.

Despite Bertha's loud protest that he wasn't to go up there, Bryson pushed her to one side and bounded up the stairs. He took a long hard look at Wynne and shook his head. 'I think she's dead, cariad,' he said in a hoarse whisper.

'No, she's not ... of course she's not,' Fern sobbed.

'I'll fetch the doctor,' he muttered, elbowing her to one side and taking the stairs two at a time.

Fern insisted on staying at her mother's side, stroking her hand and begging her to wake up, oblivious of the fact that there was no response from Wynne.

When the doctor arrived a few minutes later, he ordered them to send for an ambulance.

'She's not dead,' he told Fern, 'but she needs to be in hospital if she is to pull through.'

When the ambulance arrived Fern begged them to let her go with her mother.

'There's nothing at all you can do to help so it would be much better if you stayed here away from it all,' one of the ambulance men told her gruffly.

When she insisted, they finally agreed to let her ride in the ambulance but the moment they reached the Royal Infirmary in Newport Road her mother was whisked away to an isolation ward. They refused to let Fern see her and she was told that it was pointless to wait, so she might as well go home.

Wearily she made her way back to Tiger Bay,

not to Angelina Street, but to see if either Alwyn or Glanmor were at home.

Alwyn was there and she was shocked when she saw how pale Fern looked.

'You come and sit down while I make you a cup of tea and find you something to eat. We don't want you going down with the flu as well and you look absolutely all in, my lovely.'

Alwyn listened in sympathetic silence as Fern related all that had happened at the hospital and she immediately offered to go back there with her.

'Come on, we'll both come with you; we might be able to find out if there's any news and be able to persuade them to let you see her.'

When they reached the infirmary they were told to wait and it was almost an hour before a sister in a dark blue uniform came to speak to them.

'I'm sorry to tell you that Mrs Wynne Jenkins died shortly after she was admitted,' she informed them. 'I need details for my records, so I'd like you to answer a few questions before you leave.'

Chapter Ten

Fern was distraught and at first refused to believe that her mother was dead. She was shaking so much that Glanmor insisted that she must sit down and he would get her a drink of water.

'I don't want a drink of water, I want my mam,' she sobbed, clinging to him as if he was a lifeline.

He hugged her close, stroking her hair back from her tear-stained face as he tried to comfort her. Then he gently released her and sat her down on a bench by the wall. Patting her shoulder he went to get her a glass of water.

When he returned he handed her two small white pills. 'Take these, the sister said they will make you feel better,' he told her.

'Nothing will make me feel any better,' she sniffed.

Glanmor said nothing. He waited until she had taken the pills and her harsh sobs had eased. Placing a finger beneath her chin he clumsily wiped away her tears.

'There, that's better now, isn't it? Do you want to sit still for a bit and give those pills a chance to do their work or would you like me to take you home right now?'

Fern hesitated, looking at him in wide-eyed disbelief. 'You mean go home and leave my mam here?'

'I'm afraid that's what we are going to have to do, cariad,' he said sadly.

'We can't. Not until I've seen her and said goodbye. I'm not even sure that she's dead yet.'

'I don't think they will let you see her,' Glanmor told her.

'Why not?'

'If it was flu, then there's the chance that you might catch it,' Glanmor explained.

'I don't care about that, I want to see her,' Fern insisted.

When they approached the reception desk and asked if it was possible, the woman shook her head. 'That's out of the question,' she said sharply.

'Are you sure?' Fern persisted. 'I haven't had a chance to say goodbye to her.'

The woman frowned. 'What did you say her name was?'

'Jenkins; Wynne Jenkins,' Glanmor told her.

The woman scanned the admissions list and then looked up in disbelief. 'You mean the woman who was admitted with influenza and who has since died?' she asked in surprise.

'Yes, that's my mam,' Fern said quickly.

'No, you most certainly can't see her. Her body will have been taken to an isolation bay in the morgue by now and no one at all is allowed to go near it.'

'How do I know she is dead, if I can't see her body?' Fern sniffed miserably.

'I'm sorry, my lovely,' the woman explained in a voice full of compassion, 'but this flu is a killer. We were all hoping that the epidemic was over but this new lot, the three-day flu, as they're calling it, is so deadly that those who are brought in here suffering from it are isolated right away. We wouldn't want to take the risk of you catching it now, would we?' she added gently. Looking directly at Glanmor she advised, 'Take her on home. Those pills will help her to sleep and things may seem better when she wakes up tomorrow.'

Glanmor nodded and, putting an arm round Fern's shoulders, led her towards the door.

For the next few days Fern remained in a daze as though unable to accept what had happened. Glanmor went to see Maria and let her know what had happened and he and Alwyn did what they could to help Fern. Between them they made arrangements for the funeral. Bertha and Bryson gave no help at all; the only thing that Bertha seemed to be concerned about was whether or not Fern would be able to afford the rent now that she had only her own wages to rely on.

Fern ignored her constant carping.

'Are you deaf or daft?' Bertha shouted. She stood with her arms akimbo, her sullen face angry. 'You're not listening to a word I say. If you can't afford to pay the rent, then you'd better find somewhere else to live. Do you understand?' she added in a threatening tone.

'I've heard what you are saying,' Fern said quietly. She looked at her uncle. 'I've no money this week, but I'll be back on the stall next week, so I will pay back what I owe you as soon as I can.'

He said nothing, merely nodding with a sly grin on his face as if he knew she was heading for trouble.

The funeral was a few days later as the hospital were anxious for the burial to occur as soon as possible for fear of infection causing further outbreaks. The epidemic was subsiding but those who went down with it now seemed to develop three days of severe illness and very few of them survived.

Fern returned to the Hayes the day after the funeral. Maria was surprised to see her there but when she suggested that Fern might like to have a few days off to get over things, Fern was adamant that she was better off at work than staying at home.

'No! My moping around won't bring my mam back,' she said sadly, 'so I may as well be here working on the stall and thinking about other things.'

'True enough, my lovely,' Maria sighed. 'It's hard for a young girl like you to be left all alone in the world, though.'

'I've got you,' Fern said and her words brought a slow smile to the older woman's face.

'Yes, I'll do what I can for you, so if you've any problems, then tell me,' she added as she sorted out some of the flowers and rearranged them on the stall. 'You've got Glanmor as well,' she added quietly. 'He's been terribly worried about you, you know.'

'He's been a wonderful help.' Fern sighed. 'He must think I'm a right misery.'

'No, cariad, young though he is, I'm sure he understands what you are going through.'

'Has he lost his father?' Fern asked, her voice laced with curiosity.

Maria's lips tightened. She snipped the ends off a bunch of roses before she answered. 'Yes, I suppose you could say that,' she agreed.

Fern waited for her to explain but when it was obvious she had no intention of doing so, she sighed and picked up the off-cuts that were strewn on the stall from Maria's clippings and put them into the waste bin that they kept under the counter and which was half full of leaves and dead flowers.

'I'll take these and empty them, shall I?' It was more a statement than a question and, without waiting for a reply, she picked up the refuse bag, tied the opening with a piece of twine, and took it across to the large receptacle on the far side of the market that was kept there for rubbish.

As she returned several stallholders stopped her and said a few kindly words and by the time she was back at her own stall she felt calm and comforted.

Her day was reasonably busy so she had little time for her thoughts and by the time Glanmor came to walk her home that night, she was much more her old self.

'I'm glad I came to work,' she told him as they walked down Bute Street together. 'People have been so kind and understanding, so very different from Bertha and Uncle Bryson.'

'Oh, what have those two been saying? Not something that's upset you, I hope,' he said sharply, his handsome face darkening.

'Not really. Bertha has been ranting on about whether or not I'm going to be able to afford the rent for my room.'

'Can you?' He shot her a sideways glance.

'I think so, if I am very careful. I told Uncle Bryson that I wouldn't be able to pay for last week but that I'd make it up as soon as I could.'

'And was that all right?'

'He didn't say anything, so I suppose he accepted it.'

'Surely, under the circumstances he could have let you off paying for a week,' he muttered angrily.

'I think he might have done so but Bertha was listening.'

'Well, if you have any trouble with them about it let me know,' Glanmor told her as they reached the corner of Angelina Street and stopped to say goodbye. 'Are you sure you wouldn't rather come round and have a meal with us tonight?'

'It's kind of you to suggest it, Glanmor, but

your mam fed me all last week so it's time I tried to get back to normal. Going to work today was a good start.'

'You only eat like a bird.' He grinned. 'I don't think Mam would mind for one minute.'

Fern found that the nights were the worst. Having to sleep on her own when she'd become used to having her mother alongside her was so lonely. It made her realise afresh that her mam was gone and that she would never ever be there again.

They'd enjoyed their nightly chats, going over what had happened to them during the day, telling each other anecdotes about what had happened while they'd been apart.

It was the time, too, when they planned what they were going to do in the future. Now that Fern had started work their hopes had soared. By scrimping and saving they were both optimistic that it wouldn't be very long before they could afford their own place.

Fern wondered where her mother had hidden their savings. The room was so small that there weren't very many places to look, but so far she still hadn't managed to find them.

It did cross her mind that perhaps either Bertha or Bryson had already done so. There was no way of locking the door when she went out, so either of them could have come in at any time and searched the room if they wished to do so.

On the Saturday evening when she came home from work, Bryson was waiting in her room for the rent and money for her keep.

'I was hoping that you might say it was less than ten shillings because you have only me to feed now,' she told him boldly, her dark eyes meeting his.

'Growing up to be a proper little business-woman, aren't you?' he jested. 'Not only pretty but also hard headed as well.'

When she didn't answer he went on, 'I suppose you'd also like me to say never mind about the back money you owe,' he said with a broad smirk on his face.

She waited in silence, not knowing what to say. Of course she wanted him to let her off the rent she owed, but his manner frightened her and she had a feeling that he was going to demand something in return.

'Well, perhaps we could do that and start afresh from now and even make it a bit less each week – that is, if you were prepared to pay part of it in kind,' he added his dark eyes glittering.

'In kind?' She frowned. 'I don't understand what you mean by that. If you are saying that you want me to help with the housework, well, I already wash up after we've had our evening meal and by the number of dirty dishes there are, I think Bertha must store them up all day,' she added.

'What I had in mind has nothing to do with

Bertha or the washing-up,' he said quickly. His hand reached out and stroked her cheek. 'I mean in other ways, cariad.'

She pulled back and slapped his hand away sharply. 'I don't know what you mean.'

'I think you do.' His voice had softened and his hand went out again, this time not to touch her face but to stroke from her shoulder down her back to her waist.

As she made to move away he grabbed hold of her, pulling her very close. Her heart was thudding with fear as his mouth came down on hers, stifling her scream.

Savagely he began tearing at the front of her dress and fondling her breasts. As she struggled and fought to get away he pushed her backwards, kicked the door shut and then forced her backwards on to the bed.

As his hand moved up under her skirt she brought her knee up sharply, catching him unawares. With a raucous groan he doubled up in agony. She seized the moment to break free and was out of the room and down the stairs before he could recover from the pain she'd inflicted on him.

Without a coat, her hair flying, and oblivious that her dress was torn right down the front, she ran as fast as she could to find refuge at Glanmor and Alwyn's house.

She was so breathless when she got there that she couldn't speak as she broke into the room where they were having their evening meal.

Glanmor pushed back his chair and caught her as she collapsed against him.

'What's happened, cariad? Look at the state you are in! Who was it that attacked you?' he asked in a strained voice.

By now her sobs and tears muffled what she was trying to say. Alwyn poured her out a cup of tea from the pot standing on the table but Fern was crying so desperately that she couldn't control her sobs long enough to drink it. All the time she was clinging on to Glanmor as if she was afraid he might leave her.

Alwyn fetched a wet flannel and bathed Fern's face, mopping away her tears at the same time. She gave an exclamation of dismay as she saw the deep cut to one side of Fern's mouth and the bruising on her cheek.

'That looks very sore indeed,' she murmured. 'I'll put some salve on it right away and take another look at it in the morning because you may need to go to the hospital and have a stitch in it.'

'No, not if you put some ointment on it,' Fern gabbled. 'I never want to go back to that place ever again.'

Glanmor wanted to go round to Angelina Street and sort Bryson out there and then but his mother would have none if it.

'Don't be so daft,' she said scornfully. 'You're a mere boy and he'd make mincemeat of you. He's got fists on him like sledge hammers. No,' she went on more quietly, 'there's no call for fighting, there're better ways of doing things than that.'

'Like what?' Glanmor mumbled, his face red with anger. 'He shouldn't be allowed to get away with behaving like that.'

'Well, for a start, Fern must stay here with us. It would be far too dangerous now for her to go back there.'

'That's kind of you, Alwyn, but we both know that you haven't room for me here,' Fern pointed out. She scrubbed at her face as tears welled up again in her eyes. 'Anyway, all my things are at my uncle's place; all my clothes and everything,' she added forlornly.

'Glanmor can go with you and collect those when you know that Bryson and Bertha will both be out,' Alwyn told her.

'I won't know when that will be, though,' Fern pointed out worriedly. 'He hasn't got a job, remember.'

'I know that, but he and Bertha will both be out later tonight; they always go to the boozer on a Saturday night,' Alwyn announced.

'It's very kind of you both but even if we do manage to collect my things from Angelina Street, there still isn't room for me here,' Fern argued, looking around the crowded room that was both their living room and kitchen.

'We'll manage. We've been doing so for almost a week now, haven't we?' Alwyn told her.

'Yes, but what about at night?'

'You can stay in Glanmor's little room and he

can sleep down here. That's all right with you, isn't it, boyo?' she said turning to Glanmor for confirmation.

'I'll go along with whatever you say, Mam, as long as it means Fern is safe and doesn't have to go back there.'

'There you are, cariad,' Alwyn told her triumphantly. 'Now, don't argue any more; it's all settled. It's not safe for you to go back to Angelina Street again, except to collect your belongings, and you won't be doing that on your own.'

'Once we've collected your stuff your worries are over,' Glanmor assured her, 'and you needn't worry about a thing. Bryson Jenkins will never come looking for you here, will he Mam?' he added with a bitter laugh.

Fern wasn't so sure and she couldn't understand why they could both be so positive that Bryson wouldn't come looking for her and make her go back with him. Her head was throbbing and she felt so frightened by what had happened that she decided the best thing to do was to accept what Alwyn said without any argument.

So many things had happened to change her life in the last couple of weeks that she felt as if it was impossible to think clearly or make any decisions for herself.

Chapter Eleven

As the weeks rapidly drifted into months, Fern found that all her interest was being channelled into what went on when she was at work.

The market at the Hayes was a world in itself and she loved working there. She enjoyed the company and camaraderie of the other stall-holders and was fascinated by the variety of goods that they sold. Every possible need seemed to be catered for, from fruit and vegetables to toys, from second-hand clothing to ironmongery.

She took a great pride in her own stall and her enthusiasm for flowers increased daily. As the seasons changed so did the variety of flowers there were available. Maria had not only considerably widened the range of flowers she bought when she went to market but she now also stocked a wide variety of pot plants and decorative ferns. With every delivery they received there seemed to be something new and Fern took a keen interest in learning their names as well as how to look after them.

Maria was full of praise for her industriousness and left her more and more to her own devices when it came to arranging the displays on the stand. Twice that year she raised Fern's wages and when Christmas came she gave her a bonus that left Fern wide-eyed with delight.

Fern had very little time for doing anything other than work and going out with Glanmor. After paying Alwyn for her rent and food and buying some new clothes either because she had outgrown her existing ones or because she needed something more suitable for working on the stall than those she had worn to school, she was able to save some of her wages each week.

There was only one disappointment in her life the following year, and that was that she saw less and less of Glanmor because he had changed his job and was now working shifts in a factory. Sometimes she didn't see him for days at a time and it left a gap in her life. She had always looked forward to his meeting her after work.

Now, more often than not, he had already gone to work when she arrived home at night and in the morning, even if he was at home, there was no time to talk because she had to get to work. As a result, she spent a great deal of time with Alwyn who fussed over her as if she was her own daughter.

One bitterly cold evening in March when they were sitting on either side of the fire, enjoying a cup of hot cocoa before going to bed, Alwyn startled her by asking her if she was happy living with them.

'Of course I am. You've been like a second

mother to me,' she told her with a warm smile. 'Mind you,' she went on, when Alwyn remained silent, 'I think that it probably is time I found a room of my own. I feel so guilty about Glanmor having to sleep down here on the couch while I'm tucked up snug in his bed.'

'There's no need for you to worry yourself over that,' Alwyn told her quickly. 'These days, he doesn't always sleep down here. It depends what shift he's on. When he's here sleeping during the day he always uses my bed.'

'That's good, but it's not quite the same as having a room of his own though, is it?'

'You can hardly call it a room now, can you?' Alwyn argued. 'It's more like a partitioned-off bit of the landing.'

'It was his, though, and he managed to have some of his own personal things in there as well as his bed. Now all he has is a cupboard down here for his belongings and he has to share that with some of the pots and pans,' Fern pointed out.

'Glanmor doesn't mind, not as long as you are comfortable,' Alwyn said sagely.

'He's been very kind to me ever since I first arrived in Cardiff,' Fern admitted as she took a sip of her cocoa. 'When they bullied me at school he made them stop and it was the same when I moved in here after Uncle Bryson acted so horribly. He took my side. I think he would have gone and given him a good telling off if you hadn't stopped him,' she added with a small laugh.

'Well, he wouldn't have done himself any favours by doing that, I can tell you. If he'd given Bryson any lip, Bryson would have got nasty with him and Glanmor would have been the one who came off worse; I didn't want that happening.'

'No, and you were quite right,' Fern agreed. Staring down into her mug of cocoa she said softly, 'What I couldn't understand was why Glanmor was so sure that my uncle wouldn't come round here. He probably guessed it was where I was.'

There was such a long silence that she looked up enquiringly, but Alwyn avoided her gaze.

'I noticed that you didn't argue with Glanmor when he said it,' she added.

Alwyn drained her cup and put it down on the table before she answered. 'There's something you ought to know, Fern,' she said quietly. 'I've thought about telling you for a long time but I keep saying to myself that it isn't necessary to do so, but as I've watched the way you and Glanmor have grown closer and closer together I've come to the conclusion that it is better that you do know.'

Fern looked puzzled. 'Really? So what is it that you think I should know?'

Alwyn concentrated on pleating the front of her apron as though uncertain how to proceed. 'Glanmor has never said anything to you, then?' she asked, looking up.

'About what?'

Alwyn studied Fern intently for a moment then she said rather abruptly, 'About the fact that he's your cousin.'

'My cousin!' Fern gasped. 'Glanmor's my cousin! How do you make that out?' she asked in a puzzled voice.

'Bryson Jenkins is Glanmor's father.'

Alwyn's words hung on the air. Fern didn't know what to say. It sounded so preposterous that for a minute she couldn't take it in; when she did, she couldn't believe she had heard aright. She'd known Glanmor for almost two years now and yet he'd never breathed a word of this to her.

'Does Glanmor know that we are cousins?' she asked in a puzzled, disbelieving voice.

'We've never talked about it but he's no fool, so I imagine he's worked it out,' Alwyn stated.

'Yes, I suppose so, if he knows that Bryson is his father. Why aren't you all living together?'

Even as she uttered the words she felt a wave of embarrassment and hoped that Alwyn wouldn't think that she was being impertinent. She needed to know, though. The news had shocked her.

She tried to think back as to whether she had ever mentioned Glanmor's name when she'd been living with her uncle and Bertha. Even if she hadn't done so, it was possible her mother might have, so why hadn't her uncle said anything? Or had he mentioned it to her mother and she'd not said anything?

She wondered if Bertha knew. She was sure that if she did, she would have said something. Bertha didn't believe in keeping secrets. Everything they had ever said to her she'd reported to Bryson and most of the things he had said to her about them she had repeated to them.

'You want to know why we aren't living with him,' Alwyn's scornful voice cut through her thoughts. 'We don't talk about it because it's too painful . . .'

'I'm sorry, I shouldn't have asked,' Fern interrupted. 'It's none of my business,' she added quickly.

'No, you're right, cariad, but since I've told you so much I may as well tell you the rest. Leaving you with half a story will only set you wondering. Better to have it all out in the open so that we know where we stand.'

Alwyn reached up on to the mantel shelf above the fireplace and found a packet of Lucky Strike and selected a cigarette from the packet. Fern waited tensely until she had lit the cigarette.

'Glanmor's not a bastard, if that was what you were thinking,' Alwyn said as she blew out a cloud of smoke. 'I met Bryson when he first came to Cardiff and he swept me off my feet with his glib chatter. We married and set up home together in two rooms in Angelina Street; that's where Glanmor was born. Before I had Glanmor I was working and bringing home a good wage packet, most of which went on beer and baccy for Bryson,' she added bitterly.

'When I got pregnant and couldn't work any longer the good times were over and so was all the sweet-talking. Bryson didn't like having to be the bread winner and after Glanmor was born he certainly didn't like having to be a father.

'The minute Glanmor cried for any reason at all Bryson rammed on his cap and left the house. He spent most of the time drinking with his cronies at The Ship and when he came back home at night he was usually in a fighting mood.

'One word amiss and I'd get a back-hander; if his supper wasn't to his liking, he could be even more brutal. In the end I was black and blue all over.

'I stuck it out because of Glanmor but when he was almost five and Bryson started hammering him as well as me I decided that enough was enough.'

'So you upped and left him and took Glanmor with you?' Fern whispered aghast.

'That's right, cariad. We almost starved to death for the first few weeks but Glanmor was big for his years so they let him in at the school and I had a stroke of luck and got a job.'

'The same job as you have now, at the Seaman's Mission?' Fern asked hanging on to every word Alwyn said.

'Yes. It doesn't pay a great deal, but my wages are there every week and we've managed to scrape by,' Alwyn went on, her voice revealing her satisfaction as she let out a billow of smoke.

'Mind you,' she went on, 'Bryson didn't really miss me because that big black bitch moved in with him almost before I was through the door and they've been together ever since. Bryson has never once enquired after Glanmor and as far as I know he's never even spoken to him from that day to this.'

'You've not seen him either?'

'Oh, I've spoken to him a couple of times, but it wasn't very civil on his part.'

'So was that why Glanmor stuck up for me at school?' Fern asked in a shocked voice.

'I don't think he had any idea who you were, not until later on when he walked you home and found out where you lived,' Alwyn said with a dry laugh. 'No, cariad, that's Glanmor all over, championing the underdog. I don't even know how much he remembers of those early days with Bryson,' she added thoughtfully as she took another cigarette from the packet.

'So by right Glanmor should be called Glanmor Jenkins, then?' Fern mused.

'No.' Alwyn's voice was hard and bitter. 'Oh no! Bryson has had nothing to do with bringing Glanmor up, except to cuff him around the ears or pick him up by the arm and throw him across the room whenever he'd had a skinful and Glanmor was in his way. No, I told you I'd spoken to Bryson only a couple of times; the first was to ask him for a divorce, which he agreed to as long as I paid the solicitor's fees and the other was to tell him that I was going to change Glanmor's name to Williams. That was my maiden name and that was what I intended calling myself from then on. It's all been done legally,' she added as she puffed heavily on her cigarette.

'Glanmor's not a bit like Bryson, not in looks or temperament,' Alwyn went on, and there were pride and satisfaction in her voice. 'Glanmor is a Williams through and through. Never a day passes that I don't look at him and see my father and my eldest brother and it's a relief, I can tell you.'

Alwyn stubbed out her half-smoked cigarette and put what remained back into the packet. As she picked up the cups Fern reached out to take them from her. 'I'll wash these up,' she offered. 'I expect there are other things you want to get on with.'

'We'll do them together,' Alwyn said. 'You bring the kettle and we can use the hot water that's left in it,' she added as she preceded Fern into the scullery. 'Now do you understand why I've told you all this?' she persisted as she watched Fern tip some hot water into the tin bowl to wash the cups.

'Well, sort of.' Fern frowned as she added some cold water and swirled it round with her hand.

'Glanmor will be eighteen in a few weeks' time,' Alwyn went on. 'I don't want you getting

133

the wrong idea about him or his feelings just because he's always friendly towards you. Do you understand what I mean?'

Fern stared wide-eyed at Alwyn.

'Look, cariad, you're cousins. I don't think it's a good thing for people who are so closely related to marry each other.'

'Marry! You think that I might want to marry Glanmor?'

'If you get too close to him, you may find you have to,' Alwyn told her with brutal frankness. 'Remember, he's practically a man now and men are lustful. Good boyo that he is, I don't for one minute think he will be any different from all the others when it comes to that sort of thing. Do you get my meaning now?'

'I hear what you are telling me but I can't believe that you think I would let Glanmor, or any other man for that matter, touch me before I am married.'

Alwyn let out a sigh. 'I'm pleased to hear it, even though you'll probably change your mind when the occasion arises; most girls do and that's their downfall. Remember, cariad, that as far as I'm concerned, marriage between the pair of you is out of the question. You and my Glanmor are cousins and even though I'm not religious I don't hold with cousins marrying each other.'

Chapter Twelve

Fern wished that Alwyn had not confided in her. It seemed to place a barrier between herself and Glanmor. Whenever he spoke to her she found herself considering what he had said; going over it in her head to see if there was a double meaning to his words. Even the tone of his voice worried her in case, as Alwyn seemed to think, Glanmor might be getting too fond of her.

Until Alwyn had brought the matter up she had never given any serious thought to how she felt about Glanmor. He was a replacement for the brother she had lost in the trenches; someone near her own age who understood how she thought and acted. The news that he was also her cousin would probably have been comforting. And it would have been, if Alwyn had not gone on to say the things she had about the dangers of cousins marrying.

The easy-going camaraderie that had existed between herself and Glanmor was no more. She worried in case he misinterpreted her friendly manner towards him. When he was at home she spent a lot of time in the tiny box room that had been his bedroom, wondering how she could change things so that he could have it back.

Alwyn's bedroom was not a lot bigger but she wondered if there was room to put another single bed in there so that she could sleep in there and Glanmor could have his room back.

She wasn't sure what Alwyn would think of the suggestion. She toyed with the idea of suggesting a curtain down the middle of the room to divide her bed off from Alwyn's but was afraid that might sound as though she was the one who didn't want to share.

The alternative was to find a room somewhere else but she wasn't sure she was ready to move in with strangers. Up until now Alwyn and Glanmor had been like family, and they were.

Stop being so silly, she told herself, you're fifteen, so of course you can stand on your own two feet. You have a job and you're earning good money, so it's time you were independent; make the effort to find a room and look after yourself.

With this in mind she began counting her savings and looking around in the market to see how much it was going to cost her to buy all the bits and pieces she would need.

It wasn't simply a bed, a table and a couple of chairs; it was so many other things, such as curtains, pots and pans, cups and saucers, sheets and blankets. Even second-hand these all added up to far more than she could afford.

An unfurnished room would probably cost less but it looked as if for the present, there was nothing for it but to take a furnished room or else to go on living where she was even though it made life difficult for Glanmor.

Glanmor Williams felt unsettled. For a start he didn't like having to work shifts in a factory but so far he'd said nothing to his mam because the money was good and it made things at home easier for her. Lately, though, she kept going on about how things would be better if they had a bit more space so that he could have a room of his own. He wished she wouldn't do it in front of Fern because he was sure it was making her feel uncomfortable. He couldn't for the life of him see what was wrong with where they were.

Fair-dos, it had been his idea that Fern should come and live with them but at the time he'd been little more than a kid himself and hadn't realised all the problems it would entail. Not that she was any trouble. She got on well with his mam and he was glad that he'd been able to get her away from Angelina Street and that wicked devil Bryson Jenkins. If she'd gone on living there, heaven alone knows what might have happened to her.

It was just that now they were both older his mam kept going on about them needing a bit of personal space. He wasn't sure if Fern felt the same way or not. The box room that had once been his wasn't big enough to swing a cat round in but then she didn't have all that many personal possessions and at least she could shut the door and be on her own whenever she needed to be.

When he was working nights and needed to sleep during the day he was quite happy to sleep upstairs in his mam's bed out of her way, so why did she have to keep bringing the matter up?

Fern was taking no notice, but he wasn't sure whether it was because she was content with what she'd got or whether she was secretly saving up to move to a place of her own. He wished she would open up and tell them what she was planning to do.

He hated working at the factory and had only taken the job because his mam had said she couldn't manage on the money he was earning. Yet now he was giving her quite a bit more, and so was Fern, if it came to that, but she still wasn't satisfied. He was sure she could manage on it well enough if she wasn't squirrelling so much of it away with the idea of getting a bigger place.

When he was at home during the day, if she was there as well, he kept out of her way as much as possible. When he wasn't sleeping he went down to the Pier Head and watched the boats, like he'd done all his life for as far back as he could remember.

Going to sea was still what he really wanted to do, he reflected. He wanted to sail out over the ocean and visit all those places with strange names that were thousand of miles away.

In a few weeks' time he'd be eighteen, old enough to fulfil his dream; that was if he had the courage to do so. The fact that his mam relied on him so much and that she'd be very upset if he left home worried him. Fern would still be there to keep her company, of course, but would that compensate for his absence?

Fern. The moment she came into his thoughts he had to admit that she was the main reason why he wanted to get away. He had never in his life thought he could have feelings for anyone like those he had for Fern.

He'd noticed her the very first day she'd arrived at Eleanor Street School. When he'd seen the others teasing her he'd stepped in right away because she'd looked so defenceless. At the time he'd no idea that they were related and when he'd discovered that they were cousins, he'd been over the moon. Well, that was until his mother had started going on about it not being right for cousins to marry each other and somehow that had spoiled his friendship with Fern.

He'd still felt very protective towards her and worried about her, but he knew his mother wouldn't approve of them getting too fond of each other.

His new job had made it impossible for him to meet her every night when she finished work and to walk home with her. He'd also made it the excuse for not going out with her at the weekends as much as they used to do.

Whenever they did, whether it was for a walk or to the pictures, he had an overpowering urge to hold her hand, kiss her, cuddle her and tell her how much she meant to him. He was even ready to admit that he loved her.

Only the thought that she might inadvertently tell his mother made him keep his distance. Sometimes, though, when she grabbed his arm, or teased him by giving him one of her special looks from those expressive dark eyes of hers, he would feel his blood rising and he longed to grab hold of her and kiss her.

Perhaps if he went to sea it would be good for both of them. Being parted might break the invisible thread that seemed to keep them so close. If it didn't, if he found that she was still dominating his thoughts night and day even when he was thousands of miles away, and that he couldn't wait to get back home again to be with her, then that would make him reach a decision.

It might take a great deal of courage to defy all his mam's warnings and tell Fern how he felt about her and to ask if she had similar feelings for him. Deep down, he thought he knew what her answer would be.

There again, a long absence would prove whether he was right about that or not. The way she welcomed him when he came back would be answer enough.

His only problem was to find a ship that needed extra crew. At the moment there were so many men who'd come home from the war who were still unable to find work that he supposed he should think himself lucky that he had a job.

He kept turning the matter over in his mind but, as always, it was still unsolved when he drifted off to sleep, and it was still there, dominating his thoughts, when he woke again several hours later.

As soon as he'd had something to eat he went off down to the dockside. This time, he didn't hang around the Pier Head day-dreaming but made his way to where some of the larger ships were berthed and stevedores were busily unloading their cargo.

He spoke to one or two of the men but they completely ignored him. Moodily he perched on one of the bollards, lit a cigarette and contemplated them morosely. He didn't even rouse himself to move away when a middle-aged bearded man dressed in a merchant navy officer's uniform came briskly down the gangplank and walked over to where he was and spoke to him.

'What are you doing hanging around here?' he asked, suspicious. 'Are you looking for work?' he questioned before Glanmor could say a word.

Glanmor shrugged his shoulders. 'Not as a stevedore,' he said dismissively.

'As a deckhand?'

Glanmor looked at him with interest. 'I might be; are you taking on new crew?'

'It's a long trip, not a run round the coast,' the man answered, studying him keenly.

Glanmor felt the excitement mounting inside him. Was this the chance he'd been waiting for, the answer to all his longings as well as his present problems? he wondered.

'How long? Six months, a year?'

'Possibly even longer than that,' the officer replied. 'Perhaps eighteen months. We're setting sail for the Baltic; do you know where that is?'

'You mean you're going to Russia?' Glanmor couldn't hide the surprise or excitement from his voice. He knew that since the end of the war and the revolution in Russia all the ports there had been virtually out of bounds.

'Are you married? I'm not interested in hiring you if you are. I want some new crew with no strings or attachments of any kind. There's good money to be made if you're hard-working and adventurous.'

'Why is it that you have to take on new crew?' Glanmor asked suspiciously. 'Why aren't the men you already have staying with you for your next trip?'

The officer shrugged dismissively. 'This is our third run to the Baltic and back and one of the present crew is homesick. He's a married man and he wants to have a spell ashore with his family and the young baby he's barely seen. That decision is up to him, of course, but it's the reason why I'm looking to replace him with a young chap like you who has no family responsibilities. I'm Captain Mulligan, by the way, the master of this ship.'

'A year to eighteen months, that's a long time to be away from home,' Glanmor muttered doubtfully. He studied the ship. 'The *Saturn*. I've never heard of her and I know most of the ships that come into Cardiff,' he said dubiously.

'You need only sign on for one trip,' Captain Mulligan went on, 'that gives me a chance to see if you are made of the right stuff. We sail on the tide tomorrow night.'

Glanmor desperately wanted to go but the thought of leaving Fern behind, of not seeing her for almost a year and a half was a tremendous deterrent. The other problem was telling his mother that he was going to sea because he knew it was something she didn't want him to do.

'Wait there and I'll fetch the papers you have to sign,' Captain Mulligan told him.

Glanmor studied the long, slim shape of the SS *Saturn* more closely. It was a fine-looking vessel and, judging from the amount of cargo being unloaded on the dockside, it had a good reputation. If they were sailing on the next day's high tide, then he had to decide quickly.

Could he afford to forgo such a wonderful opportunity? he asked himself.

There would be no time for long, drawn-out farewells; no time to listen to his mother pleading with him to change his mind. He need never go back into the factory again.

Chapter Thirteen

Fern was heartbroken and Alwyn was extremely angry when Glanmor arrived home and told them excitedly about his chance meeting with Captain Mulligan, announcing that he was going to sea and would be leaving home that very night.

'Going to sea! Are you out of your mind, boyo?' Alwyn said in a furious voice. 'Whatever's put that notion into your head? You've got a good job, a comfortable home and money enough in your pocket, what more do you want?'

'I want to have some real adventure; I want to get away and see something of the great wide world before I settle down,' Glanmor said defensively.

'Settle down!' Alwyn's voice rose higher and higher and her eyes gleamed with anger. 'Duw anwyl, boyo, what on earth are you talking about? Settle down? What the hell do you want to settle down for at your age?'

'I don't. That's what I'm trying to tell you, Mam. I want to get out and see the world.'

'Why all the hurry, boyo? You haven't gone and got some girl into trouble, have you?' she questioned angrily.

'Of course not, mam!' His face flamed. 'I want to get away and do something else, though. I don't want to be stuck in a dead-end job in a factory all the days of my life.'

'I suppose if the war was still on, then you'd have been one of those headstrong young fools who'd have rushed to sign up and then volunteered to go overseas to the Front even before they sent you there,' Alwyn stated scathingly.

'No, Mam, but you know I've always wanted to go to sea and this is my big chance,' he retorted belligerently. 'Meeting up with Captain Mulligan today and his offering to take me on as a deckhand is like a dream come true.'

'I wish that's all it was, a bloody dream!'

'Yes, it does seem like that, Mam; it's what I want, and to have it handed to me on a plate like this is almost too good to be true. It's the chance I've been waiting for; the sort of adventure I've dreamed about all my life.'

'Forget it, boyo. I need you here; you're all I've got.' Her voice was no longer angry but soft and pleading. 'A good Saturday night out with your mates and a few pints inside you is all the adventure you need at your age,' she added.

'It's too late; I've already signed the papers.'

'What papers?' She glared at him, her arms akimbo, with a shocked look on her face.

'I told you, I met Captain Mulligan of the *Saturn* down at the dockside and he's taken me on as a deckhand,' he repeated.

'You never said anything about signing any papers, though,' she gasped.

'Well, I did. I'm officially one of the crew and we sail tonight at high tide.'

'Not if I can help it!' Alwyn said firmly.

'No, Mam, you're wrong. I'm not letting this opportunity pass me by. I'm going to start packing right now because I've not got all that much time left.'

'Where did you say you would be going?' Fern interrupted.

Her intervention eased the tension between Glanmor and his mother.

'I thought I told you, we're going to the Baltic, right to Russia,' he retorted a trifle impatiently. 'I'll be away for at least a year, possibly eighteen months.'

'If you must go to sea, then why couldn't you sign on for short trips; ones that bring you back into port again every couple of months?' Alwyn grumbled.

'This will be far more exciting.' Glanmor's face lit up. 'I've heard about Russia, read about it in the newspapers, but I've never met anyone before who has been there.'

'I've heard about it as well; all about the revolution that's been going on out there,' his mother stated. 'They sound like savages; men killing their neighbours sounds even worse than war between foreign countries.'

'You've got it all wrong, Mam . . .'

'Oh no I haven't. It's a bloodthirsty place and

146

you won't be safe there. I'll be out of my mind worrying about you, afraid you'll be assassinated, the same as their leader, the Tsar, or whatever he's called. Not only him; most of his family were murdered as well, by all accounts.'

'Mam, that has nothing at all to do with shipping. We'll be transporting cargo and once we've unloaded that on the dockside, the ship will be turned round and we'll be heading for home again.'

'Not much point in going all that way if that's all you're going to do when you get there,' Alwyn told him tartly. 'I thought all this talk about adventure and so on was so that you could see these foreign places for yourself.'

Fern tried not to smile. She knew that Alwyn was trying to ridicule what Glanmor was doing but she also understood how much this trip meant to him.

'We're both going to miss you but we'll be looking forward to hearing all about your travels, what you see and the people you meet, when you get home again, Glanmor,' Fern assured him.

'I'll miss you, Fern, but I know you'll take care of my mam for me while I'm gone,' he said with a warm smile.

'That's your job, not hers,' Alwyn reminded him. 'I can't understand what's got into your silly head even to be thinking of doing such a damn silly thing as signing on as a deckhand. Now why don't you get yourself washed and come and sit down and have your meal and forget all this nonsense.'

Glanmor shook his head. 'You're not taking a word of what I'm saying seriously, are you, Mam? I'm leaving tonight.'

'The SS whatever it's called sails at midnight, does it? Well, it will be sailing a man short because you'll be here tucked up safe and sound on the sofa, if I know anything about it.'

'No, Mam. My mind is made up,' Glanmor said firmly. 'It's a great opportunity and I'm not going to miss out on it.'

Alwyn made one last effort. 'Don't be such a young fool, Glanmor,' she pleaded. 'What about your job at the factory? By the time you come home again that will be gone. Some other chap will have taken it and you won't be able to get it back.'

'I don't want that job back. I can't wait to get away from it. I've hated working at that factory since the first day I started there. I'm not going to change my mind, so there's nothing to be gained by talking about it or saying anything more. I'm off to pack.'

Tears sprang to Alwyn's eyes. She clutched at Fern's shoulder. 'Go after him, tell him that you want him to stay, perhaps then he'll change his mind,' she urged.

Reluctantly, Fern did as Alwyn asked. Her own thoughts were in turmoil. She would miss Glanmor so much but she understood his yearning to get away, so was it right to put

148

obstacles in his way and try to stop him? she asked herself.

She knew Alwyn was listening as she went over to where Glanmor was taking his clean clothes out of the cupboard. As he piled them up on a chair and began looking around for something to put them in she knew that although it was breaking her heart that he was leaving she had to support him.

'I've got a fibre case you can have, if you really think you are doing the right thing, Glanmor,' she said quietly.

'Thanks, cariad!' He flashed a smile at her that made her heart beat faster and, for a moment, she wondered if perhaps Alwyn was right and she ought to try and persuade him to stay. Then, her sense of fair play overcame her own feelings. 'Would you like me to fetch it for you?' she offered.

He looked at her quizzically. 'Do you mean the one you keep underneath the bed with all your treasures in?'

'Yes, that's right.' Fern felt her colour rising. 'It will do all right, won't it?'

'It will be fine, but where will you keep all your bits and pieces if I use it? Isn't there a spare shopping bag or even an old sack that I can put what few things I have in?'

'I don't think so. Anyway, I'd like you to have it,' Fern told him. 'You don't want to turn up with your belongings in a sack, now do you?' she added quickly

'No, not really.' He grinned. 'If I had the time to do so, I'd go out and buy myself a proper canvas kitbag, the sort that I could sling over my shoulder.'

'And I suppose you'd buy a parrot as well to sit on the other shoulder,' Fern teased.

'Maybe. Perhaps I'll have both the next time I come ashore,' he retorted with a laugh.

The two women watched in silence as Glanmor started getting his things together; neither of them offered to help. Alwyn lit a cigarette but she didn't offer one to Glanmor, not even when he looked across at her expectantly.

'Are these all the shirts and underpants and socks that I have, Mam?' He frowned as he took them out of the cupboard and packed them into the suitcase.

'One on your back, one in the wash and one clean and ready to wear,' Alwyn told him. 'You're lucky there's two of everything there,' she sniffed. 'That's only because I've already done the washing and ironing for the week.'

'That's it, then,' he announced in a forced voice as he closed the lid of the suitcase. 'All my worldly belongings,' he added, patting it lightly. 'Right, I'd better be off.'

When he put his arms round his mother to kiss her goodbye Alwyn stiffened like a board. She remained unresponsive and didn't even return his kiss.

Fern wondered what she ought to do if he came over and hugged her. She didn't want

Glanmor to leave any more than Alwyn did, but she knew that he had always dreamed of going to sea. She could see that this was a wonderful opportunity for him and wanted to wish him well but at the same time she didn't want to antagonise Alwyn.

When he merely gave her a brief peck on the cheek it brought a lump of disappointment to her throat. She'd hoped he'd take her in his arms, hug her and kiss her properly. She wanted to fling her arms round his neck and cling to him and tell him how much she loved him and that it was breaking her heart that he was going, but, because Alwyn was watching, she remained mute.

The moment passed. She heard the door open, slam shut and the echo of his footsteps as, resolutely, he strode away down the road heading for the Pier Head.

For a moment neither of them spoke. Then Alwyn snatched up a shawl from the back of a chair and thrust Fern's coat into her hands, at the same time pushing her towards the door.

'Come on, after him. We must stop him. We can't let him ruin his life like this.'

The lamplighter was already putting out the lights as they went out into the street. The air was sharp but the sky was clear and there was a moon and cascades of stars to light them on their way.

Together they followed the way they thought Glanmor would be heading towards the docks,

They were walking so fast that they were both breathless by the time the Pier Head building came into view but, so far, there had been no sighting of him.

'Where do we go from here?' Fern panted. 'We don't know which dock the *Saturn* is berthed in.'

'We'll soon find out; there can't be all that many cargo boats leaving here at midnight.'

Fern leaned on the railings and looked down into the dark waters below. 'By the height of the water I'd say it is already high tide,' she murmured worriedly.

'Glanmor said they were sailing at midnight,' Alwyn repeated stubbornly. She looked up at the clock face on the Pier Head building. 'There are still a few minutes to go.'

'He said they were sailing at high tide,' Fern reminded her. 'That might be before midnight.'

Even as they argued they heard the impatient chugging of the tugs followed by the sharp response of a ship's hooter signalling that it was leaving the quayside. They watched in silence as a long, slim vessel moved out into the narrow channel that would take it out into the open sea.

'That's it; we're too late, Alwyn. I'm sure that's the *Saturn*,' Fern whispered.

They clung together, shivering in the sharp night air, watching the ship disappear into the darkness, carrying with it the man who was so close to both their hearts.

152

Chapter Fourteen

Fern and Alwyn both missed Glanmor although neither of them openly admitted it.

Fern accepted that he had hated working in a factory. She also suspected that he had dreamed so much about going to sea that he knew he would never be able to settle down until he had finally achieved his ambition and his need to see more of the world was out of his system.

Alwyn felt bitter and angry that he had been so ungrateful as to desert her after she had worked so hard and sacrificed so much to give him a good, stable home life.

Frequently she took her frustration out on Fern, even going as far as to infer that Glanmor had left home because she'd taken over his room.

'It was Glanmor's idea that I should use his room,' Fern protested, when Alwyn brought the matter up.

'Well, that's Glanmor all over, isn't it?' Alwyn sighed. 'I suppose it's because of the way I've brought him up, always making sure that he behaved unselfishly and put others before himself. Not me, his own mam, of course. He took me for granted. Always expected me to be able to sort things out and do everything for myself. Now look at the state things are in.'

'I don't know, you seem to be managing quite well,' Fern said encouragingly.

'You don't know what you're talking about,' Alwyn said dismissively.

Whenever she said this Fern wondered if perhaps it was time she left. She had saved hard ever since she'd been working in the market and she was sure that now she had enough money saved to be able to rent a room of her own. The only thing that stopped her from doing so was that she was afraid that if she did, then when Glanmor came home from sea his mother wouldn't tell him her new address.

She kept telling herself that he knew where she worked, so what did it matter? But at the back of her mind was the thought that she'd like to wait and find a place with Glanmor, not on her own. Even if he had to go back to sea for another trip she would know he was coming back to her and that she was waiting for him.

Sometimes, when she was feeling very depressed or worried and it had been a long time since she'd heard from Glanmor, she wondered if he had found another girl. It was a well-known fact that sailors were supposed to have a girl in every port and she knew she would be heartbroken if he told her that he'd found someone else.

Although he wrote to them separately, Fern

often wondered if his mother received more letters than she did. Glanmor wasn't much of a letter-writer and he said very little about where he was or what was happening to him. He seemed to have no idea when he would be back in Cardiff.

When she tried to talk to Alwyn about Glanmor she found the older woman seemed to know even less than she did.

'It's no good talking to me about him; you probably hear from him more than I do,' Alwyn muttered.

'I think we are both missing him, though,' Fern sighed.

'It's all very well for you; it's not your responsibility when things go wrong here. This is where Glanmor should be. We need a man about the place to knock in nails, move heavy furniture, and the hundred and one other small jobs that need doing, like putting a new washer on the tap,' Alwyn went on in a disgruntled voice as she tried to turn the tap off and stop the irritating drip.

Every night when she arrived home Fern found that Alwyn had a fresh moan about something. At first she offered to help but this only made Alwyn even angrier.

'You do it,' she'd say in a scornful voice. 'You wouldn't know which end of a hammer to use.'

Although Fern knew that Alwyn was probably right she was willing to try but Alwyn made it so clear that it was beyond her capabilities that in the end she said nothing and after a while stopped offering her services.

When one evening she arrived home and found a broad-shouldered middle-aged stranger in the kitchen fitting a new washer on the leaking tap she gave an inward sigh of relief that Alwyn had at last called someone in to mend it and would no longer be grumbling about it all the time.

To her surprise, when they sat down for their evening meal, he sat down with them. Alwyn introduced him as Jake Tomlinson. 'He's one of the sailors from the Seaman's Mission where I work and he offered to come and mend it,' she explained.

From then on, Jake became a regular visitor. When he'd finished whatever little job it was that Alwyn had asked him to come and do, the pair of them would go off to the pub so that she could buy him a beer or two.

'I'm not in the habit of going to pubs, but it's the only way I can recompense him for his services since he refuses to take any money,' she explained to Fern.

The friendship between Alwyn and Jake seemed to grow apace and soon he was eating with them every night. Most evenings he and Alwyn went out to the pub but occasionally he brought a bottle of rum with him and they stayed in. Whenever this happened Alwyn made it quite clear that she expected Fern to either go out or take herself off to her own room.

It was times like this when Fern really did miss Glanmor. He was the only real friend she had; the only one who had ever taken her out to the pictures or for a walk.

When she had started working at the market one or two of the younger men who worked there had invited her out but she had always turned down their invitations, preferring to spend any leisure time she had with Glanmor.

She had rebuffed them so often that now, when she would have welcomed the opportunity to go out with them, they no longer showed any interest. They were still quite friendly, though, and would always keep an eye on her stall for a few minutes while she was absent if she asked them to do so.

It was shortly after Christmas when she came down with a heavy cold. She managed to keep going but as soon as the morning rush was over outside the railway station on Saturday, Maria took over and sent her home for the rest of the day.

'Off to bed with a hot-water bottle and a drink of hot lemon when you get there, mind, and stay there all day tomorrow if you are no better,' Maria advised.

When she woke up the next morning she had such a sore throat and aching head that she felt even more ill than she'd done the day before. Thankfully it was Sunday, so she decided to do as Maria had told her and stay in bed.

She lay there for several minutes hoping that she might hear Alwyn moving around and could call out and ask her if she would make her a cup of tea. Then she remembered that Alwyn would have gone to work, preparing the vegetables for the men's midday meal. Shivering, she pulled her coat on over her nightdress and padded down to the kitchen to make herself a drink.

To her surprise, Jake was in the kitchen. He was wearing only a singlet and trousers and from the tousled look of his hair and the stubble on his face he had only just woken up himself.

'Another one who has slept in,' he grunted as she went into the scullery. 'There's tea in the pot, I've just brewed it.'

She felt uncomfortable as he stood there breathing heavily, scratching his chest and watching her as she took down a cup from the shelf and filled it from the big brown teapot.

'Taking it back to bed with you, are you?' he questioned.

'Yes, I am.'

'Do you want someone to come with you to keep you company and give you a cuddle?' he leered as he moved closer to her.

Fern didn't answer but she edged as far away from him as she could.

'You've only got to say the word,' he persisted moving closer to her. 'There's no point in being lonely.'

'I don't need any company. I've got a bad

158

head cold and I want to have a lie-in,' she said stiffly as she pulled her coat more tightly together.

Jake turned away, pulled a cigarette out from a packet in his pocket and began to light it. 'In that case, if you've got a snotty nose I don't think I'll bother,' he muttered as she hurried past him on her way back upstairs.

Fern didn't answer but she found she was still shaking when she reached her narrow little room. With a feeling of panic she looked around for something to push up against the door in case he decided to follow her.

From then on, when she discovered that Jake had more or less moved in, and was sleeping with Alwyn three or four nights a week, she was careful to avoid him as much as possible. Nevertheless, she was aware that he seemed to be watching her all the time and it made her feel uneasy.

Fern wondered how Jake and Glanmor would hit it off when Glanmor came home and wondered what he would have to say when he found out how much his mother had changed now that Jake was more or less living with her.

Alwyn really was a completely different person, Fern reflected. She had not only put on a great deal of weight but she'd also taken to using lipstick and powder and had started to dress up in the evenings when she went out drinking with Jake.

Fern tried to ignore what has happening at

home and to concentrate instead on what went on at the Hayes. Business was steady but far from brisk because spring was late. When at last it did start to warm up, the air was heavy and oppressive and every so often there was the rumble of thunder and everyone's nerves seemed to be on edge waiting for the storm to break.

Alwyn complained about the heat at work and often when she came in from work Fern found her pottering around barefoot in the kitchen, wearing only her under-slip. Jake was usually lounging against the sink in only his string vest or else with his shirt unbuttoned all the way down.

'You should try taking your dress off, Fern,' Jake told her. 'You'd feel a lot cooler if you did, especially if you also took those clumpy shoes and your thick stockings off as well and sat with your feet in a bowl of cold water.'

'I'm sure I would feel cooler and I would do, if I had some privacy,' Fern told him. 'There's not much chance of that here though, is there?' she added pointedly.

Although Alwyn said nothing she raised her eyebrows and gave Jake a puzzled look.

Fern pretended not to notice it but she was well aware of the atmosphere in the room. As soon as she'd eaten her meal and helped to clear everything away she went off to her room.

Here at least she could strip off and get cool, she thought thankfully as she took off the heavy navy-blue cotton dress she'd worn to work that day and then peeled off her lisle stockings and lay down on the bed.

The air in the tiny bedroom was stagnant and although she had opened the sash window as wide as she possibly could the air was so heavy that she felt drowsy and in next to no time she had drifted off into a light sleep.

She was wakened by the feel of someone's hand sliding the straps of her slip down off her shoulders. For a moment the light breeze across her naked flesh was deliciously cooling but when she felt the hand move down her neck and then start to fondle her exposed breasts she drew in her breath sharply. Shocked into alertness she opened her eyes.

For a moment she thought she must be still asleep and having a bad dream. She blinked rapidly and ran her hand over her eyes to try and clear her head.

It was no dream. She found Jake Tomlinson was on her bed and kneeling over her, his face so close to hers that she choked on his stale breath.

Petrified, she opened her mouth to scream but immediately his hand clamped down over her face, effectively silencing her. She struggled to breathe and she felt so scared that she couldn't stop shaking.

'Got you at my mercy now, haven't I?' he gloated as he looked down at her.

There was such a look of lust on his face and

his dark eyes glittered in such an evil way that when she felt his hand slide up her bare leg she was only too aware of what was in his mind and she struggled desperately.

His cruel laugh at the ineffectiveness of her attempt to free herself gave strength to her endeavours. She knew she was powerless against his strength so she bit down hard on the side of the hand he was still holding over her mouth.

He yelped with pain as her teeth pierced his flesh and momentarily relaxed his hold of her.

Taking a deep breath she brought up her knee and managed to catch him not in the groin, as she'd intended, but in the soft flab of his stomach and that momentarily winded him.

'You spiteful little bitch, I'll get even with you for this,' he panted as he pulled away from her.

'Alwyn will get even with you when I tell her about what you've tried to do,' Fern sobbed. 'She won't be welcoming you here again in the future.'

'If you say one word to her, you'll find yourself in trouble,' he warned. 'You'd better watch out. Make sure you know who's walking behind you when you come home at night.'

'You wouldn't dare attack me,' Fern challenged. Her breath caught in her throat as spasms of fear took hold of her.

He laughed coarsely. 'I'm not the only one who'll be out to get you one of these dark nights.

Keep looking over your shoulder, if you know what's good for you.'

His threats made her feel so vulnerable that she decided the time really had come for her to move out. She couldn't stand the atmosphere any longer. She had enough saved up and although her original intention was to do nothing until Glanmor came home, she decided she couldn't wait any longer for that to happen.

She dressed quickly, determined to act right away before she changed her mind. Her savings were tucked away under the bed in one of Maria's stout canvas purses so she wedged a chair against the door in case either Alwyn or Jake should hear her moving the mattress and come to see what was going on.

She breathed a deep sigh of relief as she pulled the purse from its hiding place. Then she straightened the room before opening it. When she did so she gave a gasp of dismay. It was completely empty. Every penny of her hard-earned savings was gone.

She couldn't believe it. She wondered if she had mistakenly taken it out and counted her savings and then put the purse back under the mattress without putting the money into the purse. Or whether she hadn't closed the purse properly and the money had fallen out. Once again she removed the mattress; this time completely so that the springs were bare, but there was no sign of any money or anything else hidden there.

Tears of self-pity streamed down her face. Who had taken it, she wondered? It had to be either Alwyn or Jake, but how had they known it was there? She'd always been so careful; counting it and then secreting it away when Alwyn was out of the house. She knew every coin and note that was in the purse. She knew exactly how much should be there.

The more she thought about it the surer she became that Alwyn was the culprit. All the new clothes she'd been buying; the good food she was putting on the table whenever Jake was there for a meal. Alwyn must also be the one paying for their nights out at the pub because Jake had been out of work ever since he'd started coming there.

The only thing that mattered was that she was now as penniless as she'd been when she'd first moved there from Bryson and Bertha's place. All her plans, whether to rent a room right away or wait until Glanmor came home were dashed.

There was nothing for it but to go on living with Alwyn and Jake and she didn't take his threats lightly. From now on she'd have to barricade herself into her room at nights and always be on the alert for his next move.

Chapter Fifteen

Jake's revenge, when it came, was so unexpected that Fern was quite unprepared and at first didn't even associate it with him.

It happened on a Friday night; Maria wasn't feeling well and after the morning rush at the station was over she'd come across to the Hayes to let Fern know that she was going home.

'I think that's very sensible of you,' Fern told her. 'Go home and put your feet up and take it easy for the rest of the day and then, with any luck, you'll feel as right as rain tomorrow.'

'Yes, cariad, if you say so, but when you get to my age and your rheumatics start playing up it usually takes more than one day's rest to get over them. Still,' she added with a warm smile, 'it will help. Now, you sure you can manage without me?'

'Of course I can,' Fern assured her. 'You get off home and have some rest.'

'Yes, that's what I'm going to do.' She lowered her voice and whispered, 'Can you handle the money? It means you'll have to take it home with you tonight, so put it inside this purse and make sure that you tie it on good and proper underneath your top clothes,' she added as she discreetly pushed a canvas bag into Fern's hands.

'Put it out of sight, now, and mind you don't let anyone see you putting the takings in it or see you putting it on.'

'Of course I won't,' Fern whispered in reply. 'Hardly likely to do so if I have to put it on underneath my clothes, now, will I?' she added with a broad smile.

'Will you be able to manage to do that all right?' Maria persisted worriedly.

'Of course I will,' Fern assured her.

The rest of the day went well and when it was time to go home and the other traders were all packing up their stalls Fern asked Rhodri, a tall gangling young man who worked close by, if he would keep an eye on her stall while she went to the ladies.

In the seclusion of the underground toilet cubicle she secreted the day's takings away into the canvas bag Maria had left her. It made an uncomfortable bulge underneath her dress but she managed to disguise it as much as possible before she went back up the narrow steps and walked across to her stall.

By the time she'd finished packing everything away Fern was almost the last to leave the market site so she set off briskly to walk to the tram stop in Bute Street.

There was a long queue of people waiting and when the tram finally came it was packed with home-going shoppers and workers. As she tried to elbow her way on she was pushed back on to the pavement even before the conductor had given three tugs on the bell to signal to the driver that they were completely full.

Knowing there would not be another tram for perhaps ten minutes or longer, Fern felt vulnerable with all the money she was carrying. Because there were so many other people standing there waiting she decided to start walking to the next stop.

When she reached it there was still no sign of a tram so she decided she would carry on walking. She had just passed John Street when she was aware that there was a man walking on either side of her. As they reached the corner of Bute Street and Herbert Street they moved in closer and tried to make her turn down the side street. When she resisted they grabbed hold of her arms and tried to force her down there. Immediately she screamed and fought to get free from them.

Aware that she was attracting attention and people were hurrying towards them, they each grabbed her by an arm, lifting her clear of the ground, and tried to run with her. Fern lashed out with her feet, kicking at their legs as hard as she could. One of the men stumbled and all three of them ended up in a heap on the ground. By then other people had reached them and were helping Fern to her feet.

'Duw anwyl, there's louts you are, attacking a woman in that condition,' one said in shocked tones.

Fern was aware that everyone was staring at her. In the rumpus, the canvas purse she was wearing under her skirt had bunched up in such a way that it made her look as though she was pregnant.

Her attackers fled and as the people who'd stopped and helped her to her feet, dusted her down and murmured words of comfort, she said nothing to correct them.

'You're shaking like a leaf, do you want us to call a copper, cariad?' one woman asked.

'No,' Fern shook her head, 'I don't think there's much point. They've gone, haven't they?'

'True, but there're witnesses, so we can tell the bobby what they looked like.'

'I don't think I want to make a fuss,' Fern murmured. 'Thank you so much for helping me. I'll get the next tram home and I'm sure I'll be safe enough now.'

A couple of people walked with her to the tram stop, one holding her arm as if afraid she might fall.

Once she was on the tram she discreetly moved the purse so that it was no longer making her skirt bulge out and she was more comfortable. What on earth would she have done if those two men had found it and taken all the money? she wondered.

She was still shaking when she arrived home. Jake stared at her in open-mouthed disbelief. He seemed to be surprised to see her yet he made no comment at all about how dishevelled she looked or that her face had a bad cut on it. His reaction made her suspicious and she wondered if he'd had something to do with the attack.

Remembering his threat she wondered if he had arranged for the two men to attack her. If he had also been hoping they would have money to share with him when it was all over, he was going to be very disappointed, she thought with a degree of satisfaction.

She went straight up to her bedroom and barricaded the door before she removed the purse. Then she emptied out the contents and counted it to make sure that it was all there.

As she looked at the money spread out on her bed she realised that it was more than double the money she'd managed to save up towards moving out of Margaret Street and into a place of her own. With this much she could do it right now and not wait for Glanmor to come home. For one moment she was tempted to do that and then when she told Maria about being attacked to let her think that all the day's takings had been stolen.

The moment the idea came into her mind Fern felt thoroughly ashamed that she had even thought it. Maria was struggling to make ends meet as it was because the stall was not nearly as busy as it had once been. Flowers and potted plants were one of the first things that people cut back on when they were trying to eke out what little money they had. Food came first and next was replacing their clothes when the ones they

169

were wearing wore out. All the little luxuries of life like sweets, cakes and flowers were right at the bottom of the list.

She would have to tell Maria about the attack, of course, and she intended to do so first thing the next morning before any of the other stall-holders or one of the customers told her first.

Maria was relieved to hear that the day's takings had not been stolen but she was very concerned about Fern's cuts and bruises.

'You should have called the police and reported it,' she admonished. 'Thugs like that deserve to be punished. Did you see them hanging around the market at any time during the day?'

'No.' Fern shook her head. 'I'm pretty certain that I know who they were. Well,' she corrected herself quickly, 'not who the two men were, but I know who told them to accost me.'

Maria's mouth dropped open and she looked at Fern in astonishment. 'Whatever do you mean, cariad?'

When Fern told her about Jake and how he had behaved Maria looked shocked. 'Does Alwyn know what's going on?'

'Heavens no! She wouldn't believe me; she thinks so highly of Jake. If I told her, then she would probably say I had to move out and I can't do that.'

'Why not? I pay you well, so are you saying that your wages aren't enough for you to live on?'

'No, of course not.' Fern sighed. 'I want to move out of Margaret Street and get a room of my own. I've been saving up to do that ever since I started work but I was hoping that Glanmor would come home and then we could find a place together.'

She stopped and bright colour flooded into her face as she saw the expression on Maria's face. 'I don't mean live together, not in the way you are thinking,' she assured the older woman.

'I thought you meant that you were expecting him to ask you to marry him,' Maria said mildly with a twinkle in her dark eyes.

'Well, he probably will; we do care a lot about each other and he knows I'll be waiting for him,' Fern said defensively. 'I thought that if I went on living with his mam it would give me the opportunity to save up a nice little nest egg and then we could rent a couple of rooms and even buy all the countless other things we would need to set up home.'

'So what stopped you from using the money you'd saved to move out and find yourself a place when Jake Tomlinson started making a nuisance of himself?' Maria asked as she busied herself arranging the pots on the stall. 'I'm quite sure that is what Glanmor would expect you to do if he knew that you were having trouble of that sort.'

Fern was quiet for so long that Maria stopped what she was doing and asked her again, this time keeping her eyes fixed on Fern's face so that she had no option but to answer.

'After Jake attacked me I knew I couldn't go on living there so I decided I would go ahead and find a room,' Fern said quietly. 'I had almost twenty pounds saved up; more than enough to do what I wanted to do, but when I went to get my money from where I'd hidden it underneath my mattress, I found that it had gone'

'All of it?'

'Every penny piece had been taken.'

'And you think that Jake Tomlinson took it?'

'Well, it must have been him. At first I thought it was Alwyn, but now I'm not so sure that she would do anything like that.'

'No, I'm quite sure she wouldn't,' Maria agreed. 'So what did you do when you found it was missing?'

'Nothing at all. What could I do? If I told Alwyn, it would have caused a rumpus and if I'd accused Jake, he would have denied it.'

'So why do you think he set those two men on you?'

'He couldn't do it himself, could he, that would have put him out of favour with Alwyn and he probably knew I would have told her all about everything else.'

Maria looked puzzled. 'Why would he want to be revenged on you like that?'

'Because I'd rejected him, I suppose. And because I'd bitten his hand rather badly when he held it over my mouth to stop me screaming after he'd forced me down on the bed.' She stopped and a smile lit up her face. 'It made him yelp, I can tell you.'

'Fair-dos; he was annoyed by that but why send those men to attack you, I wonder?'

'I don't know. The only thing I can think is that he wanted to get me into trouble with you. He probably thought that if I lost all the takings you would sack me.'

'Yes, maybe he did. He sounds a right evil devil,' Maria agreed. She sighed. 'Alwyn never did have much luck with men. Look at that Bryson.' She stopped and held up a hand. 'I know he's your uncle but he's a bad lot in more ways than one.'

'Whatever do you mean by that?' Fern frowned.

'Well, for one thing, he managed to get himself out of the army by claiming that he had a bad back. They tried to prove that he was hoodwinking them but he's a clever rascal and he managed to convince the army doctor that he really was in pain. Two or three times they attempted to draft him but in the end they simply gave up.

'The recruiting people told him he'd have to go and work in munitions but after a couple of weeks in a factory he managed to have an accident and was off sick. They could see that he was going to be more trouble than he was worth and so they didn't insist that he must go back there. In my opinion they were glad to see the back of him.'

'Yet hard-working young men like my brother

Barri were sent to fight over in France at the Front. Barri was only eighteen when he died,' Fern said bitterly.

'That's the way of things,' Maria commented. 'The bad 'uns always seem to get away with everything while the honest, upright chaps are the ones that take the brunt. Anyway, enough of that, we can't undo what's happened in the past so there's no point in dwelling on it. What we can do is make some plans for the future. To start with, I think the best thing for you to do is to come and live with me.'

Fern smiled gratefully. 'That's awfully kind of you, but I couldn't put you out like that.'

'You won't be putting me out at all,' Maria assured her. 'I've got a spare bedroom; it's not very big, but there's a bolt on the door,' she added with a dry smile.

'If you are quite sure that it won't be upsetting you,' Fern murmured doubtfully.

'It's upsetting me far more to hear what's going on where you are now. When we finish here tonight I'll come back to Margaret Street with you. I can help you move your few bits and pieces and deal with Alwyn if she starts making a fuss.'

'You won't tell her what I told you about Jake, will you, because I don't want to cause trouble; she is Glanmor's mam after all.'

'I won't say a word about that. I take it she knows about you being attacked last night?'

'Yes, but by the time Alwyn came home from work I'd sorted myself out so I don't think she knows the whole story. She certainly doesn't know that Jake had anything to do with it.'

'Well, leave it like that,' Maria advised. 'The least said the better. If she does ask questions about you leaving there, then I'll tell her that I need some company.'

'I think that would be best,' Fern agreed.

'Come on, then,' she added briskly. 'We had better get cleared up here so that we can leave good and early, otherwise it will be midnight by the time we get back to my place and have a bite to eat.'

'You are quite sure about all this?' Fern asked anxiously. 'You are so used to living on your own that I'm sure you will find it difficult to have someone else staying with you.'

'If I find you too much trouble then I'll send you packing and since I don't think you want to have to go back to Margaret Street I'm pretty sure that you'll behave yourself.'

'Thank you, Maria, I am grateful.' Fern smiled, hugging the older woman.

'Now stop chattering and let's get things moving,' Maria told her. 'With any luck you'll be settled in and we'll have everything ship-shape before you go to bed tonight.'

Chapter Sixteen

Fern found that living with Maria was like turning the clock back and that her life was almost as comfortable as it had been before she came to Cardiff.

Maria's flat was at the top of a three-storey house in Loudon Square and looked out on to the park and trees. Fern could occasionally even hear birds singing and that conjured up fond memories of her old home in Blaenafon.

After a couple of days of awkwardness while they found their way around each other, they settled down into a pleasant routine that suited them both. They made an excellent team. Down the week Fern tidied around and made herself useful in a hundred and one ways while Maria cooked their evening meal. At the weekends she helped with the cleaning, washing and ironing.

As they worked they talked. Maria regaled Fern with stories of her own childhood in Tiger Bay and her struggle for independence after her husband was killed in the Boer War.

'My own mam and dad were both dead and I felt I had no one, so I was determined to make my own way in life. Selling flowers outside the railway station has kept a roof over my head and food in my belly but having a stall in the Hayes has always been my dream and thanks to you, cariad, it has come true, though how long it will last is another matter.'

Fern looked at her in alarm. 'Whatever makes you say that, Maria?' she asked.

'We're in troubled times, cariad. There are still a lot of men who came back from the war who can't find work and, added to that, there's a lot of unrest in the Valleys.'

'Do you mean amongst the coal miners?' Fern questioned.

'That's right, my lovely. A lot of them think they should be paid better wages because of the dangerous work they do. They're probably right, but the coal barons are a greedy bunch. Unless they manage to come to some sort of agreement with the men there'll be a strike, you mark my words.'

'Surely that won't affect us down here in Cardiff, will it?' Fern frowned.

'It most certainly will do, cariad. Cardiff's wealth depends on the amount of coal shipped from here, surely you know that. If the miners go on strike then the docks will be practically at a standstill and there will be even more men out of work than there are now. If that happens, there won't be many people buying flowers, or any other little luxuries, I can tell you.'

Fern fell silent, thinking not only about the effect of a miners' strike on them but also of how it might affect the rest of the shipping. If the docks came to a standstill, how would Glanmor's ship fare, because surely they must return to port very soon.

'Come on, cariad. I didn't mean to depress you,' Maria told her. 'We won't be going out of business yet. Christmas is only just around the corner and business is always brisk then. This year you can try your hand at making up the holly wreaths that folks like to buy to hang on their front doors.'

'I bet you get scratched to bits making them, is that why you are going to let me do it?' Fern said teasingly.

'I'm sure your fingers are more nimble than mine so you'll make a better job of it than I can.' Maria smiled.

Despite Maria's prophesy about a strike pending, Christmas 1920 was a bumper one for them. It seemed as if people were determined to throw off the lingering gloom from the war days and to enjoy themselves and hope for better things to come in the new year.

By the time they closed the stall late on Christmas Eve both of them were so tired that they told each other they intended to lie in the next morning until midday.

'That's the one good thing about Christmas Day falling on a Saturday, you get both Saturday and Sunday to recover from the hectic rush like we've had today,' Maria sighed exhaustedly.

'We shouldn't really grumble because we've

probably done a week's business in one day,' Fern reminded her. 'All the holly wreaths have sold,' she added, 'and I won't have to face another batch of prickly holly for a whole year.'

'Yes, they've sold extremely well.' Maria nodded. 'In fact, since you did such a good job of making those wreaths, you can do them again next time.'

They spent a very quiet Christmas. As they'd agreed they didn't get up until late morning and so they had their celebration roast chicken with all the trimmings later in the day.

'You really are a splendid cook, Maria,' Fern congratulated her as they cleared everything away and washed up. 'I've eaten so much that I won't need another meal for days.'

'That's good, because I won't be cooking tomorrow,' Maria told her. 'A complete day of rest is what I have in mind.'

'Why don't you have Monday off as well?' Fern suggested. 'I'm sure I can do the station as well as the stall at the Hayes.'

'If you can manage the stall on your own, then I will,' Maria agreed. 'There's not much point trying to sell flowers outside the station. The sort of men who buy buttonholes won't be going to work and most of the other people will be coming back from visiting friends or family and they won't have any money left over for flowers.'

'That's settled, then,' Fern agreed. 'I'll be as

179

quiet as a mouse when I get up so as not to disturb you,' she promised.

'Good. I'll come along to the stall late afternoon to walk home with you.'

'You don't need to do that,' Fern admonished. 'Surely you trust me not to run off with the takings,' she said, smiling.

'I trust you, cariad, but I've never forgotten what happened to you when I did leave you to look after the money. I don't want you being attacked again.'

'I think that's all in the past, don't you?' Fern said confidently. 'I've never seen anything of Jake or Alwyn since I moved in here with you so I don't think we'll ever have any more trouble from them.'

Maria's words echoed in Fern's head when it came time to close down the stall and Maria still hadn't turned up as she had promised, to walk home with her.

There was snow falling and she felt so nervous as she fastened her coat over the bulky purse and wound her thick scarf around her neck to keep out the cold that when Rhodri from the adjacent stall said half jokingly, 'Do you want me to walk home with you, Fern?' she readily agreed.

The moment she did so she regretted it because she saw the eager look on his face. For months he had been trying to persuade her to go out with him and she had steadfastly refused.

She knew he had taken a liking to her and she didn't want to lead him on. Her heart was already taken and all she wanted was for Glanmor to come home so that they could plan their future together.

'I'm only letting you walk with me because this snow is turning into a blizzard,' she warned him.

'I know, I know, there's no need for you to be as frosty as the weather.' He grinned. 'I only live one street away from you now that you've moved into Loudon Square so I'm not putting myself out in any way.'

'I thought Maria was coming to meet me,' she added as they walked to the tram stop.

'In this weather! She shouldn't be working at all at her age, she's not looking at all well, is she?' he stated.

Fern looked at him in surprise. She knew Maria had slowed down in the past few months but she didn't think she looked ill. Or did she? Fern felt worried. Was she so caught up with her own life that she hadn't noticed? she wondered.

'Living with her like you do, you probably haven't noticed it as much as I have,' Rhodri commented.

'No, that's true,' Fern murmured as she looked up at him. 'I'm surprised you have,' she added.

'I've probably known her a lot longer than you have,' he said cryptically. 'I've known her all my life and she seemed quite old when I was a little boy.'

'Well, that wasn't all that long ago,' she teased.

'I'm twenty-six, a lot older than you, and I'm ready to settle down,' he told her seriously.

'I hope you find yourself a nice girl, then,' Fern responded in an equally serious voice.

'Oh, I've found one,' he sighed, 'but she doesn't want anything to do with me, except to let me walk her home when it's snowing.'

Fern felt uneasy; their banter was going too far and she was sure he was leading up to asking her out again so she was relieved when they reached Loudon Square.

'I'll come right to the door with you,' he stated when she paused on the corner and thanked him for seeing her home.

'There's really no need,' Fern said firmly.

'I want to see Maria, to wish her a Happy New Year,' he said stubbornly.

'You can do that when she's on the stall tomorrow,' Fern told him abruptly.

'I want to see her tonight,' he insisted. 'I want to make sure she's all right,' he added as an explanation.

'There's no need, Rhodri.' I'll make sure she is; I promise you.'

'Well, we're here now so I may as well have a word with her,' he insisted.

'I thought you said you were quite capable of walking home on your own,' Maria chided as they entered the flat together.

'We walked together, Mrs Roberts, because it's snowing quite heavily,' Rhodri told her.

'Anyway, I only live in the next street so it wasn't taking me out of my way.'

'So why haven't you gone on home, then?' Maria asked tetchily.

'I wanted to wish you a Happy New Year,' he said, smiling.

'That's days away, couldn't it have waited?'

'I suppose it could have done.' He shrugged his shoulders. 'Well, now I've done so I'll be on my way.'

'Thank you for walking with me, Rhodri,' Fern said with a smile, trying to ease the tension between the three of them.

As soon as he'd gone she turned to Maria. 'Did you forget you'd insisted on coming or aren't you feeling well?'

'I don't know what you're talking about,' Maria said crossly. 'It's snowing out there and I didn't want to risk slipping and breaking my leg or my arm or something. Anyway, you're home now so why the fuss and all the questions?'

Fern bit her lower lip as she studied Maria. Rhodri was right, she thought worriedly. Maria wasn't looking well. She was so thin that she looked frail and Rhodri's remark about her being old made Fern realise how lined Maria's face was.

'I think Rhodri wanted an excuse to see that you were all right,' she said gently. 'He said he thought you didn't look too well,' she added tentatively.

'I'm as well as I'll ever be,' Maria said as she

moved to the table and began rattling the plates as she set them out in readiness for their meal. 'Now get your hat and coat off or this meal that I've spent all day cooking will be ruined.'

The hot pie made from the leftovers of the chicken and vegetables from Christmas day was both warming and filling and Fern enjoyed every mouthful.

'You go and sit down and I'll clear everything away,' Fern volunteered after they'd finished eating.

'Don't you want to have a mince pie and a cup of tea first?' Maria asked.

'No, I'll do the washing-up first and then we can sit and enjoy that in front of the fire. It will give my dinner a chance to go down and make room for it,' she added with a laugh as she began collecting up their dirty plates.

To her surprise, Maria didn't argue or protest but went straight to her favourite armchair which Fern noticed was pulled right up close to the fire.

When she finished the washing-up Fern made a pot of tea and carried it in but when she went to hand Maria a cup she noticed that she had already fallen asleep so she put it down on the table without trying to waken her.

She'd already finished her own drink and was leaning forward to put some more coal on the fire when she noticed that Maria had slumped forward in her chair and was sitting at such an awkward angle that she was in danger of falling out of it. Gently she tried to prop her up into a more comfortable position but realised it was impossible to do so without waking her.

'Maria.' Gently she shook her arm but there was no response. She tried again but the older woman appeared not to hear her and remained slumped forward.

Fern felt thoroughly alarmed. Maria was not responding; her face looked crumpled and saliva was drooling from one side of her mouth. She wasn't sure what to do and wondered if she ought to call someone to help her.

Struggling desperately, Fern managed to move the armchair with Maria in it away from the fire in case she slid forward. Then she found Maria's heavy black shawl and wrapped that round her, tucking it well down into the sides of the chair in the hope that it would prevent her falling out.

She wasn't sure whom to ask for help. Maria was such a proud, independent woman that Fern was pretty sure that she would hate it if any of the other people in the house saw her in such a stressful condition so, remembering that Rhodri lived only a street away, and that he had great respect for Maria, she pulled on her hat and coat and ran to get him.

By the time she reached his home in Loudon Place she was breathless. Rhodri looked concerned when she told him what had happened and, without even stopping to pick up his coat, he took her by the arm and hurried her back to Maria's flat.

When he saw the state Maria was in he shook his head sadly. 'She's had a stroke. We'll have to get a doctor and if we can't find one then I'll go for an ambulance.'

'Surely she isn't that bad?' Fern exclaimed worriedly. 'She cooked us a lovely meal and we'd just finished eating and she was having a rest while I washed up . . .' her voice petered out as she saw the worried expression on Rhodri's face.

'Will you be all right here with her if I go and see if the doctor is on duty?'

'Yes, of course I will. You ought to go home first and get your coat, though, Rhodri, or you'll end up ill as well,' she advised with a watery smile.

The waiting time seemed endless. Fern sat holding Maria's hand and talking to her in the hope that perhaps she was only in a deep sleep and would wake up and ask where her tea was.

Rhodri was gone for almost half an hour and apart from her heavy breathing there was no movement at all from Maria.

When she heard the sound of an ambulance siren a shiver went through Fern because it meant that either Rhodri had not been able to get a doctor to come out or else the doctor had ordered an ambulance even without seeing Maria, because he felt she needed to go to hospital.

Chapter Seventeen

An hour later, after they'd given all the details they knew about Maria to the admissions clerk at the Cardiff Royal Infirmary, Fern and Rhodri were told to go home and come back again tomorrow.

'Could we see her before we leave?' Fern pleaded.

'No, I'm afraid not,' the clerk said briskly. 'Mrs Roberts has been admitted to Ward Three and is in good care so there is nothing more you can do.'

As they walked to the tram stop in Newport Road Fern wondered how she was going to manage to look after the flower business on her own until Maria was well again.

As if reading her thoughts, Rhodri said, 'Don't worry about things, I can give you a hand on the stall.'

'That's kind of you, Rhodri, but you have your own stall to run,' Fern said, smiling at him gratefully. 'I'll have to give up the station pitch; I can't possibly run both.'

'You could take someone on to help you,' he suggested.

'Not without asking Maria first,' Fern said quickly.

'No, I suppose not,' he agreed. 'Perhaps we can arrange something, though.'

Their conversation was interrupted by the arrival of the tram. After they had both found seats and the conductor had taken their fares Rhodri asked, 'Which is the busiest time outside the station? I mean, is it in the morning or the afternoon?'

'In the evenings,' Fern said quickly, 'especially at the weekend. Friday night is the busiest because that's when all the office workers are paid and a lot of the men buy their wives or mothers a bunch of flowers on the way home.'

'Then why not let me look after your stall each evening and you go over to the pitch and keep that going.'

'It's a great idea, but I couldn't expect you to do that.' Fern smiled. 'You'd be losing business on your own stall, especially on a Friday night, because that's when you are extra busy. It's when all the young boys have money in their pockets to buy a new gramophone record or a piece of sheet music.'

'OK, then simply close the stall down early on Fridays, put a notice on it to say where they can find you, and I'll make a point of redirecting people whenever necessary.'

'I suppose I could do that,' Fern said thoughtfully. 'The big problem is that I would have to take the day's takings with me and I wouldn't feel safe if I had so much money on me, not after what happened to me a few weeks ago.'

'Then don't take it with you; leave it with me and I'll meet you when I close down and walk you home. You do trust me, don't you Fern?' he asked when she remained silent.

'Of course I do, Rhodri,' she said quickly. 'I'm just mulling it over in my mind.'

Before they parted Fern agreed to give some thought to Rhodri's idea. She was anxious to keep things going for Maria.

'It's the only way you'll be able to do it,' Rhodri emphasised, 'because you can't be in two places at once.'

'I know, but I want time to think about it,' Fern argued. She laid a hand on Rhodri's arm, 'I really am grateful; for your concern and your offer of help,' she said quietly.

His face lit up and the frown that had furrowed his brow vanished. After a moment's hesitation he leaned forward and rather awkwardly kissed her on her cheek.

Fern tried not to pull away but she wished he hadn't done it. She didn't want any boy except Glanmor touching her, and she suspected that Rhodri's kiss was more than a show of friendship.

Although the stall at the Hayes and the pitch outside the station were only a matter of minutes away from each other, as Rhodri had pointed out, she couldn't be in two places at once so running them both would call for careful planning, Fern thought worriedly.

The only thing she didn't like about the plan

was that it meant she would have to rely on Rhodri's help and she was afraid that it was unfair to encourage him to think that she cared for him when all she wanted was to be friends and nothing more.

She lay awake that night for a long time trying to reason out what to do. In the end she decided that the welfare of Maria's business was of more importance than her own feelings and unless she did as Rhodri suggested, by the time Maria came out of hospital she might find her financial future was in serious trouble.

Maria was in hospital for two weeks and by the time she came home again Fern felt exhausted. Rhodri had been a wonderful support but most of the responsibility and organising had fallen on Fern's shoulders because she was the one who knew what to do, where to buy and how to price and display flowers.

Maria was very weak and frail. The stroke had left her unable to use her left hand properly. She had hardly any grip and her arm appeared to be so thin that it looked as if it was withered.

She was grateful and astonished when Fern told her how she'd managed to keep both the stall and pitch running, and amazed when she heard how Rhodri had cooperated and helped.

'He'd never have done all that if he hadn't taken a real shine to you, cariad,' she remarked shrewdly. 'You know, you could do worse than marry a chap like that,' she added sagely.

'Me marry Rhodri Richards?' Fern said in a

disparaging voice. 'Never! I'm surprised you even mention it when you know quite well that I've promised to wait for Glanmor.'

'Promises are made to be broken,' Maria pronounced. 'He's been away for a long time and you've no idea when he's coming back. He might never return to Cardiff.'

'Oh he will,' Fern said confidently. 'You'll see – any day now, I expect,' she added hopefully.

'You can't be sure about that, cariad. You've not heard a word from him in a while, have you?'

'No, that's true enough, but then how can he get in touch with me when he doesn't know where I am living? He's probably written lots of times but the letters have gone to Margaret Street, because he doesn't know that I've moved in with you.'

'Well, that's true enough,' Maria admitted.

'In fact,' Fern went on, her voice full of self-pity, 'he probably thinks I've let him down and gone off with someone else because I haven't replied to any of his letters.'

'Duw anwyl, do you always have to look on the black side of everything?' Martha said crossly.

Fern didn't answer; she was too occupied by her own thoughts of how much she missed Glanmor and felt close to tears as she thought he might come home to Margaret Street expecting her to be there to greet him only to be told she'd gone. Because they'd parted on such bad terms Alwyn probably wouldn't tell him where she was living now.

Nevertheless, even if she never saw Glanmor again, she still wasn't interested in marrying Rhodri. He was nice enough and she was grateful for the way he'd helped her, but she thought of him only as a friend and nothing more.

'Don't take on, cariad,' Maria said softly. 'I'm just a silly old busybody trying to do a bit of matchmaking. Of course Glanmor is the one for you, we both know that. He'll be back, and when he finds you aren't living in Margaret Street, then he'll come looking for me to see what I can tell him. He always knows he'll find me outside the station. Which is another reason why I must pull myself together and get back there,' she added stoically.

It was early summer before Maria was well enough to return to work.

'You're not well enough, but your regular customers are missing you and constantly asking after you.' Fern sighed. 'I suppose a couple of hours a day on the stall would be all right.'

'If I'm well enough to do a few hours each day on the stall, then I am well enough to be outside the station,' Maria argued.

'It's too draughty there for you,' Fern told her.'

'Rubbish! It's the middle of summer!'

'Yes, and you'll find it exhausting standing there in the hot sun,' Fern argued.

'One minute it's too draughty and the next it's too hot. Make your mind up, cariad,' Maria said crossly.

'I think you'd be better off on the stall where there are other people around if you need help.'

'You mean like that nice Rhodri Richards,' Maria said, her eyes twinkling mischievously.

'Most of the stallholders would help if they saw you needed it,' Fern answered, refusing to rise to the bait.

'Very well, I'll work on the stall for a few weeks as long as you promise that I can go back to my pitch the moment I feel strong enough to do so.'

'Not for at least another month or two. What is more, I want you to promise that once the weather starts getting colder again you'll switch back to the stall,' Fern insisted.

She knew Maria was still hoping that she would take up with Rhodri and was constantly telling her what a fine-looking boyo he was, but although she agreed with Maria about that she had no intention of going out with him. She was only interested in Glanmor and he was constantly in her thoughts, especially in those quiet moments before she drifted off to sleep.

She tried to visualize what he must look like now. After almost two years he'd be a full-grown man and probably look quite different.

Maria seemed to take on a new lease of life once she was back working her pitch and even when the autumn winds became chill she refused to let Fern take her place outside the station. Maria was still working there the week before Christmas even though it was horribly cold and wet.

'I'll wrap up really warm; I'll put on two of everything. I'll even put two shawls round my shoulders then, if the top one happens to get wet, I can take it off,' Maria told her.

'What about your feet, though? Standing there for hours – they'll be like blocks of ice,' Fern persisted.

'Nonsense, cariad.' Maria shook her head. 'I'll be wearing two pairs of thick woollen stockings and they'll keep my legs and feet snug and warm. You make up plenty of holly wreaths and don't forget I'll want some as well as sprigs of mistletoe. Don't go keeping back all the best bits for your stall,' she added as an afterthought.

'Those as well as flowers will make the tray too heavy for you to carry,' Fern warned.

'Not a bit of it. I'll only have mistletoe and posies in my tray and Rhodri can bring over a bigger one with all the wreaths on it and stand it on the ground by my feet.'

'You might turn giddy bending down to pick them up,' Fern said worriedly. 'Do you think we could put up a trestle table?'

'No, cariad, the station people wouldn't allow it. Now don't worry, I'll tell the customers to pick out the wreath they want so they'll be the ones doing the stooping down, not me.'

For the few days leading up to Christmas,

Fern was so busy on the stall that she hadn't time to worry too much about Maria. A couple of times she asked Rhodri to keep an eye on things while she dashed over the road to make sure that Maria was all right.

'Of course I'm all right. Now, get yourself back to your stall and stop worrying about me,' Maria told her crossly.

When they finally packed up on Christmas Eve, Maria was far from well. She claimed it was just a touch of the sniffles but Fern could see that she was having trouble breathing.

Maria tried to make light of it, talking about what good business they'd done, but by the time they reached home she was not only shivering but coughing and wheezing.

'You'd better take off all those damp clothes and go straight to bed,' Fern told her. 'I'll bring you some hot soup.'

'That's no way to spend Christmas Eve,' Maria panted. 'There're dozens of jobs to be done. I haven't stuffed the chicken yet.'

'I'll see to it, so don't worry. Go on, get yourself undressed and into bed. As soon as the kettle boils I'll make you a cup of hot cocoa and I'll fill a hot-water bottle to warm up your feet.'

'I don't want to go to bed. I was planning to make some mince pies tonight,' Maria protested.

'You've already made a Christmas cake so we can eat that instead.' Fern smiled.

'Christmas isn't the same without a mince pie,' Maria grumbled. 'Supposing someone should

195

call round to see us tomorrow – we'd have nothing at all to offer them.'

'We'd have the Christmas cake,' Fern reminded her. 'Anyway,' she added with a light laugh, 'we're not likely to get any visitors, now, are we?'

'I don't know; we might have a visitor. I did tell Rhodri to call round for a cup of tea and a mince pie if he felt like it. It was only my way of saying thank you to him for all his help over the last few days,' she added quickly as she saw Fern frown.

'Then I'll make some mince pies tonight, if that's what it is going to take to make you go to bed.'

When she took Maria a hot drink Fern felt concerned about how ill Maria looked. There were two bright flushes of colour on her cheeks and her forehead was burning hot.

'I really think we ought to call in a doctor,' she said worriedly. 'He could give you something to stop you getting any worse.'

'Rubbish! We don't want to waste the money I've struggled to earn on a doctor,' Maria croaked.

By next morning, however, there was no question of whether or not to send for a doctor. Maria's breathing was so terribly laboured that she could barely speak.

Fern had no idea where to find the nearest doctor on duty so, pulling on her hat and coat, she ran down the road and round the corner to Rhodri's house to ask him if he knew.

'You get back home and take care of Maria and I'll go and fetch one for you,' he offered.

'Do you mind? It's Christmas Day, you must have plans of your own,' she added shyly.

'Oh I have,' he grinned, 'I'll be sitting down to a meat pie and a bottle of beer for my Christmas dinner.'

'You mean you are all on your own?'

'That's right. In fact, I was thinking of taking up Maria's invitation and dropping in to see you both this afternoon.'

'Then it's a good job I did as Maria asked and made some mince pies last night.' Fern smiled. 'I would ask you to our Christmas Dinner, if you like. We're planning on having roast chicken and there will be Christmas pudding with custard. Doesn't that sound better than a pork pie?'

'It most certainly does!' he agreed, his face creasing into a broad smile as he pulled on his cap and wound a muffler round his neck. 'Perhaps we'd better wait and see what the doctor has to say first, though. You mightn't have time to cook a fancy dinner if you have Maria to look after.'

Chapter Eighteen

Maria had developed bronchitis and was ill for several weeks. At first the doctor was afraid that it might turn into pneumonia and that she would have to go into hospital again, but with Fern's careful nursing she slowly began to make a recovery.

Throughout the difficult weeks of trying to look after Maria and run both stall and pitch, Rhodri was a tower of strength. Fern knew she could never have managed without his help. She and Maria were so grateful to him that they invited him to come to their place for a meal when he'd finished work each evening.

'Duw anwyl, you don't need to go to that much trouble. I'm used to looking after myself so you don't have to feed me every night; you've got enough to do as it is,' he told Fern.

'Maria likes to see you. She says it's as good as a tonic to talk to you,' Fern said, smiling.

'Oh, does she indeed! Well, all she talks about is you, cariad. You and your future,' he added.

'I see. I did wonder why you wanted to come every night,' Fern joked.

Although she tried to keep the banter between them light she was well aware of his feelings.

His eyes seem to follow her every movement and she wondered what else Maria had said to him. She hoped that she hadn't brought up the subject of marriage because, much as she liked Rhodri and was grateful for his help, she simply wasn't interested in him other than as a friend.

It was the beginning of February, though, before Maria was fit to work again and then she agreed that she would take things easy. Fern insisted that for a short while Maria should serve on the stall on Fridays while she took her place outside the station.

'If you are working on the stall then I won't have to worry about you because Rhodri will be alongside you and he will keep an eye on you.'

'Yes, and he'll be worrying about you instead,' Maria commented dryly. 'I don't like the idea of you selling out in the street while it's dark so early.'

'There's no need for either of you to worry; I cut my teeth on the pitch, remember.'

Their conversation went through her mind as she loaded up a large trug with plants and flowers and a second, lighter, tray with small posies and buttonholes.

She had almost finished for the night and was putting the few remaining posies into the trug to make it easier to carry them back to the stall when a tall bearded man came up to her.

'I'm afraid there's not very much choice left

199

this late in the evening,' she murmured without looking up from what she was doing.

'Oh, I've seen what I want,' he said, and at the sound of his voice Fern looked up, startled.

'Still selling flowers then,' he commented, his blue eyes twinkling.

'Glanmor?' Fern stared at the broad-shouldered man in disbelief. 'Glanmor! Is it really you?' she gasped as she studied the tanned, bearded face.

'I was hoping I would find you here. My mother said she had no idea where you were living these days.'

They stared at each other for a moment longer, each taking in the changes in the other's appearance and then she was in his arms and he was holding her so tightly that she could hardly breathe.

When he kissed her, she laughed and pulled away. 'That tickles,' she told him.

'Really!' He affected mock surprise. 'Perhaps, then, it's a good job I've only grown a beard and not a moustache as well.'

'If you had then I wouldn't have let you kiss me,' Fern told him.

'Are you saying you want me to take it off?' Glanmor questioned, pretending to look hurt. 'It's taken me almost two years to grow it and I'm very proud of it.'

Fern looked serious and then, experimentally, she stroked it. 'No, perhaps not. It does make you look different, though; quite grown-up, in fact,' she teased.

'I am grown-up.'

'Oh, Glanmor, it's so wonderful to see you.' Her arms went round his neck and her lips sought his. This time, as he responded, she didn't draw back but gave way to her pent-up passion.

'Hey! Steady on! You'll be getting us arrested.' Glanmor smiled but he kept his arm firmly round her waist, pulling her as close to his side as he could, and giving her a tight hug.

'Are you home for good?' Fern asked anxiously, her eyes searching his face.

Glanmor shook his head. 'No, cariad, I'm only ashore for a month or two. Well, that is if I want to rejoin the *Saturn*. She's in dry dock for repairs at the moment but as soon as those are done we'll be making another trip to Russia.'

Fern bit her lip and said nothing but she wished she hadn't asked. Knowing that he would be leaving again so soon in some ways ruined everything.

'Come on; don't let's worry about that at the moment, cariad. I'm here now and you're more lovely than ever,' the arm round her waist tightened and she felt his lips against her cheek. 'I've been dreaming of this moment all the time I've been away; I've missed you so much. We've an awful lot of catching up to do. For a start, you'd better tell me where you are living now.'

'With Maria in Loudon Square.'

He frowned. 'I thought you got on well with my mother; what made you move?'

Fern bit her lip and was silent for a moment. 'It wasn't your mother, it was him; that Jake Tomlinson, It was all right at first but then things became unpleasant.'

Glanmor looked taken aback. 'I haven't met him yet, but you mean he caused trouble between you and my mother?'

'Far worse than that! He attacked me and tried . . .' She looked embarrassed. 'Oh, you know what I'm trying to say. Your mother didn't believe me so I simply had to leave. When I went to work next day, Maria saw the state I was in and the bruises I'd got in the struggle to get away from him, and she suggested that I move in with her.'

'Cariad! I'm so sorry.' He pulled her into his arms again and hugged her close, smoothing her hair back from her brow and then kissing her tenderly.

'He wouldn't have dared to lay a finger on you if I'd been around,' Glanmor assured her.

'That's what Maria said but you weren't here so you couldn't come to my rescue. She was nearly as upset as I was,' Fern smiled, 'I expect she will tell you all about it when she gets the right moment. You are coming home with me to see her?'

'Isn't she here with you?' he asked looking around as if expecting to see her.

'We have a stall in the Hayes as well now,' Fern reminded him. 'Normally I run that and Maria is here. She hasn't been too well so I thought it was better for me to stand out here than for her to do so. In fact, at the moment we only sell here on a Friday night because I found it was so difficult running both of the sites while Maria was so ill.'

'So Maria is at home?'

'She will be by now; she's been on the stall today. She's going to be very surprised to see you. We've barely heard from you in all the time you've been away.'

Glanmor raised his eyebrows. 'I've written to you but you've never replied. The letters were all addressed to Margaret Street, of course, because that was where I thought you were still living.'

'I've not had a single one of them and couldn't write because I had no idea where you were.'

'You could have addressed it to the *Saturn* and the name of the shipping company and they would have sent it on.'

'Maria didn't think that there was any point in doing that because we didn't know your destination.'

'Utter rubbish!' he exclaimed angrily as they began walking in the direction of Loudon Square. 'I'm surprised Maria told you a tale like that. I did write to you, Fern, dozens of times, until the last few months and, as you'd never answered, I thought you'd lost inerest and found someone else.'

Fern shook her head, her eyes bright with tears as she realised Alwyn must have kept all the letters Glanmor had sent to her and how near she had come to losing him.

'So there is no one else?' he questioned as they turned into the Square.

'Of course not!' She squeezed his hand. 'It's been so lonely without you; please don't go away like that again.'

'I don't want to give up the sea,' he said stubbornly.

'No, I know that, but can't you sign on for a shorter trip? I wouldn't mind you being away for a month or two but this time you have been gone for years.'

'If I stay with the same ship, then it will be Russia again,' he told her. 'You could come with me, of course.'

'Go to Russia with you?' Fern stopped dead and stared at him in disbelief.

'Why not?'

'I couldn't leave Maria in the lurch. It wouldn't be fair after all she's done for me. Wait until you see her and you'll understand what I mean. She's still quite frail after her illness and she wouldn't be able to manage the stall or the pitch on her own.'

'I'm sure she could find someone else to help her; no one is indispensable, you know.'

Fern bit her lip and didn't answer. She was uncertain about what to say but as they were already in Loudon Square and he would be seeing Maria in a few minutes, she thought it was better to say nothing. Once Glanmor saw

Maria then he'd realise why it was impossible for her to leave.

Maria was overjoyed to see Glanmor. For a brief moment she stared at him as if she was seeing a ghost, then she held her arms wide and he was hugging her and she was kissing him, both of them crying.

'You bad boy,' she scolded, 'why have you never written to Fern all the time you've been away?'

'It's a long story. Fern will explain.'

'If she believes it then there must be a grain of truth in it,' Maria commented. 'Do you want a cup of tea or can you stay and have a meal with us?'

'I'll stay if there is enough to go round because by the smell of it you're having cawl. I've dreamed about your delicious soup and Bara Brith while I've been away,' he added with a deep sigh.

'Get away with you!' Maria chuckled but Fern could see her eyes had lit up at the compliment.

As Maria went towards the kitchen Fern caught her by the arm and stopped her. 'I'm sure everything is more or less ready, so while I dish up, why don't you sit down and talk to Glanmor and catch up on what he's been doing.'

Maria hesitated, then smiled and nodded. 'Yes, very well, I am feeling a bit tired. Call out if you need any help,' she added as Fern went into the kitchen.

As she strained the potatoes and cut some

chunks of bread she could hear them talking. Glanmor was expressing concern that she had lost so much weight and was looking thin and frail.

'I'm getting old, boyo. None of us last for ever and I've had one thing after the other. I've had the doctor here so many times I've lost count and I've been in hospital twice.'

'You mean Fern isn't looking after you as well as she should?' he joked.

'Oh, she's been wonderful; she's looked after me, all right. In fact, I don't think for one minute I'd be here today if it wasn't for the way she nursed me back to health. She's been an absolute wonder even though she's had troubles of her own.'

'She did mention them briefly when I asked her why she was living with you,' Glanmor murmured.

Fern felt uneasy; she didn't want Maria talking at length about Alwyn and Jake. After all, Alwyn was Glanmor's mother and for a time, until Glanmor had gone to sea and Jake came into her life, she had been very good to her.

'Right, come on, take your seats,' she said briskly as she took four hot plates into the living room and arranged them on the table so that she could ladle out the soup. As the savoury smell permeated the room Glanmor sniffed the air appreciatively.

'We really are going to have Maria's special

cawl,' he exclaimed. 'There's absolutely nothing in the world to beat it.'

'So you said before,' Maria laughed. 'If it's all that good, then why has it taken you all this time to come back for a bowl of it?'

'Perhaps the pair of you had better stop jabbering and come and sit at the table before it all goes cold. There's nothing worse than cold cawl – even Maria's.'

'Does she always bully you like this, Maria?' Glanmor teased, smiling across at Fern as he helped Maria out of her armchair and towards the table. 'Hey!' He looked around the table in surprise. 'Were you expecting visitors?'

As if in answer to his question the door opened and Rhodri burst into the room. 'Sorry if I'm late. I hope you haven't been waiting and let the cawl go cold.'

'I've dished ours out but you sit down and I'll fetch yours,' Fern told him as she hurried back into the kitchen.

'I don't suppose you two have met.' Maria beamed. 'This is Rhodri Richards, he works on the next stall to ours at the Hayes and he has helped Fern so much. I don't know how she would have managed without him.'

Chapter Nineteen

Fern held her breath as the two men shook hands and took stock of each other. They were of similar height but Rhodri was very thin and wiry whilst Glanmor was more solid. Glanmor was so tanned and weather beaten that he looked much stronger and fitter than Rhodri, even though he was the younger of the two men.

Fern sensed that they seemed to be wary of each other as they shook hands and there was a hint of caution in their voices as they greeted each other.

As the meal progressed their distrust of each other became even more apparent. Maria tried to draw Glanmor out by asking him to tell them more about his time in Russia but he was very reticent. Rhodri was equally dismissive of what he'd done to help Maria and Fern when she tried talking about that.

The moment they'd finished eating Rhodri pushed back his chair and stood up. 'Thanks for the meal, Maria. I have to rush. I'll see you on the stall tomorrow,' he said turning towards Fern. 'Don't be late,' he added abruptly.

Fern bit back the sharp retort she was about to make and merely nodded.

'Rhodri seems to be in a great hurry tonight,' Maria commented as the door closed behind him.

'Perhaps he is taking his girlfriend out and he doesn't want to keep her waiting,' Glanmor commented.

'No, he hasn't got a girlfriend or anyone else, poor boyo,' Maria said sadly. 'Rhodri lives on his own and has done ever since I've known him. You'd think a nice-looking chap like that would have found a wife and have settled down and become a family man long before this,' she added.

Her remark was met by silence. Fern began collecting up the plates to take them through to the scullery to wash up.

'No,' she protested as Glanmor started to help, 'you go and sit by the fire with Maria. I'll make a pot of tea and bring it in as soon as the kettle boils.'

As she scraped the leftovers off the plates and then plunged them into hot soapy water, Fern's mind was in turmoil. She tried to reason out why the two men had been so hostile towards each other. She hoped it was because both of them thought so much of Maria and so were jealous of each other, and not because of their feelings for herself.

As she brewed the tea and arranged three cups and saucers on a tray ready to take through to the other room she resolved that as soon as she and Glanmor were on their own she would explain the situation more plainly to him. She hoped it would clear the air if she made it clear to him that she'd only accepted Rhodri's help because it had been an emergency and she'd had no one else to turn to.

She would also have a word with Maria and ask her to have a quiet word with Rhodri and explain exactly who Glanmor was in the hope that they could all be friends.

Glanmor still looked rather put out when she took in the tea and although she tried to ask him questions about his long trip the conversation always seemed to come back to the subject of the stall. Maria kept singing Rhodri's praises and going into details about how helpful he had been and how much he had helped Fern while she had been unable to go to work.

Fern wondered if she was doing it deliberately or simply not thinking about what she was saying since it was obvious it was information that Glanmor didn't want to hear. His scowl deepened and in the end he delved into his pocket and brought out his cigarettes. He offered the packet to them and when they both declined he lit up his own cigarette and drew deeply on it.

Fern watched his face and the tight lines around his mouth slowly softened as he exhaled and relaxed. As their eyes met he managed a smile and once again she resolved to tell him at length how and why Rhodri was treated as a special friend.

For another hour or so they chatted amiably

enough. Glanmor related anecdotes about his trip that drew astonished gasps from Maria. Then she struggled up from her armchair and announced that it was time she was going to bed.

'Don't be too late, Fern,' she cautioned. 'Remember, it's Saturday tomorrow and that means a long, busy day. Mind you make sure the door is locked after Glanmor leaves before you come to bed. I expect to be seeing a lot more of you, boyo, over the next few weeks,' she added as she reached the door. 'We've both been lonely without you.'

'Nos da, Maria. Don't worry, you'll be seeing me every day while I'm on shore leave,' he promised. 'I'll not only be dropping in on the stall but also coming around in the evenings as well, if that's all right?' he added.

'Of course it is,' she told him with a warm smile. 'If I'm not working, then I'll be at home here resting and it would do me good to see you and have a heart-to-heart,' she added meaningfully.

'You mean you trust Fern to manage the stall all on her own?' he joked.

'Not completely on her own, Rhodri's always on hand to keep an eye on things and to give her a hand when she needs it.'

The smile faded from Glanmor's face. 'Yes, of course, I'd forgotten about that.'

The moment Maria was out of the room Fern said quickly, 'I want to explain about Rhodri. I

211

don't think you understand what the situation has been and I don't want you getting the wrong impression.'

'Whatever makes you think I'm doing that?'

'I'm not sure. Maria does go on about him a lot and how helpful he is; which is true, of course,' she added quickly.

'So what else is there that I should know?' he quizzed, his gaze holding hers.

'I'm not sure how much Maria told you while I was out in the kitchen doing the washing-up,' she said hesitantly and then waited for him to speak.

'Well, she's told me all about her illness; it sounds as though she's been pretty bad. She also said how much you'd done for her. In fact she couldn't praise you enough for all your care and attention,' he added with a warm smile.

'And of course she was bound to mention how much Rhodri did to help us both?'

'Yes.' He nodded. 'It seems he's been a tower of strength but whether it was because of Maria being ill or because he wanted to help you, I wasn't too sure,' he added curtly.

'Probably both.' She smiled gently. 'Look, Glanmor, there was no way I could have managed both the stall and the pitch on my own; you do understand that, don't you?'

Glanmor nodded but he was still frowning. 'Do you still need his help, though?' he questioned.

'On Friday afternoons Maria looks after the

stall while I do the pitch outside the station. Rhodri keeps an eye on her and helps her if she needs any of the heavy stuff lifting and so on. As a reward, because he won't accept money for his services, Maria invites him to come back here for his evening meal.'

Fern crossed over to where Glanmor was sitting and perched herself on the arm of his chair. 'Why does it worry you so much?' she asked softly, burying her fingers in his thick hair.

Looking up he caught her hand and then pulled her forward so that her eyes were on a level with his. 'Because the pair of you seemed to be so close that I wondered if there was anything going on between you,' he stated fiercely.

'Glanmor Williams, I do believe you are jealous,' Fern exclaimed laughingly as she slid down on to his lap, twining her arms round his neck.

'Only if I have cause to be,' he said, holding her shoulders as her lips sought his.

'There will never be anyone else in the whole world for me except you,' she breathed softly and this time her lips were on his, conveying their own tale of her longing to be with him.

Glanmor responded with a passion that both thrilled and frightened her by its intensity. Their need for each other was overwhelming. Gasping, they slid from the chair to the rug in front of the fire.

He murmured tender words of love and

waves of desire flooded over her. He peeled away her clothes and began stroking her body, and as he caressed her breasts her breathing became ragged and she longed for release.

Her intense reaction to his touch seemed to heighten his own desire and as they consummated their passion Fern felt that it was a blissful culmination of her months of dreaming and desire.

'We shouldn't have done that, cariad,' she whispered, nuzzling his neck.

'I've thought of nothing else all the time I've been away from you,' Glanmor groaned. He propped himself up on one elbow and lovingly traced the outline of her face with his forefinger. 'You will marry me?'

'Marry you! Of course I will ... one day, perhaps next time you come on leave.'

'No, I mean now, right away, we've both waited long enough,' he told her firmly.

'How can I? I'm only seventeen. I would need permission and now Mam's dead it would probably mean asking Uncle Bryson because he's my nearest relation.'

'Then go round to Angelina Street tomorrow as soon as you finish work and ask him,' he said. 'I suppose I'd better come with you in case he starts being awkward in any way,' he added rather reluctantly.

'Uncle Bryson would never agree to us marrying each other,' Fern said worriedly.

'Why ever not?'

'Well,' she wrinkled her nose, 'he is your dad, and that means we are first cousins and you know as well as I do that it wouldn't be considered right for us to marry.'

Glanmor laughed harshly. 'I don't think it would bother him what I did – or what you did, for that matter. It's only a legal thing. If you don't want to ask him, or he won't fill in whatever form it is he has to sign, then we'll live together and say we're married.'

'You've been away from civilisation for too long,' Fern laughed. 'Can you imagine what your mother would say if we did that?'

'She couldn't say very much since she has that fellow Jake Tomlinson living there with her these days, now could she?'

Fern shook her head. 'He's only supposed to be her lodger. We'd end up in trouble if we did anything like that. Even here in Tiger Bay they don't break those sorts of rules.'

'We don't have to stay here in Cardiff,' he said stubbornly. 'You could come back to Russia with me. They're far more lenient over there. This fellow Lenin who is running the country now has made sweeping changes about all those sorts of things. We could live together and no one would raise an eyebrow or turn a hair.'

'So how do I get to Russia? Do I stow away on the *Saturn*?' Fern giggled.

'I'm quite serious, so think about it,' Glanmor told her as he kissed her long and hard before pulling away and standing up. 'Come back to

Russia with me and then we can be together,' he repeated as he began to pull his clothes back on.

'It means leaving Maria in the lurch.'

'She'll understand when you tell her the reason you are leaving. You can't stay with her for ever, now can you? Anyway, she wouldn't expect you to do so,' he added without waiting for her to reply.

'Maria's been very good to me and I feel it's up to me to look after her now she's so frail,' Fern protested.

'She's much better now. You said yourself that she's even started coming back to work on Fridays.'

'She's not well enough to work on the stall all week, though. If I left, she'd have to give up either the stall or the pitch. As it is, it's difficult coping with both of them.'

'I'm sure she'd soon find someone else to take your place,' Glanmor insisted. 'In the meantime, this Rhodri boyo would give her a hand and keep an eye on her.'

'It takes time to learn the job, though, and you said you might be leaving again in a couple of months,' Fern went on, ignoring his jibe about Rhodri.

'I'd better be going now because it's well past midnight and you have to be up early in the morning. You mustn't be late or you'll be getting told off by Rhodri.'

'You will look in on the stall sometime during the day?'

'Of course I will. I'll come at lunchtime and whisk you off to the Milk Bar for a snack while Rhodri keeps an eye on things, since he's so good at doing that.'

Fern's mind was so full of all that had happened that evening and the things she'd talked about with Glanmor that although it was so late she was sure she would never sleep.

After she'd locked the door behind him and made sure that the room was tidy she crept into bed as quietly as possible so as not to disturb Maria.

As she snuggled down under the bedclothes, however, it was not all their future problems that filled her mind as she drifted off to sleep: as she put her head on the pillow all she could think about was the wonderful love-making she'd experienced when she'd been in Glanmor's arms.

Maria's voice calling out to her that it was time to get up seemed to come within minutes. Bleary-eyed, she pushed back the bedclothes and forced herself to get out of bed and to go and put the kettle on to make a cup of tea for herself and Maria before she went to the Hayes.

Had Glanmor being there last night and making love to her all been a dream? she asked herself as she washed her face under the kitchen tap and, shivering in the cold morning air, went back to her bedroom to get dressed.

Chapter Twenty

For the next few weeks, Fern found that life seemed to settle into a comfortable routine. Glanmor was as good as his word; he came to the Hayes at midday each day and whisked her off to the nearest Milk Bar for a hot drink and a snack while Rhodri kept an eye on her stall as well as his own.

Glanmor also came to meet her each evening and walked back to Loudon Square with her. On Friday evenings he came to the station to meet her and walk her home, leaving Rhodri to escort Maria home from the Hayes even though at first he resented the fact that Rhodri stayed to share the evening meal as well.

The atmosphere between the two men was cool although, reluctantly, Glanmor accepted that Rhodri was a very good friend to both Fern and Maria and meant nothing more than that to Fern. They had very little in common and the atmosphere on Friday evenings was nowhere near as easy-going as it was on other evenings.

Occasionally, Glanmor and Fern went out in the evenings but because it was winter and the weather was so cold and unpleasant they usually preferred to sit by the fire, drinking tea and talking until Maria went off to bed at around nine o'clock.

After that, once they were on their own, they wasted no time but enjoyed those magic moments that Fern looked forward to and which meant so much to both of them.

When she was in Glanmor's arms, when he was telling her how lovely she was and how much he loved her and needed her, all her other problems simply vanished. She wanted things to be like this for ever; she never wanted him to go away again.

Their passionate lovemaking had come to mean so much to her. The guilt she had felt the first time they'd made love had long since been overcome. How could it be wrong to give and receive so much joy and pleasure? she told herself.

The evening when Glanmor told them that the work on the *Saturn* had been completed and that once their new cargo had been arranged and stored on board they would be ready to sail for Russia, Fern felt that the bottom had dropped out of her world.

He'd waited until they'd finished their meal and Fern had brought in the tray of freshly brewed tea and they were all sitting round the fire, relaxed and comfortable.

'So does that mean that you are going to sail away without another care in the world?' Maria asked.

'Sail away, yes, but I won't be carefree, Maria. I do have a very big problem.'

Maria looked at him sharply. 'Oh yes, and what's that, then, boyo?'

'I want to marry Fern before I sail; I want to make sure she's here waiting for me when I get back.'

'Good. I'm pleased to hear you say that. I was beginning to think that you were just playing fast and loose with her affections and simply out to break her heart. So what's the problem, then? Surely she hasn't turned you down.'

'No, it's nothing like that at all, Maria,' Fern said quickly. The trouble is that I'm not old enough to get married without the permission of a parent or guardian. That means asking Bryson because he's my nearest male relative. I don't think he would agree to it because Glanmor is his son and that means he's my cousin.'

'Perhaps you could sign the forms, Maria, and say you were Fern's guardian,' Glanmor suggested.

'Oh yes? I suppose you do realise that I would be perjuring myself if I did that?' she chuckled.

'I couldn't let you do that, much as I wish to marry Glanmor,' Fern told her with a despairing sigh. 'Anyway,' she added, 'by the time Glanmor comes back from his next trip I will probably be old enough for us to go ahead without having to ask anyone's permission.'

'Several years of separation is a long time,' Maria mused. 'They can be years of frustration

220

and worry in case one of you finds someone else,' she added.

'Let's talk about something, else shall we?' Fern said uneasily.

'Not yet, because there is something I want to say to you both.' Maria paused and held out her cup to Fern for a refill.

'I've been waiting for the right moment to tell you this and now seems to be as good a time as any other. I went to see the doctor this morning' – she held up her hand as Fern was about to speak – 'hear me out, cariad, it's hard enough to tell you this as it is,' she paused and took a sip of her tea.

'The doctor told me that unless I give up the flower business and all the strain and work it entails then I am going to find myself back in hospital again in next to no time. My heart is not what it was and he says I'm far too old for all the worry of running a business. He advised me to give it up and put my feet up.'

Fern and Glanmor looked at each other. Fern felt that receiving two body blows in one evening was too much. She wondered what was going to happen next. Glanmor saying he would be leaving within the next few weeks was bad enough, but this was even more serious. It sounded as though her job on the flower stall was at stake and it was the only kind of work she'd ever done.

'I'm sorry you feel worn out, Maria but can't you give up the pitch and let me go on running the stall? Rhodri will always give me a hand if I need it,' Fern said lamely.

'No, cariad, it's not as simple as that. There's the buying and selling to be organised as well as preparing and pricing up all the flowers and plants ready for sale. I know you do a wonderful job serving on the stall but there's all the other work that's entailed, the ordering and the keeping of the books.'

'If you showed me what to do, I'm sure I'd manage,' Fern said eagerly.

'Yes, you probably would, but to tell you the truth, I'm at my wits end trying to find the money to pay for everything on time. I'm so behind with settling all the bills that I'm very worried that I'll be in serious debt very soon and have the bailiffs knocking on the door.'

'Oh Maria,' Fern said in a shocked voice. 'Why ever didn't you tell me about all this before now? We might have been able to make some changes or something,' she added vaguely.

'There didn't seem to be any point in doing so, cariad. Now don't worry, I'll make sure we keep going one way or the other until you've found yourself another job. You're bright and efficient and I'll give you a good reference so you shouldn't have too much trouble. One of the other stallholders at the Hayes might be glad to take you on so start putting the word around.'

'There's no need for Fern to do that,' Glanmor told her. 'I want her to come with me, back to Russia. We could be together there.'

'Really?' Maria looked so relieved that Fern felt close to tears. 'So what's stopping you doing that, Fern?'

Fern shrugged her shoulders and shook her head, she couldn't speak; at that moment she felt it was all too much for her. Life seemed to be rushing past her and so many things were happening all at once that she couldn't take them in.

'She didn't want to leave you in the lurch, Maria,' Glanmor said bluntly.

'Well, she needn't worry about doing that,' Maria exclaimed forcibly. 'In fact, she will be solving the biggest of all my problems. Telling you both has been hard enough because I was worried about what would happen to you, Fern, but if I know you are going to be with Glanmor, then it's all working out for the best.'

'Surely there's something we can do to keep things going,' Fern said worriedly. 'I know how much the business and especially the stall means to you.'

'Not any more, my health is what matters to me most of all,' Maria told her.

Fern bit her lip. She didn't know whether or not to remind Maria that several times in the past Maria had hinted that she hoped in time that she would take over the business.

'I might be able to help you out with money,' Glanmor offered. 'I've saved up quite a bit while I've been at sea.'

'And you are going to need every penny of

it to meet your expenses now that you're going to have to look after Fern as well as yourself. No, I don't want either of you worrying about me. Giving up the stall and, if I'm lucky, possibly managing to sell the business, will bring in enough to cover all I owe,' Maria assured him.

'I feel terrible about going away and leaving you with so much to deal with on your own when you are still not well,' Fern murmured.

'Well, there's no need to be concerned, cariad. In fact, it's solved my biggest headache of all knowing what you're planning to do. I hated the thought of having to tell you that you'd have to find another job and now you've saved me the trouble.'

Fern wasn't altogether sure if Maria was telling the truth. She knew how much the flowers meant to her; it had been the one thing she'd worried about when she'd been in hospital.

Perhaps if she talked to Rhodri about it he would be able to suggest a way of helping Maria to keep the stall going even if she wasn't there. Then she remembered about all the debts Maria said she had and how selling up would take care of them and she felt even more bemused than before.

The SS *Saturn* was due to sail in less than a week and Glanmor had said that if she was going with him then he wanted her belongings ready a couple of days before they sailed so that he could stow them away on board. Over the next few days she would have to decide what to take with her and what to leave at Maria's until they came back. It meant that she hadn't very much time to talk to Rhodri about the situation or to go into it further with Maria.

Glanmor brought along a kitbag for her to pack her things in. Once she'd done this and he had taken them back to the ship she really felt as though the die was cast and she was virtually on her way.

Saying goodbye to Maria was a tearful affair. The older woman tried to remain stoic but her wrinkled cheeks were wet with tears as were Fern's as they hugged and kissed before they parted.

'Now mind you take good care of Fern,' Maria told Glanmor as he hugged her and said goodbye. 'Remember this time to write and let me know how you are both getting on.'

It was a bitterly cold night and Fern shivered as damp mist swirled around them as they made their way to where the ship was berthed. For one brief moment Fern wished she was still sitting in front of the fire, drinking tea with Maria.

As they walked down Bute Street towards the Pier Head Glanmor seemed to be so much on edge that Fern wondered if he was having second thoughts about taking her with him.

'I'm freezing,' she whispered as she slipped her arm though his and snuggled up to his side.

He said nothing and he seemed so tense that

it was almost as if he was rejecting her. 'Is something wrong? Would you sooner I wasn't coming with you?'

'Heaven's no!' He stopped and took her in his arms and kissed her. 'Of course I'm pleased that you are coming with me but there is a slight problem,' he murmured.

'Go on. Tell me. I don't like it when you are in such a pensive mood like this.'

'I'm not in a mood,' he told her gruffly as he released her and, tucking her arm though his again, began to walk quickly. 'I'm a bit worried though.'

'What about?'

Again he was silent and seemed withdrawn. Then, as the Pier Head came in view he headed towards a Milk Bar. 'Come on, let's stop and have a hot drink to warm you up and I'll try and explain things while we're drinking it.'

He found a secluded corner seat but he remained silent until their drinks were served. Then, avoiding her gaze, he said in a hard, flat voice, 'I'm not sure how you are going to take this. You see, the *Saturn* doesn't carry passengers.'

'Yes, I know that. It's a cargo vessel,' she murmured as she sipped her drink.

'That's the point. Cargo and crew – that's all. No passengers whatsoever.'

'What are you trying to tell me? Are you saying I can't come with you?'

He stared down into his mug of steaming hot cocoa. 'Not openly, you can't.'

'I don't understand.' Fern frowned. 'You've already taken all my things on board.'

'Yes, I know that, but no one knows they're your things; they think I have another kitbag of stuff. I'm going to have to smuggle you aboard and you will have to stay hidden in my cabin for the whole of the journey,' he said gruffly.

'You mean that no one at all must know I'm travelling on the ship?' Fern exclaimed in a shocked voice. 'Why on earth didn't you tell me this before?'

His hand sought hers and squeezed it. 'I was afraid you wouldn't come,' he told her.

'So however am I going to get on board?' she asked, bemused.

'I'm planning to smuggle you aboard somehow and into my cabin. And then you must stay there. Like I've said, no one must know you are on board.'

'I don't see how you can keep me hidden for the whole of the voyage,' Fern argued worriedly. 'That could be two years.'

'I don't either, but once we are well on our way I'll own up that you are on board. We don't put into port until we reach Russia so there's no possibility of the captain ordering you off the ship.'

'What about you, though. Will you be punished?'

'I probably will be, but I'm not worried about that because it will be worth it.'

'So what kind of punishment do you think you are likely to get?' Fern persisted.

'I don't know.' He shrugged. 'I'll have to wait and see what the captain decides on.'

'You won't be given the cat-o'-nine-tails, will you, Glanmor?' she shuddered.

He laughed. 'No, I wouldn't think so. That used to be one of the punishments in the Royal Navy in the olden days but I don't think they use it any more.'

'If they take you away and put you in irons or shut you up in isolation somewhere, then I will be on my own and I could even starve to death.'

'It won't come to that. I'll be punished but Captain Mulligan is a pretty reasonable sort of man so I'm hoping I will be able to make him understand why I had to break all the rules and smuggle you on board. Anyway,' he went on quickly, 'if I'm being punished, they'll know you are on the ship and the captain wouldn't let you starve, so you have nothing to worry about.'

Chapter Twenty-one

The fine drizzle that had been falling when they'd left Maria's had now turned to sleeting rain. As they made their way from the Pier Head through the maze of the docks to where the SS *Saturn* was berthed Fern was afraid of slipping into the dark murky waters on either side of her. In desperation she clung on to Glanmor's arm.

He was so concerned that there was no one else about that he kept looking back over his shoulder to make sure they weren't being followed, which made her feel all the more nervous.

When the outline of the ship came into view he stopped and whispered, 'Don't speak; don't say a word now until we are on board and in my cabin. Do you understand?'

Fern nodded and remained silent but she felt petrified, wondering what might happen next.

Holding her arm tightly Glanmor waited until he was quite sure that there was no one about then hurried her towards the ship. The climb up the gangplank to the deck seemed to Fern to be mountainous. The steps were slippery from the rain but Glanmor's tight hold on her arm steadied her.

As she stumbled on to the deck she stopped to regain her breath but Glanmor looked around nervously and hurried her towards another set of steps. She found that these led down below deck and they looked far more perilous to her mind than the steps they had just negotiated.

Without a word of explanation he twisted her round so that she was facing the gangway, with her back to the steps. Then he began to descend them and, holding her ankle he guided it on to the first rung. Keeping close behind her he helped her down to the deck below.

Fern gasped with relief when she was on even ground again but it was by no means the end of her ordeal. Quickly he propelled her forward to another gangway and repeated the process of helping her descend to the level below.

Once they were in the bowels of the ship he hurried her along to where his bunk was situated. It was in a very small cabin towards the prow of the ship. It was so tiny that they were barely able to close the door once the two of them were inside.

Speaking in a whisper, Glanmor told her she must wait there while he went and reported to the first mate.

Left alone, Fern looked round in dismay. There was no bed, only a hammock slung between two hooks, and it took up the entire width of the cabin. There was one small cupboard and a large chest which she supposed must act as a seat as well as a means of storage. On the wall above it was a small piece of mirror, positioned almost too high for her to see her reflection and so miniscule that she wondered why he bothered having it there at all.

She shuddered at the thought that this was to be her home for the whole of their journey to Russia. She had no idea how far away that was or how long it was going to take to get there.

She took off her wet coat and looked for somewhere to put it. The only thing she could find was a single hook high up on the wall near the chest, so she draped it on that.

As she was doing so there was a sudden deafening noise and the cabin began shaking and rocking. She clamped her hand over her mouth to stop herself from screaming in fright; then she realised that it must be the ship's engines being started up.

Still trembling, she moved across the cabin with the intention of sitting in the hammock but the juddering of the ship made it impossible for her to get into it. Each time she tried to sit it seemed to tip and throw her out again. She wondered how on earth anyone could actually sleep in it. The slightest movement of the ship and they'd be out on the floor.

The room was hot and smelled fusty and she longed for a breath of fresh air. There was a tiny porthole window so she went over to it to see if she could open it but there seemed to be no way of doing so. As far as she could make out it was simply a small circle of thick glass set into the hull. She tried to peer out through it but the glass was so obscure that she could see nothing.

Her heart pounding, she sat down on the chest and put her head in her hands. It was like a nightmare, she thought unhappily. Taking a deep breath and pushing her hair back from her face, she tried to blank out all her fears and concentrate on thinking of other things as she waited for Glanmor to come back.

If she had known it was going to be like this would she have come? she asked herself.

In her heart she knew the answer was yes because more than anything else in the world she wanted to be with Glanmor. Yet, even so, at this moment she couldn't help wishing that she was back on the flower stall in the Hayes, serving customers and exchanging friendly banter with Rhodri.

The wait for Glanmor seemed endless. Fern began to panic in case he never returned. When he did he was carrying a plate of food and a mug of tea.

'Come on, tuck in,' he said as he placed both of them on the chest alongside her.

She shook her head. 'I'm not hungry,'

'Well, drink the tea while it is hot and you can eat the food later. Make the most of it, I might not get the chance to bring you any more for quite a while.'

Fern gave him a wan smile and picked up

the tin mug. The tea was sweet and almost black; so strong that she almost choked as she swallowed it.

Hugging the mug between both her hands she enjoyed the feeling of warmth that emanated from it far more than she did the contents. In an attempt to appear grateful she picked up one of the sandwiches. The bread was very thick and coarse and the chunk of beef in between the two slices was so tough that she found she couldn't bite into it.

She made a pretence of eating, then put it to one side. 'I'll enjoy that later,' she promised.

Glanmor nodded. 'Whatever you think best, but we'll be leaving port quite soon. Have you ever been to sea before?'

'You know I haven't. Why do you ask?'

He frowned. 'Well, the first part of the journey can be a bit choppy. The ship might roll quite a lot.'

'What has that got to do with whether I eat this now or later on?' Fern asked.

'Most seasoned sailors say you feel much better if you have some solid food inside you. They claim that it helps you to stop feeling queasy,' he added quickly.

'You mean you think I'm going to be seasick?'

'It's quite possible that you might be. I was for the first few days. I found that once the ship reached calmer waters and settled down then so did my stomach. I'm simply warning you about what to expect,' he added with a grin.

'I'm finding everything is so different and strange and nothing at all like I thought it was going to be that I don't suppose being seasick will make all that much difference.'

She looked round the tiny cabin. 'I thought I was going to have a lovely little cabin all to myself and have my meals with you and your friends and it would be all friendly and exciting. I don't know how I am going to survive in here even for one night.' She sighed. 'You haven't even told me how long the journey will take,' she added looking at him.

Before he could reply a klaxon sounded and he moved to the door. 'I must go. I'm needed on deck.' He gave her a quick kiss. 'Stay in here and keep the door shut. Don't answer if anyone knocks. I'll be back again as soon as I possibly can.'

Left alone and remembering what Glanmor had said about eating, Fern picked up the sandwich again. This time she took it apart, ate some of the bread and then tried to break the meat into smaller pieces. She had no cutlery so she was forced to tear it apart with her fingers. Even then, when it was in manageable chunks, it was still so tough that she could hardly chew it.

The noise from the engine as well as from other parts of the ship had now increased and she could feel severe rocking movements as the tugs started pulling the SS *Saturn* from her mooring place and headed out to sea with her.

Within a very short time it felt almost as if

the floor beneath her feet was moving independently and she assumed they'd now reached the open sea. She clung on to the side of the chest to try and steady herself as the ship was buffeted around and tilted first one way and then the other. She tried to stand up but the swaying was such that she felt that if she did she would lose her balance completely.

As Glanmor had warned her, the ship's motion soon made her feel queasy. All she wanted to do was to lie down but she knew that if she hadn't been able to sit in the hammock when they were in dock then she certainly wasn't going to be able to climb into it now with everything swaying from side to side.

Gingerly, she edged forward and crouched down on to her knees so that she could lie down on the floor. It felt better, but the floor was so hard that it was far from comfortable.

She wished she'd spread her coat or something down first but it was too late to do anything about that now. She knew that if she tried to sit up, let alone stand up, she would probably be sick. The only thing she could do was lie there until Glanmor came back.

It was three days before Fern felt well enough to even sit up. Glanmor did his best to make her as comfortable as possible by spreading one of his blankets on the floor for her to lie on and covering her over with another one to try and stop her shivering.

It meant that he had no bedding at all for

himself so he slept in the hammock fully dressed and spread his coat over his shoulders to try and keep warm.

To Fern the journey seemed endless. She was tired and weary, hungry and thirsty and had never felt so ill in her life. Glanmor did what he could for her but it wasn't enough. When her temperature started to soar and she was verging on delirium he was so worried that he told her he was going to tell the captain that she was on board.

'No, you mustn't do that,' she begged. 'It will get you into trouble and you'll be severely punished.'

'I can't leave you in this state any longer. This isn't mere seasickness; you need to be seen by the ship's doctor.'

Captain Mulligan was more than annoyed; he was absolutely furious and delivered a scathing reprimand. 'It's considered bad luck having a woman on board, you should know that; it could have caused a riot amongst the crew. I'll mete out your punishment later,' he told Glanmor. 'For the moment, we must give priority to treating this young girl.'

Fern was transferred from Glanmor's cabin to Captain Mulligan's own quarters. She was so weak that she was unable to stand let alone walk so Glanmor was instructed to carry her there. He was then assigned by Captain Mulligan to watch over her twenty-four hours a day until her fever abated.

When he heard that Fern was on the road to recovery he gave permission for her to use the facilities in his cabin so that she could have a bath.

Fern almost cried with relief as she lay back in the tub of hot water. She washed her hair which was stiff with sweat from the last few days. As she emerged from the bath and towelled herself dry she felt thoroughly refreshed.

She was also relieved to find that the sway of the ship no longer made her feel queasy. As she dried and combed her hair she felt she was ready to face Captain Mulligan and accept whatever punishment he might impose.

'Captain Mulligan has invited you to eat at his table to night,' Glanmor told her. 'I hope you realise that he is doing you a great honour,' he told her with a smile.

'Feeding me up before he claps me in irons, is he?' She grinned as Glanmor helped her to the table where Captain Mulligan was already sitting.

'Have you heard what your punishment is to be yet, Glanmor?' she whispered as they walked towards the captain's table.

'No,' Glanmor shook his head, 'but as long as he is lenient with you that is all that matters.'

Captain Mulligan looked so stern, and his mouth above his massive beard was set in such a tight line, that Fern felt a tremor of fear. When he indicated to Glanmor that she was to sit in the chair right next to him she knew she was shaking like a leaf.

237

Apart from acknowledging her presence with a formal 'Good evening', he didn't speak to her again until after the meal was over. She tried valiantly to eat what was placed in front of her but she felt so tense with foreboding that she could barely swallow.

At the end of their meal Captain Mulligan turned to her and asked her if she had anything to say. He listened in silence as, in a trembling voice, Fern explained that the reason she'd stowed away was because she was too young to marry without parental consent and she knew it would never be granted.

'Glanmor decided the only way we could live together without shocking everyone we knew was for me to return to Russia with him. I love Glanmor so much that it seemed to be the perfect solution,' she added with a shy smile.

'So you persuaded him to smuggle you aboard my ship?' Captain Mulligan said sternly. 'You must have known that you were bound to be discovered. Surely you realised that it was against the rules and that it would get Glanmor into serious trouble? Why didn't you ask if you could travel with us?'

'Your ship doesn't carry passengers, it was as simple as that,' Fern sighed.

'Humph! It seems we've got one now whether we want her or not,' Captain Mulligan growled. He took a sip of his drink. 'I could cast you over the side, I suppose. That would be a quick and easy way of dealing with the matter.'

'If you did that, then I would probably drown and you'd feel responsible,' Fern said in a shaky voice.

'Hmm! I suppose you have a point. What about if I set you adrift in a lifeboat? Do you think you would manage to survive long enough to reach land?'

Fern shook her head. 'I'd die of fright long before I reached the coast,' she told him.

'Well, in that case, I suppose I'll have to consider letting you to stay on board. If that is what you want to do, then you will have to earn your passage.'

'Willingly. I'll do anything you tell me to do,' Fern told him eagerly.

Captain Mulligan's bushy eyebrows went up as he regarded her contemplatively.

'Well,' he said at length, 'what about scrubbing the deck every morning at five o'clock, or would you prefer to go on watch every night from midnight until six the next morning?'

Fern quailed at the thought of either of those tasks but she squared her shoulder and tilted her chin defiantly. 'You are the captain, so it is up to you to decide which one you want me to do,' she parried.

He laughed uproariously and slapped his fist down on the table. 'A feisty young lady; I like that. Perhaps those tasks are rather daunting, but what else can you do. Can you cook?'

'Not really.' Fern shook her head. 'I can cook for myself and I often prepared a meal for Maria,

239

the woman I lodged with, but I wouldn't be any good at cooking for as many people as there are here. I could help perhaps in other ways.'

Captain Mulligan nodded his head thoughtfully. 'Well, there's always room for another one in the galley. If you can't cook, then I suppose there are plenty of other things you could do to help like preparing the vegetables and washing up all the dirty plates and the greasy pots and pans afterwards.'

'If I do that, will you let Glanmor off without any punishment?' she asked boldly.

Captain Mulligan scowled and then sat stroking his beard as he considered what she'd requested.

'You're asking a lot, young lady,' he boomed. 'He knew full well that he was contravening all the ship's rules when he smuggled you on board. If you hadn't been taken so ill that he was worried about your welfare he would never have said anything. In fact, I don't suppose either of you would have done. He'd have smuggled you ashore when we reached Russia without saying a word to me.'

'If he'd been able to do that you would have known nothing at all about it so there would have been no question of punishing him. He meant well, he was only trying to make me happy. Please don't punish him for doing that,' Fern begged.

'I'll think about it and also about what is the most suitable punishment for you. In the meantime, keep out of my sight and perhaps I can forget I ever saw you.'

Fern nodded. Although his tone was harsh she saw the twinkle in his piercing blue eyes as, nervously, she held out her hand and thanked him for being so considerate.

Chapter Twenty-two

Fern waited in trepidation for a summons from Captain Mulligan to let her know what he had decided her punishment task was to be. As each day passed and she heard nothing she breathed a little more easily. Nevertheless, she remembered his warning and made sure she kept well out of his way.

Glanmor brought her meals back to the cabin. Now that it had been acknowledged that she was on board he no longer had to scrounge leftovers or save part of his own rations for her.

He was no longer permitted to sleep in his own cabin, however. Instead, he had been told that for the rest of their journey he was to sleep on deck. Knowing how cold and uncomfortable this must be Fern wondered if this was intended to be his punishment for smuggling her on to the ship.

She found being in such a confined space on her own all day and all night was very claustrophobic. Rather daringly she began taking a walk on deck each evening at the time when she knew Captain Mulligan would be having his evening meal.

She wished Glanmor could walk with her but

they knew that would be forbidden so they'd agreed that he would keep an eye open and alert her if there was any change in the captain's routine. Normally his mealtime lasted for well over an hour and it was a time Fern looked forward to all day.

She revelled in the feeling of fresh air on her face and even though the temperature dropped lower and lower as they sailed across the Baltic and drew nearer to Russia it did not deter her from her daily constitutional.

As they sailed across the Baltic Sea and entered the Gulf of Finland Glanmor explained that they were now not very far from their journey's end.

'Very soon now we'll be approaching Petrograd,' he told her. 'We'll be going into dock there and once our cargo has been unloaded we'll be given shore leave.'

The closer they got to Russia, though, the more Fern worried about what was going to happen once she left the *Saturn*. While she was still on board she felt fairly safe but Russia was a foreign country and the people would speak a language she didn't understand. Even the food would be strange and the people probably very different from those she'd grown used to in Cardiff's Tiger Bay.

Constantly she thought of Maria and wondered how she was. Had she managed to sell her business, or had she changed her mind and was she struggling to keep going? She hoped that Rhodri was taking care of her as he'd promised to do.

Occasionally she mentioned what she was thinking to Glanmor when he brought her meals to the cabin but he always hushed her to silence.

'Stop worrying about the past; you're embarking on a new life now. Everything will be fine because I'll be there to take care of you,' he always assured her. Then he would take her in his arms and the moment his lips met hers she was lost to the real world. All her worries and other thoughts went out of her mind as she made the most of their brief, passionate moments together.

Every night as she settled down to sleep she found herself shivering with the intense cold. She tried to imagine she was in Glanmor's arms, safe and warm, cocooned in his love, and it helped her to find peace with herself and the world around her.

It was only during the long lonely days that the dark troublesome thoughts returned to plague her. If she knew more of what lay ahead she would probably feel more confident, she told herself. As it was, she knew so little about Russia that she couldn't formulate any plans or even indulge in any dreams about what sort of future she and Glanmor would have.

Never mind, she told herself, as long as Glanmor was there at her side looking after her then all would be well because he'd make sure of that.

When finally Glanmor was able to tell her that they would be entering the Port of Petrograd sometime within the next two days Fern felt elated.

They were there; it was the real start of their great adventure. There was no turning back now. The die had been cast. Within hours she would be setting foot in Russia. At first she felt jubilant but then her fears and uncertainty grew apace.

Memories of the stories she'd heard about the revolution that had taken place there surged into her mind. There had been an uprising and people had killed their ruler the Tsar, so what sort of place was it? Was it going to be as lawless as it sounded?

She tried to concentrate on all the good things Glanmor had told her, about this new man Lenin who was now in charge of the country and all the wonderful things he had done for the ordinary people. They thought so much of him that they were even talking of changing the name Petrograd to Leningrad and she found that all very confusing.

Fern wondered how long the *Saturn* would be staying in Petrograd after they'd unloaded the cargo they'd brought. She felt sure that it would not take more than a few days at the most and she felt very concerned about what was going to happen after that.

Glanmor had mentioned shore leave but he didn't seem to know how many days or weeks that would be. Anyway, did it matter? Although he had not made it clear, she was sure he intended leaving the *Saturn* and staying ashore in Russia.

He must be intending to do that, she mused, because he had talked incessantly of the better life they would have there. It was why she had agreed to come with him, so surely he wouldn't simply leave her there all on her own?

The whole object of coming to Russia, she reminded herself, was not only so that they could be together but also so that they would be able to live together openly without breaking the law or being condemned as being sinful. Where would they live and how long would their money last if he couldn't get a job?

As she waited for Glanmor to explain things in more detail, she became increasingly frustrated. She felt so alone; so vulnerable. If only there was someone she could talk to, or something she could do to pass the time constructively, she mightn't feel so bad. She collected together her few possessions, sorted them and packed them into the kitbag.

When she woke the next morning the entire atmosphere on the ship had changed. The pulsing of the engines was gone; she could hear a confusion of shouts and orders coming from below deck as well as from the top deck and the shore.

She waited impatiently for Glanmor to bring her food so that she could find out what he knew, but the time ticked by and he didn't put in an appearance.

Since the strict daily routine seemed to have been abandoned Fern wondered if she dared go up on deck so that she could see for herself what was happening – even though Captain Mulligan had told her to stay in her cabin.

The hours passed but still there was no sign of Glanmor or of her food and she became increasingly concerned about what was happening. She could only assume that he was so busy helping with the unloading that he didn't have time to come and see her. Surely, though, they must stop for food? She felt hungry so the men unloading the cargo must be starving by now.

She kept opening the door of the cabin and peering out. There seemed to be a lot of activity but she couldn't see what was going on. She wondered what would happen once all the cargo had been unloaded. Did they turn the ship round and go back to Cardiff right away or would it have to go into dry dock for a thorough overhaul before embarking on another long journey?

It was late evening before Glanmor came with food for her. He looked exhausted.

'Don't I get a kiss and a hug?' she asked as he handed her the plate of food and then stepped back as though to leave. 'Have you had something to eat?'

'No,' he shook his head, 'we've only just completed the unloading of all the cargo. I brought yours along first because I thought you'd be hungry.'

'I'm starving, but I'm also concerned about what is going to happen next.'

'Captain Mulligan has sent for me and I have to go and see him right away so I should be able to tell you after that,' he said, smothering a yawn. 'I'm dog-tired,' he added ruefully.

Fern tried to eat the food Glanmor had brought her but suddenly her appetite had gone. She pushed the meat and potatoes around on her plate but although they looked and smelled appetising enough she didn't really want them.

It was almost an hour before Glenmor came back again and when he did his tiredness seemed to have vanished and his face was wreathed in smiles.

'It's all fixed,' he told her jubilantly. 'The *Saturn* has to go right around the coast to Nakhodka Port, which is away to the East, to pick up the next cargo and Captain Mulligan has said I can stay here in Petrograd while they do that. I will then rejoin the ship when she returns and puts in here again on her way back to Cardiff.'

'So how long will that take?' Fern asked in bewilderment.

'I'll be in Petrograd quite long enough to find somewhere to live and for you to be settled in properly.'

'You mean you are going to rejoin the ship and leave me behind all on my own in a strange country!' Fern exclaimed, her eyes widening with fear.

'I will be back again in next to no time. Now, don't worry, cariad. I will make sure that we have found you somewhere nice to live. You will be sharing with another couple or family so you won't be lonely while I'm away,' Glanmor assured her.

Fern looked doubtful. 'I don't like the idea of being with complete strangers, especially since I don't understand their language and they probably won't know mine. Couldn't you stay here until the *Saturn*'s next trip?'

'What would we live on? I need my job to earn the money to keep us,' he pointed out.

'Surely you could find work here in Russia; can't you stay ashore for six months or even a bit longer, until we are properly settled in?' she begged.

Glanmor was about to refuse to even consider such an idea but then, when he saw how frightened Fern appeared to be, he promised to give it some thought.

'First things first,' he hedged. 'We have to go ashore and find somewhere to live. After that, we'll see how things go. I'm off to get something to eat but I'll be back within the hour, so have all your things ready.'

'You mean we have to leave the ship tonight?'

'Yes, we do. They will be sailing on to Nakhodka on the early morning tide.'

It was well after midnight before Fern and Glanmor managed to find somewhere to stay and then it was just temporary accommodation for the one night.

They slept in each other's arms, but they were far too exhausted to make love. By the time they woke the next morning, the sun was already high in the sky. Remembering the urgency to find somewhere permanent to live before nightfall Glanmor was anxious to start looking.

They discovered that Petrograd was an impressive city but they were not on a sight-seeing tour. After wandering through some of the more impressive streets they returned to the dockside where there was a network of side streets rather similar to what they were used to in Tiger Bay.

As they began making enquiries they found their lack of Russian and the difficulties they were having in understanding what people said was a great handicap.

Finally, utterly exhausted and dispirited, they went into a small café for some food. To their immense relief they found that the young couple who ran it understood a smattering of English. Even more importantly, they could even speak it sufficiently well for Fern and Glanmor to know what they were saying.

When Glanmor and Fern told them they were looking for somewhere to live, to their immense delight the couple said they were looking for someone to share their apartment with and introduced themselves as Jacob and Dairvy.

Jacob, a swarthy-looking Russian, had once

been a ship's cook and Dairvy, who was very young, told them she came from Finland. She was expecting a baby in a few weeks and wanted to stop work and they were more than happy that Fern and Glanmor should come and share their home.

Dairvy took them to see the apartment, which was in a high block overlooking one of the many canals that formed a network that eventually linked up with the River Neva.

As they were shown around Fern was rather taken aback to discover that they were already sharing the apartment with another couple.

'You two will have a bedroom all to yourselves but everything else you will share with the rest of us,' Dairvy explained. 'Both of you will be very happy and quite comfortable here,' she assured them with a bright smile.

Fern wasn't sure about that but Glanmor seemed to be very pleased with both the accommodation and the rent that they would have to pay so she said nothing.

When Glanmor said that he would be sailing again very soon Jacob frowned and became concerned.

'We cannot afford for you to be absent. We want to share with someone who will pay their share of rent and so on each week,' he pointed out.

'Fern will be here, she will not be coming with me.' Glanmor assured him.

'Aah, so does that mean she will be working

and have the money to pay us?' Jacob asked anxiously.

'Fern has to find a job first but, rest assured, she will pay her way,' Glanmor promised him.

Jacob was not so easily reassured. 'What sort of work do you do?' he asked Fern and then shook his head dubiously when she told him about the flower stall.

'Perhaps you would like to take over my job while I am having the baby?' Dairvy suggested.

'You mean as a waitress? I've never done anything like that,' Fern said worriedly.

'We were going to advertise for someone but if you want the job and to work here at the Korsky Kafe, then it is yours,' Dairvy told her with a smile. 'I do not have to stop work for a while yet, so I will be able to show you all you need to know. When I have the baby then Jacob will be on hand to tell you what to do if you forget.'

It seemed an ideal solution so Fern agreed to give it a try. 'I need a few days to get settled in here and I want some free time to be with Glanmor before he has to sail again,' she explained.

'I have several weeks before I will give up working so that seems to be ideal for us all round,' Dairvy beamed.

Jacob seemed to be equally pleased about the arrangement and as Glanmor handed over the first instalment of their rent they shook hands all round to seal the deal.

Chapter Twenty-three

The apartment in Fontanka Street was not very large and the small windows looked out on to a busy road. It consisted of three bedrooms and a living room, kitchen and bathroom. The kitchen was a narrow slip of a room and apart from open shelves for their crockery and a built-in cupboard in which to store food, it seemed to have no proper cooking arrangements other than a gas ring.

When Fern commented on this Dairvy explained, 'Here in Petrograd we share everything. Women are out at work so much that they have no time for cooking so people use the communal kitchens. There are washhouses as well to take your dirty clothes to; it is not the practice to wash them at home.'

The bedroom that was to be theirs was sparsely furnished and although the metal-framed bed was only a large single it took up most of the available space. A cupboard was built into one wall and alongside it there was a shelf with a small oval mirror above it. The only other furnishing in the room was a plain wooden chair.

When Dairvy left them on their own Fern and

Glanmor looked at each other in dismay and then they both started laughing.

'It shouldn't be difficult to keep tidy,' Glanmor chuckled as he pulled her into his arms and kissed her. 'Are you happy now?'

'Well, at least we have a roof over our heads and I have the promise of a job, so I don't think we could hope for anything more, do you?' Fern smiled as she raised her lips to his.

'You're right, but it's not exactly what I had in mind for our first home together,' he said ruefully.

'No, but it is better than still being out on the streets looking for somewhere to stay,' Fern pointed out.

'As long as you're happy about it then that's all that matters,' Glanmor murmured as he stroked her hair back from her face and kissed her again.

'I like Dairvy, I think we will be good friends,' Fern stated as Glanmor released her and they sat down on the edge of the bed. 'I wonder what the other couple who live here are like,' she said and frowned.

Glanmor stood up and held out a hand to pull Fern to her feet. 'It's not what I want to do right this moment but I suppose we had better go and find out.'

To their surprise the other occupants were both men. Boris was tall dark and wiry and Vladimir was of medium height and barrel-chested. One of them was a professional dancer and the other a singer who was very proud of the fact that he sang with the Leonid Utyosov Jazz band that had only just been founded and was considered by the Russians to be an exciting innovation.

Fern and Glanmor spent the greater part of the first two weeks they were in Petrograd exploring the city and marvelling at all the wonderful buildings. On his previous visit Glanmor had not been free to leave the port area. Now that he had the opportunity to roam around to his heart's content he was impressed by all the sculptures and statues to be found in every park.

'I had no idea that Russia was like this,' Fern admitted. 'I thought everything would be grey and drab and very utilitarian. Most of the buildings along the banks of the Neva near the Palace Square are breathtakingly beautiful.'

'So you think you are going to be happy living here, do you?' Glanmor stated.

There was such relief in his voice that Fern felt she had to agree with him even though in her heart of hearts she would have preferred to be back in Cardiff.

'It's wonderful sightseeing with you but I'm not too sure that I will like it quite as much when you have to sail away and leave me here all on my own,' she admitted.

'You'll have Dairvy for company. Once she's had her baby then the two of you will be able to take it out for a walk. There are so many parks here that you can go to a different one each day of the week if you want to.'

'I don't suppose I'll have much time for walking in the parks; I'll be working in the café, remember,' Fern said as they strolled hand in hand along Nevsky Prospect – the long avenue on the left bank of the Neva – pausing every now and again to admire first one and then another of the splendid buildings.

'I'm sure Jacob will give you some time off, especially if he knows that you want to go out with Dairvy and the new baby,' he told her confidently.

'I wish you didn't have to leave,' she murmured. 'Couldn't you stay and let the *Saturn* go back without you? I don't mean for ever,' she added hastily as she saw his mouth tighten, 'you could rejoin them when they come back again with their next cargo.'

'It's a good job that Captain Mulligan isn't around to hear you making such suggestions,' he laughed, putting an arm round her shoulders and hugging her tightly. 'He thinks he is being very benevolent as it is in letting me stay with you until it is time to sail and making the other members of the crew do all the work and preparation for our return journey.'

Fern knew he was right about that so she said no more, but as the last few days flew by she felt very depressed and worried. Not only because she would be left there without him but also because of the prospect of starting work at the café.

Dairvy had been trying to teach her a few basic words of Russian but Fern found it difficult to understand them and even harder to pronounce them. She was sure she would never be able to understand what the customers were asking for. She was also worried in case she wouldn't be able to speak the words distinctly enough for them to know what she was saying.

The night before Glanmor's departure, as they lay in each other's arms, she knew it would be the last time for many months. She tried not to cry but her heart was so heavy that even their lovemaking didn't seem as wonderful as it usually did.

He left before dawn, creeping out of the apartment as quietly as possible so as not to disturb any of the others. Before he left he tucked the bedclothes tightly in around Fern as though to replace the warmth of his own body. Then he kissed her gently on the lips and again on the forehead and he was gone.

She held back her tears until she heard the echo of his footsteps on the pavement outside fade away into the distance, then she gave way. She sobbed until her pillow was wet with her tears and she fell into a sleep of utter exhaustion.

It was mid-morning when she woke and she knew that by then the SS *Saturn* had not only left port but also would be well on its way back through the Gulf of Finland and heading into the Baltic Sea, homeward bound for Cardiff.

Fern found that working at the café was exhausting. The day started very early because they were near enough to the docks for many of the stevedores and other port workers to call in on their way to work for breakfast.

Most of them were big burly men, some from Russia, and others from one of the surrounding Scandinavian countries. They expected immediate service and were quick to complain if their food wasn't piping hot. Fortunately, most of them ordered the same set breakfast each day and Jacob knew them all so well that there was rarely any problem. He dished it out on to the plates and Fern found that all she had to do was carry it over to the table and smile in a friendly manner as she put the plate down in front of them.

There were not a great many customers later on in the morning and those who did come in usually only wanted a hot drink. From midday onwards, however, there were sailors who had come into port and agents who were visiting the ships in dock regarding their cargo, and this was when Fern found that her lack of language was a problem.

Jacob helped her out as much as he could but every minute of his time was taken up in cooking the food the customers asked for and dishing it up.

While Dairvy was still working and able to help, things went fairly smoothly but Fern was dreading the time when Dairvy would have to stay at home and get things ready for the baby.

As it was, Dairvy went into labour before she could take any time off at all. It all happened so quickly that they were all taken off guard and for a brief spell panic ensued.

There was good advice from all sides and then Dairvy was whisked off to hospital to give birth and Fern and Jacob were left to run things on their own.

They were so busy that there was no time to stop and worry about what was happening to Dairvy. Jacob knew that he couldn't leave Fern to run things on her own so he had to wait until after they closed that night before he could visit the hospital and find out whether he was the father of a boy or a girl.

When he returned to the apartment he was beaming with pride as he announced that they had a son. Egor was a big, bouncing baby and he was doing well; so was Dairvy, and he was confident that they would be home again within a couple of days.

'Very soon she will be back to help us at the café, so do not worry. You will manage fine until then,' he told Fern reassuringly.

'Dairvy won't be fit to come back to work again for several weeks,' she warned him.

'Serving customers, no, perhaps not,' Jacob agreed. 'But she will be there to tell you things

259

that you do not know and to help you to understand what the customers are saying and what
they want. The baby will be with her, of course.
It will lie there asleep and be no trouble at all.'

Fern thought he was talking nonsense. At
home, even in Tiger Bay, it was customary for
women to rest for at least a couple of weeks
before they felt strong enough to do any sort of
work again. If the woman had no relations to
care for her and her family then the neighbours
usually rallied round and did whatever was
necessary.

Also, there was the question of feeding the
baby. How on earth was Dairvy going to manage
to do that unless she did it in the small poky
kitchen behind the café? That wasn't a very
suitable place for a baby at all because it was
always hot and steamy in there.

Within a week, though, Dairvy proved Fern
was wrong and Jacob right. Dairvy was back at
the café proudly showing off the baby to all the
customers.

When the baby needed feeding she sat at one
of the tables in the far corner of the room, undid
her blouse and let the baby suckle, crooning to
it all the time it was feeding. Customers came
and went and no one seemed to take any notice
at all of what was going on.

Egor thrived. Long before Fern had mastered
even a smattering of Russian, baby Egor was
being gradually weaned on to a bottle. He spent
most of his day sitting propped up, looking

around and gurgling happily at the attention he was receiving from the regular customers – many of whom were family men who were used to young babies.

Fern had anticipated that there would be disturbed nights from the baby crying but she found this was far from the case. The baby slept in a crib alongside Dairvy and Jacob's bed and there was rarely a sound from him, even when he started teething.

On Sundays, as Glanmor had suggested, she accompanied Dairvy on a walk. They had no pram so she showed Dairvy how to carry the baby Welsh-fashion in a big shawl that she wrapped round her body as well as round the baby.

'If you carry him like that it not only keeps the baby warm but also leaves your hands and arms free and takes most of the weight of the baby as well,' she pointed out.

Once the baby was fully weaned Fern occasionally looked after it for an evening while Jacob took Dairvy out. They were both enthusiastic about jazz and enjoyed going along to hear Vladimir sing.

'One night, perhaps, you will come out with me and we will go dancing,' Boris suggested.

'I can't dance,' Fern told him laughingly.

'Then it will be my privilege to teach you,' he told her with a solemn bow.

Fern shook her head. 'I don't think it would be a very good idea,' she told him.

'Why ever not?' Boris asked in mild surprise.

'You are a professional dancer,' Fern pointed out.

'I would still like to teach you,' he told her gravely. 'It would be a great joy for me to do so.'

Fern found that he was as good as his word and after one or two stumbling attempts she found she actually enjoyed the experience. She even began to look forward to their night out and her next lesson with him.

'I think that one night you should come and hear me sing,' Vladimir told her. 'Afterwards, who knows, perhaps you will want to sing to the jazz music.'

Fern smiled and shook her head, saying that she enjoyed music but she knew nothing about jazz.

Vladimir was not to be discouraged. 'You take lessons from Boris, so it is only right that you should come and listen to the jazz music and sing,' he insisted.

Finally, she capitulated but emphasised that she had no intention of singing.

'You come from a land that is famous for its singers and they are held in high regard so there is probably no need for me to teach you at all,' Vladimir told her.

'Wales is certainly the land of song,' Fern agreed. 'Nevertheless, it is something I am not able to do,' she added wistfully.

Vladimir appeared to accept this and suggested that, even so, it might make an enjoyable evening for Dairvy if he invited her to come along as well.

Dairvy was delighted when they suggested this and Jacob was easily persuaded to stay at home and take care of little Egor for the evening.

'We will dress up in our best clothes and make an occasion of it,' Dairvy told Fern, her face glowing with excitement.

It proved to be an evening that both of them thoroughly enjoyed. When they returned home afterwards they both agreed that they couldn't wait to do it again.

'Not every week, but most certainly when it is a special occasion, or when Boris invites us because he knows it is going to be an outstanding event,' Dairvy declared.

Although there was now plenty going on in her life both socially and at work, Fern was still missing Glanmor and still counting the weeks until he would return to Petrograd.

She wished she was sharing all her new experiences with him but she consoled herself that there would be so much to tell him when she did see him again.

Chapter Twenty-four

Fern and Dairvy had enjoyed a night of opera in which Vladimir had sung one of the leading parts and, along with Boris, who had escorted them there, they'd joined in the celebrations with Vladimir and several of the other singers afterwards.

Normally neither of them drank apart from the occasional vodka at their apartment when it was a celebration of some kind. Because this was a special occasion, they'd both had more than one drink and had returned home extremely merry.

As the four of them entered the apartment, loudly shushing each other to silence so as not to waken Egor, they stopped in surprise because Jacob was not alone.

For a moment Fern thought she must have celebrated far too well and that she was hallucinating. Rising from a chair and holding out both hands to greet her, was Glanmor.

He looked taller, broader and even more handsome and bronzed than she remembered. She shook her head as if seeing him through a mist. 'Is it really you?' she gasped before rushing towards him and flinging her arms round his neck.

He embraced her enthusiastically and then kissed her rather chastely, looking questioningly at the two men as if he was not sure who they were or what they were doing there.

'Surely you remember Vladimir and Boris,' Fern giggled. 'We've all been to the opera to hear Vladimir sing,' she added by way of explanation of why they had arrived home together. 'Didn't Jacob tell you where we were?'

'No, but then I've only just this minute walked in,' Glanmor told her. He looked somewhat relieved by her explanation as he shook hands with both the men and then greeted Dairvy with a warm hug and a kiss on the cheek.

'Your homecoming, Glanmor, is an occasion that calls for a celebration,' Jacob declared as he went over to the corner cupboard and began taking out glasses.

'Not for me, Jacob. I've already had more than enough to drink already,' Fern protested.

'I don't think I'd better have any more vodka either,' Dairvy giggled. 'I feel quite light-headed as it is.'

'Nonsense! We must all raise our glasses to welcome Glanmor home,' Jacob insisted as he began filling their glasses. 'I must also introduce Glanmor to my son Egor.'

'Surely that can wait until the morning,' Dairvy frowned, 'I think it would be better to leave Egor where he is since he is sleeping soundly,' she added quickly, putting a detaining hand on Jacob's arm as he moved towards the door of their bedroom.

Jacob was not to be deterred. He went through into the bedroom and within a matter of minutes had brought out the sleeping child wrapped in a blanket.

Egor stared around wide-eyed, blinking and rubbing the sleep from his eyes with a chubby fist then, shyly, he buried his face in his father's shoulder and it was several minutes before he could be coaxed into giving Glanmor a smile.

Almost an hour passed before Egor was asleep again and they were all ready to retire to their separate rooms. Fern wanted to be on her own with Glanmor but now, as they closed their bedroom door, she felt as if her head was about to split in two. In a few hours' time she knew that she would have to be ready for work at the café and all she wanted to do was sleep.

Glanmor, on the other hand, was wide awake and not only wanted to talk about all that had happened during his absence, but was also eager for them to make love.

Glanmor's homecoming had been something she'd dreamed about for so long. The thought of being once again in his arms, feeling the sweetness of his lips on hers as the prelude to his body possessing hers had been like an insatiable hunger. Yet, now that he was actually here and they were alone at last, all Fern felt she wanted to do was to curl up in his arms and go to sleep.

She struggled to respond to his caresses but her eyelids felt so heavy that she knew that at any moment she was going to fall asleep. Perhaps it was all a dream and she was imagining his hands sliding over her bare skin and his lips seeking out the most sensitive of places, she told herself.

Sensing her lack of response Glanmor finally abandoned his tender ministrations and took her almost roughly. Then, satiated, he turned his back towards her and almost at once was asleep.

For a long time Fern lay awake, conscious of his nearness and wanting to make amends. She felt bitterly humiliated even though she felt it was her own fault. By now her head was one massive raging pain which was almost blinding her, and her bitter tears because she felt she had failed Glanmor made it throb even more.

Glanmor was still sleeping when Jacob knocked on their door and called out that it was time to leave for work. For one moment Fern thought of saying she wasn't feeling well enough to do so. Then, common sense prevailed. Perhaps it was better to go to work, she reasoned, and then, by the time she saw Glanmor again, things between them might be back to normal.

They were so busy all morning that she had little time to dwell on the events of the previous night. Dairvy was also very withdrawn and said very little except when work demanded that she must do so. As a result of having had his sleep disturbed the night before Egor slept most of the morning.

'I expect you would like to have the afternoon off,' Jacob suggested to Fern when the midday rush was over. 'Run along with you, then. Your Glanmor will probably only be here for a very short while so it is understandable that you will want to make the most of your time together,' he said, smiling.

'That is kind of you, Jacob, but can you manage?' she asked, looking towards the corner of the room where Dairvy was spoon-feeding food into Egor's hungry mouth.

'Supposing I come back again in an hour and take Egor to the park? I'm sure Glanmor would love to do that with me,' she added quickly as Dairvy looked up and Jacob raised his eyebrows questioningly to know how she felt.

After that it became the regular procedure for the next couple of weeks. Fern worked in the mornings while Dairvy had some time off and then, early in the afternoon, Glanmor would come and the two of them would go off together for the rest of the day. Occasionally, they went on their own but more often than not they would take Egor with them.

Egor had taken a special liking to Glanmor – so much so that at times Fern felt almost jealous of the rapport between him and the child. It made her eager for them to have a proper home together and a family of their own.

When, rather shyly, she mentioned it to Glanmor, he smiled in agreement. 'Very soon,' he promised. 'Do you want us to stay here in Russia or to go back home to Cardiff?'

His question set her thinking. Petrograd was a beautiful city and she had grown used to living there. Now that she had mastered a smattering of Russian she felt more at ease yet, nevertheless, she was often homesick for the more familiar surroundings where she'd grown up.

As the time for Glanmor's departure drew nearer her unease about staying in Russia increased. Every day in the café she heard heated discussions between the customers about what might happen in the future – not only in their own city but also in Russia as a whole.

The revolution after the war had brought about a great many changes but there was an increasing air of dissatisfaction everywhere. Lenin had done some great things but many people were still discontented and it seemed possible that there would be another uprising before very much longer.

The thought of being involved in something like that worried her. She wanted to be with Glanmor and in her heart of hearts she knew then that she wanted them to go back to Cardiff.

The original reason for coming to Russia, so that they could be together without being married, no longer mattered. She was eighteen now, so there was nothing to stop them being married if they wanted to be.

When she told him she wanted to return with him, Glanmor shook his head. 'It's not possible

269

for you to come with me, Fern, because, as you very well know, we don't carry any passengers on the *Saturn*.'

'Surely Captain Mulligan would make an exception. He did before,' she reminded him.

'That was under duress. What else could he do? He could hardly throw you overboard.'

'There you are, then,' Fern persisted. 'Why don't I stow away again this time? We more or less know what he will do if we are unlucky and he does find me.'

'I very much doubt that he would be as lenient next time,' Glanmor said dryly. 'No, it is not a good idea. You stay here while I do one more trip and then, I promise you, we will be together. You quite like working at the Korsky Kafe, don't you?'

'You know I do, and I love little Egor and I couldn't ask for better friends than Jacob and Dairvy—'

'And Vladimir and Boris?' Glanmor butted in.

'Well, I like them as well, of course. They've been very good friends. Boris has taught me to dance and Vladimir is always eager for me to go and listen to him singing.'

'Do you ever go out with either of them on your own?' Glanmor questioned.

Fern looked at him in surprise. 'I go dancing with Boris sometimes,' she admitted and then felt uncomfortable as she saw the scowl that darkened his face.

She bit her lip as she tried to work out exactly what he was thinking. Surely he couldn't be jealous. He had only to look in the mirror to see that he was twice the man Boris was and, as for her having feelings for either Boris or Vladimir ... well, that was laughable.

She liked them well enough but neither of them could ever be her soulmate. That special accolade was reserved for him and him alone. Surely after all this time and all they'd been through together, Glanmor must know that.

He was still looking at her questioningly. Uneasily she recalled how jealous he had been of Rhodri and how hard it had been then, even with Maria's help, to convince him that there would never be anyone else. She didn't know what to say or do. For one brief moment she was tempted to let him think that she was attracted to one of them, then perhaps he would agree to let her accompany him back to Cardiff as she had suggested.

Glanmor seemed to take her hesitation to heart, and even when she laughed and told him he was being ridiculous his face remained gloomy. In desperation she flung her arms round his neck and pressed her lips against his.

For a moment he was stiff and unresponsive then, with a deep groan, he hugged her close and kissed her hungrily. 'I hate being parted from you,' he muttered savagely. 'It's torture every moment we are apart but I've signed on and I can't break my contract.'

'Surely Captain Mulligan would understand if you said you wanted to stay here,' she pleaded.

'It would leave him shorthanded, so of course he wouldn't understand and there would be serious repercussions. It might also mean that I would never get another boat ever again.'

'Why would that matter? You don't want to spend the rest of your life at sea, surely, Glanmor. I thought you were planning to find a job ashore so that we could settle down together and have a place of our own and start a family.'

'Of course we are, but it's not possible yet. If I leave the ship, I have no job to go to and what little money I have saved up would last no time at all.'

'If we stay here in Petrograd, you would soon find work,' she told him.

'You were extremely lucky. We were very fortunate to meet up with Jacob and Dairvy on our first night in Petrograd and to have been offered both accommodation and a job for you. The chances of something like that ever happening again are remote.'

'You should have started looking for a job the minute you came ashore,' Fern told him.

'It's not only a question of finding a job but also needing somewhere else to live before we could contemplate having any children.'

Fern looked at him in surprise. 'What's wrong with living here with Jacob and Dairvy and little Egor? I thought you liked them?'

'We could hardly have a family in that one

small room, now, could we?' he reasoned. 'No, we must be patient. Another trip will mean I have much more money and that will make all the difference to the sort of life we can have together.'

Their lovemaking that night was tender and deeply satisfying. It made her all the more desperate to be with him. She knew it was pointless harping on the matter and, deep down, she knew he was right and that Captain Mulligan would probably take very severe measures if she attempted to stow away again.

There was nothing for it but to be patient. It would mean that she would have to stay in Petrograd for at least another year, possibly even longer, but as long as she knew they would be together at the end of that time, she could wait.

Instead of moping, she would plan ahead and decide whether they would have a better life if they stayed where they were or if they returned to Cardiff.

Chapter Twenty-five

Fern felt extremely depressed after Glanmor had left but she put it down to the fact that she was missing him so much. Three weeks later, when she was still feeling so wretched that all she wanted to do when she came home from work was eat her meal and then go and lie on her bed, she started to worry.

She slept badly and several mornings when she woke and forced herself to get up and go to work she felt so unwell and bilious that she was sure she must be sickening for something.

Finally, in desperation, she mentioned it to Dairvy, hoping she could offer some advice or suggest something she might take to alleviate the feeling. Far from being sympathetic, Dairvy simply laughed and clapped her hands excitedly.

'Surely you don't need me to tell you what's the matter with you,' she chuckled, 'you're expecting a baby!'

Fern stared at her aghast. 'I can't be,' she gulped. 'We're not ready to start a family yet.'

'All the signs are there.' Dairvy smiled. 'I thought you would be pleased. Your Glanmor seems to love children; he certainly took to little Egor. I think he will make a wonderful father.'

'So do I,' Fern agreed, 'but I don't want a baby yet; not until the time is right.'

'There is never a right time,' Dairvy said sagely. 'Babies come when they come and if they are born out of true love, then what is wrong with that?'

Fern sighed and shook her head. 'We had plans. This will be a long trip for Glanmor as they are delivering cargo to places in Australia and South Africa. After that there may be a stop-off in dry dock in Cardiff for an overhaul before they return to Petrograd. It means he will be gone for perhaps two years. The next time he comes ashore we planned to set up home and start a family,' she explained.

'So, in the meantime, he works for the money and when you meet up again you will greet him with the baby, and he will be overjoyed and you will then be a family.'

'Do you really think it will work out as perfectly as that?' Fern asked dubiously.

'Of course. By then you will know how to be a mother and that is a very hard part to learn. The men do not really like all the fuss and trouble of a young baby no matter what they say. You will have his child ready to greet him and that will be splendid.'

'I want Glanmor to be with me when the baby arrives, though. The thought of going through it all on my own frightens me,' she added with a sigh.

'You will not be on your own,' Dairvy laughed

275

as she put her arms round Fern and hugged her. 'I will be at your side like you were at mine. I will help you; I will show you all the things you have to do. You will enjoy every moment and you will be so proud to be able to have a fully grown baby, one who can smile and coo and take notice of his father when he arrives home.'

Dairvy made it all sound so feasible that Fern felt more resigned to accepting what fate had thrown at her. Even so, no matter how helpful and caring Dairvy might be, Fern still longed to share her news with Glanmor and for him to be with her when the baby was born. Although she wrote to him right away, she knew it would be weeks before he received her letter and several more until she had a reply.

The thought of what having a baby entailed hit her so forcibly that for several weeks she was so quiet and immersed in her own thoughts that both Dairvy and Jacob were worried about her. Even some of the customers noticed that her bright, welcoming smile was missing and that although she now knew a smattering of Russian she no longer stopped to chat or make some friendly remark as she served their meals or cleared the tables afterwards. So many of the customers commented and asked why she was so gloomy that in the end Jacob decided to have a word with her about it.

'When customers come in here they like a cheery greeting,' he reminded her. 'You were popular with them all because you smiled and quipped with them. Now, apart from a mumbled *Dobraye utro* when they arrive and *Dasvidaniya* when they leave, you say nothing, not even when they try to speak to you in English.'

'I'm sorry.' Fern pushed her hair back from her face in a gesture of despair. 'These days I can think of nothing but this baby I am having. I will try and be more cheerful and greet them more affably,' she promised.

It took considerable effort but after a few days she found that taking more notice of the customers did seem to divert her thoughts from her problem.

By the time she was four months pregnant, the baby was already taking second place in her thoughts. She even resumed her social life and went dancing with Boris and occasionally went with Dairvy to hear Vladimir sing.

As the months progressed, she did begin to feel very tired at the end of the working day, but Dairvy was well aware of this. Little by little she increased her own working hours so that Fern could go home and rest after the midday rush.

'I'll take Egor with me and after he's had his nap then I can take him to the park,' Fern suggested when Dairvy told her about the new arrangement.

'Oh no, the extra time off is so that you can rest and you won't be able to do that if you have Egor with you, not now that he's toddling,' Dairvy told her.

'He's as slippery as an eel these days and even Dairvy finds him tiring,' Jacob laughed.

Fern was grateful for their concern and she did take advantage of the arrangement to lie on her bed and rest. The only problem was it gave her even more time to think about Glanmor and wish that they could be together.

She knew the route the *Saturn* was taking and she had written to him several times but she knew there was always the chance that her letters would not arrive until after the ship had left port and might not reach their next point of call in time for him to get them.

More and more, she wanted him to find a shore job and she didn't mind whether it was in Petrograd or in Cardiff. Nothing mattered as long as they could be together and he was able to come home every night. She resolved that next time he came ashore she would tell him that these long partings were more than she could stand.

Fern's baby was born without enough time for her to go to hospital on the last day of 1924 after a short, intense labour. Dairvy acted as midwife and afterwards claimed that it all went exceptionally well, even though Fern disputed this and said she had never experienced such agony in all her life.

'Nonsense; there was nothing to it. You should think yourself fortunate that everything was so easy,' Dairvy assured her.

Afterwards, when she brought Fern a

refreshing cup of tea and helped her to settle the newborn child to suckle, she added, 'I suppose you know that being born on New Year's Eve is considered to be very special for the child.'

'She most certainly is very special,' Fern agreed as she looked down proudly at the baby lying against her breast, her tiny hand curling and uncurling as she suckled. 'I only wish Glanmor was here to welcome her into the world.'

Once again she sent a letter, this time to tell him about the arrival of their baby and to ask him what name he would like to give their little daughter.

Dairvy and Jacob pressed her to give the child a name and Vladimir and Boris both came up with suggestions but Fern refused to even consider them.

'I'm not deciding on a name until I hear from Glanmor. I'm simply calling her "Baby", because it is only right that Glanmor is the one to choose the child's name,' she insisted.

The morning rush was over and Fern had settled down in a corner of the café to enjoy a cup of coffee and feed Baby when Dairvy and Egor arrived. Egor toddled over to where she was sitting and gave her something he was holding in his hand.

Fern's heart thudded as she saw that it was from the shipping line and she looked up questioningly at Dairvy.

'It arrived at the apartment after you'd left this morning,' Dairvy told her excitedly. 'I can't wait for you to open it. It could mean that Glanmor is coming home sooner than you expected. Here, let me hold Baby while you read it.'

Her hopes rising by the minute, Fern extracted the thick sheet of paper inside the envelope and then she gave a gasp. Her body stiffened and the colour drained away from her face. In silence she handed the letter over to Dairvy.

Frowning, Dairvy scanned the contents then with a gasp of concern she put her arm round Fern who was shaking with shock.

'What's going on? What's the matter?' Sensing that it was bad news, Jacob came hurrying over to them.

Without a word Dairvy held out the letter to him and as soon as he'd read it his face registered disbelief.

Within minutes Jacob had gone into the kitchen and come back with a bottle of vodka and three glasses. 'Drink this,' he ordered, handing Fern a strong measure.

'Falling overboard is terrible enough,' he commented, 'but to be— Surely there was no need to tell you such gruesome details,' he said angrily.

Fern shook her head, her eyes wide with distress. She still couldn't believe what she'd read and she reached out again for the letter but Jacob shook his head. He folded it carefully and put it back inside the envelope. 'I will put this somewhere safe,' he mumbled. 'You do not want to keep reading it over and over again.'

Fern felt too upset to argue. He was probably right, she thought. Perhaps the best thing to do was to forget she had ever read those horrible words. Perhaps they'd got it all wrong. Glanmor might have swum round to the other side of the boat and been picked up later on.

'There's daft you are, girl,' she scolded herself out loud. 'Duw anwyl, they'd all be looking over the side of the ship watching and wondering what they could do to help Glanmor, so they'd know exactly what happened. No one would have written such a terrible letter unless it was true.'

She wished she could cry and release the hard knot in her heart and the lump in her throat, but there were no tears. It was as if the shocking news had dried her up completely.

She looked down at the sleeping child in her arms, wondering what the future would hold for them now. It had been frightening enough finding she was pregnant without Glanmor being at her side. Now the thought of having to look after Baby and bring her up all on her own filled her with a feeling of trepidation.

Jacob and Dairvy were kind and helpful but they weren't her family. She didn't want to stay in Russia for the rest of her life but how was she ever going to manage to get away on her own?

She suddenly felt desperately homesick for

Cardiff. Would she ever walk those familiar streets again and be able to understand everything that was said to her? she wondered.

For the moment, there seemed to be nothing for it but to knuckle down and make the best of things. She supposed she ought to think herself lucky that she had such good friends as Dairvy and Jacob and a roof over her head as well as a job.

She had been prepared to stay in Petrograd for another year or so, until Glanmor returned from his trip. When he came back, they were to have planned their future together. For the moment, nothing had changed really, she tried to tell herself.

But in her heart she knew full well that it had. Knowing that Glanmor would be coming back had kept her hopes bubbling. Now they had been dashed and she had nothing to look forward to and it was impossible to make any plans whatsoever for the future.

The news of Glanmor's tragic death spread quickly amongst the customers. In so many instances it brought back vivid memories of unexpected deaths they'd known in their own families during the revolution. The expressions of sympathy expressed in Russian and broken English were so heartfelt that they released Fern's pent-up tension and brought tears to her eyes.

She tried hard not to give way to her emotions while she was at work but at night she sobbed into her pillow.

Dairvy and Jacob said nothing about Baby's crying but Fern knew that in the confines of the flat it was almost bound to waken them. She tried to control her grief but she sometimes wakened from a deep sleep to find herself sobbing and Baby crying because she'd been disturbed.

In the stillness of the night the baby's cries seemed incredibly strident. Anxious to quieten her down, Fern would take her into her own bed.

As she cuddled her fatherless child she found holding the tiny body close gave her comfort. By the time Baby was calmed and sleeping once more, Fern found her own eyelids drooping.

Cautiously, so as not to waken her daughter, she would slither further down in the bed still cradling the sleeping baby in her arms, hoping they'd both sleep for another few hours.

Chapter Twenty-six

Fern found that Glanmor's death affected her deeply and she wondered if she would ever get over it. There were days when she was convinced that it had all been a dream; a very bad dream but, nonetheless, something that had occurred inside her mind.

Then someone would commiserate with her, or say something that struck a chord in her heart, and she would be overcome with such an immense feeling of desolation that the world around her would suddenly become alien.

She didn't know what to do. The thought of working at the Korsky Kafe for ever depressed her. At the same time she knew full well that she was lucky to have a job where they made her baby welcome and allowed her to work the hours that best suited her.

Her one consolation was Baby. She still hadn't decided on a name for her and, as no one insisted that she do so, she still called her Baby and so did all the customers.

Baby went everywhere with her – cradled in the crook of her arm or carried in a shawl Welsh-fashion – and they were inseparable. Fern no longer took the trouble to make her sleep in her crib at night. Instead, she took her into her own bed knowing that when she had her child alongside her they both settled better, gaining comfort from their closeness to each other.

Fern's other solace was vodka. It had started when Jacob had given her a strong measure when she'd first heard the terrible news about Glanmor. After that, when the nightmares became too frightening to bear, she found that a small tot of vodka would calm her down and drive them away.

As the weeks passed, however, the small tots became more frequent and gradually she found they needed to be larger in order to drive away the ghosts of the past; especially last thing at night before she settled down to sleep.

Jacob warned her that she was drinking more than was good for her, especially since she was still feeding Baby herself, but she ignored his advice. It was far better to go to bed in a slight haze, knowing that she would fall asleep within minutes of her head hitting the pillow, than to lie there haunted by thoughts of what sort of future she might have had if Glanmor hadn't died.

Baby was a sickly child; Fern worried endlessly because she wasn't thriving as well as she ought to be. She blamed the intense cold of the Russian winter even though Dairvy argued that the cold had made Egor strong and resilient.

'He's a boy and he has both his mother and father to nurture him,' Fern told her gloomily.

'I think Baby would thrive better if you let her sleep on her own in her crib at night,' Dairvy kept pointing out gently but Fern refused to listen to her.

'She needs feeding during the night and if she was in her own crib, I'd have to get out of bed to pick her up and attend to her. By the time I did that she'd have wakened the whole lot of you with her screaming.'

The accident happened on a Friday night. They'd had a very busy day in the café and they were all exhausted. When Jacob suggested they should all have a vodka to help relax them after they'd finished their evening meal that night, Fern was the first to accept.

'Not for me,' Dairvy said, shaking her head and smothering a yawn. 'If I drink vodka this late at night I sleep like a log and I can't wake up in the morning. You're drinking far too much these days, Fern,' she added reprovingly.

'That's the way I like to sleep,' Fern told her as she picked up her glass and drained it down in one gulp. Then with Baby cradled in her arms she said goodnight to them both.

When Fern didn't appear at breakfast the next morning, Dairvy scolded Jacob. 'It's your fault for giving her so much vodka last night,' she chided.

'She'll be here at any minute; leastways I hope she will, because she's on early shift at the café.'

When, ten minutes later, Fern still had not put in an appearance Dairvy became worried. 'Do you think I should knock on her door and waken her?'

'Do whatever you think is best,' Jacob said with a shrug. 'If she is still sleeping, then perhaps you should come down to the café this morning instead of her.'

'No, that is not the arrangement,' Dairvy protested. 'I need to be at home with Egor this morning.'

Dairvy knocked twice on Fern's bedroom door but there was no answer. She called out her name, but there was still no response. She tried the handle but the door was bolted. In desperation she called to Jacob to come and force the door open because she was sure there was something wrong.

Jacob wasn't at all keen to break into Fern's room but Dairvy was so concerned that when there was no response to his own repeated knocking and shouting he put his shoulder to the door. The flimsy bolt gave way instantly.

It was clear to both of them as they went into the room that Fern was in a deep sleep. Dairvy went over to the bed and shook her by the shoulder. As she did so, Fern stirred but still didn't waken; not until Dairvy let out a scream.

Startled out of her deep sleep by the intrusion Fern sat up in bed, rubbing the sleep from her eyes and pushing her hair back from her face as she did so.

As she stepped towards the bed Dairvy pointed down to Baby who was lying half underneath Fern. Her little arms were blue and when Dairvy picked up the child, Baby's body remained completely limp.

Dairvy drew back and put a hand over her mouth as she gave a cry of horror.

'What's happened to her?' Fern gasped as she tried to move Baby and there was no response at all from the child.

There was fear on her face and her voice was a distraught whisper as she stared from the baby to Dairvy and back again.

Gently Dairvy lifted the little body; it was cold and as floppy and lifeless as a rag doll.

'My God! Your child is dead,' Jacob gasped. 'You've rolled over and slept on her.'

The horror in his voice brought Fern to her senses. She reached out for Baby, snatching her back, cradling her and crooning to her as she chafed the little arms and legs desperately trying to restore the circulation.

'Do something, fetch someone, Jacob,' Dairvy pleaded, her face wet with tears.

'It's too late for a doctor,' Jacob exclaimed hopelessly.

'It will have to be reported, though, because the baby is dead,' Dairvy pointed out.

'You stay here with Fern and I will go and open up the café. Perhaps one of our customers will know what we ought to do.'

How they all survived the next few days

none of them ever knew. There were so many questions asked that Fern thought she must be going completely mad.

Her grief over losing the baby was such that she couldn't even cooperate when Jacob asked her to give it a name before the burial service. 'I only ever called her Baby,' she said sadly, 'won't that do?'

To add to her distress Jacob and Dairvy refused to let her have any vodka. They blamed themselves for encouraging her to drink it in the first place because they were sure it was what had led to the terrible accident.

Dairvy was so upset by what had happened that she couldn't stop crying. Fern remained like a zombie, dry-eyed and silent, taking no notice of what was going on around her.

She remained impervious to all the investigations, and even left Dairvy and Jacob to make the funeral arrangements. She watched impassively as Jacob carried the tiny white coffin containing Baby's body for burial.

Afterwards she stayed in her bedroom refusing to eat or drink or talk to anyone for almost a week, leaving Dairvy and Jacob to manage the café and look after little Egor the best they could.

When she finally returned to work, apart from looking pale and tight-lipped, Fern acted almost as though nothing at all had happened. One or two of the regular customers tried to express their sympathy but she ignored their words and merely shrugged and got on with what she was doing. For the most part they accepted her stoical reticence without comment.

Within a few weeks it was as if Baby had never existed. Fern worked hard in the café, managing to smile when it was necessary to do so but remaining rather aloof. She continued to look after Egor as she had always done.

The only change in her routine seemed to be that since Jacob would not allow her to drink vodka when she was in the flat, then, whenever she was not needed to look after Egor in the evenings, she became restless and went out.

At first it was with Dairvy to hear Vladimir sing or occasionally to watch Boris dance as they'd done in the past. Gradually, however, when Jacob wasn't able to look after Egor or when Dairvy said she had jobs she had to do around the home, Fern started going out on her own.

She still went to the same places but now that she was on her own she no longer wanted merely to sit and watch. As a child she'd always loved to dance and she was eager to take part.

At first, because they felt sorry for her, both Vladimir and Boris arranged for her to participate in some minor way. Within a very short time she was so appreciated by the audiences that the management of the theatres where they performed began including her as an independent act.

Although she claimed that she couldn't sing

her voice was pleasant, and when she sang popular songs in her own tongue some of the audience who understood the words were delighted and many of them tried to join in.

Her dancing was even more successful than her singing. She was happy to partner Boris in demonstrations of ballroom dancing but she preferred to perform solo and again the audience was pleasantly receptive.

As she spent more and more of her evenings either dancing or singing she began to resent having to work in the café. For one thing, with so many late nights, she was constantly tired; for another, she found her work as a waitress was not nearly so stimulating as being part of the entertainment scene.

When she told Jacob she would like to work less hours at the café so that she would have more time for her other interests, he was most annoyed.

'I'll still look after Egor each day, so that will mean that Dairvy can work longer hours at the café whenever you want her to do so,' she promised.

Jacob was not happy with such an arrangement. Dairvy expressed no opinion whatsoever; she merely listened, smiled and nodded. Whether she was in agreement with what Fern had said or with what Jacob decreed Fern was never quite sure. The tension in the flat increased daily. Jacob started finding fault with Fern's work at the café and this led to angry exchanges. When she asked

Dairvy to talk to Jacob and point out that her work was as good as ever Dairvy merely shrugged.

'Jacob, he is the boss,' Dairvy explained. 'Here at home and in the café. Whatever he says is right.'

Fern felt they were both being unreasonable. Matters came to a head when they expressed the opinion that she was not showing them the gratitude they felt they deserved. Fern decided that since there was no way of mollifying them she had no option but to make some changes whether she wanted to do so or not.

When she voiced her feelings to Vladimir and Boris she was dismayed to find that because of their longstanding friendship with Dairvy and Jacob they were not very supportive. They even went so far as to try and make sure that she no longer appeared in any shows they were in.

Piqued by their attitude Fern felt that she was more or less forced to make a choice about her future. Although she knew she was taking a considerable risk, she decided to stop working at the café and become an entertainer.

'If that is your decision, then I think it would be best if you also found yourself some other accommodation,' Jacob told her.

'I am perfectly happy to stay here and I will pay you whatever rent you ask,' Fern told him. 'What is more, since I will be at home a great deal more during the daytime, I can look after Egor for you most days,' she told them both.

She felt sure that Dairvy would find this quite acceptable because it meant that she would be able to put in more hours working at the café and that would mean a better life for herself and her family. Jacob, however, didn't approve.

'No, that is not a satisfactory arrangement. If you are not working at the café, then I will need your room for whoever takes your place there as a waitress,' he insisted.

'They may not want to rent a room from you; they may still be living at home or in lodgings nearby, and can walk to work each day,' Fern pointed out.

'If that is the case, then that will be very good,' Jacob told her. 'It will mean that little Egor can at long last have a room of his own instead of his bed being in a corner of our bedroom,' he added.

'You mean you want me to go?' Fern frowned, trying hard not to let him see how worried she was by his decision.

'That is correct,' Jacob affirmed in a very formal voice. 'Please do so as soon as you can.'

Fern looked at him in dismay. She'd had it all planned out in her mind that she would go on living with him and Dairvy virtually for nothing in return for looking after Egor until she had managed to become established as a full-time entertainer. If she had to move into other lodgings where she would have to pay rent and buy her own food, what little money she had would be gone in next to no time. She wanted to ask

293

Jacob if she could wait a little longer but pride wouldn't let her.

There was another problem: she could still only understand a smattering of Russian and on the few occasions when she had ventured into the heart of the city without Dairvy she had felt nervous about asking for directions when she was uncertain of her whereabouts.

Listening to the talk that went on in the café each day, especially when there were sailors there who spoke in English, she knew that there were still a great many revolutionary factions in the city. The thought of being on her own worried her. She had no idea how she would cope if she was ever involved in an uprising, no matter how small it might be.

When she was in the café, or accompanied by Vladimir, Boris or Dairvy, she felt safe enough. Now, when they were all turning their backs on her and leaving her to her own devices, she was not at all happy with the situation she found herself in.

Her longing to be back in Cardiff was now stronger than ever but she could see no way of getting there. Even if she could find a boat to take her home, the cost of a passage was far more than she could pay out of her meagre savings.

The only other way she could manage to return to Cardiff would be to travel back overland, through Europe.

It was an idea that she and Glanmor had once

discussed when they had first talked about coming to Russia. He'd been afraid that they might encounter difficulties with customs and the police when they wanted to move from one country to the next, so she was not sure if she could undertake such a journey on her own.

Chapter Twenty-seven

Fern was left in no doubt that Jacob was keen for her to leave their apartment so that he would no longer be responsible for her in any way. He had no interest in her welfare and expected her to make her own plans for her future.

Since Russia had given women the same powers as men, all the normal courtesies had vanished; many no longer felt in any way responsible for the welfare of even their own womenfolk.

Gone were the days when men were protective, made way for women, held doors open for them or offered to carry their heavy shopping. Women had insisted on equality with men and that was what they were getting. Fern felt that in so many ways it had made life much less pleasant for them.

Since the revolution, communal eating places had come into existence and cafés were no longer as popular as they'd once been. She suspected that was why Jacob could manage without her working at the Korsky Kafe and was quite relieved that she would be leaving without him having to ask her to stop working there.

When she asked Boris and Vladimir if either

of them could help her by asking their managers if they could take her on so that she would automatically be considered when they were negotiating new programmes with theatre companies, they were both very hesitant.

'It is up to you to audition the same as we had to do,' they told her. 'If you are good enough, then maybe you will be included in the roster, otherwise . . .'

The unfinished sentence and the shrug of the shoulders told her all she needed to know. She was on her own and her future depended on whatever she was able to achieve with her own talents.

Suddenly, she was not only afraid of living in Russia on her own but she had also decided that she hated it there because she felt lonely and isolated.

Although the people appeared to accept her, she was still a foreigner in their midst and one more in the rising figure of unemployed women. Since employers were forced to pay women the same rates as men, then men were automatically given preference in the jobs where their skills were considered to be superior.

Fern wished she had tried harder to learn the language and become involved in Russian politics as she'd intended to do when she first arrived in Petrograd. Had she done so, then she could have applied for work in the medical section or in general educational work, where women still seemed to be predominate.

Her resolve to return to Cardiff grew ever stronger, only she didn't know how to set about it. If she couldn't afford her passage by sea, then she would have to travel overland and that meant a tremendously arduous journey. Once through the Baltic States and on into Germany she would then have to travel across Holland and Belgium to France. After that it should be fairly straightforward to cross to England and, once on British soil, making her way back to Cardiff should be simplicity itself.

Could a woman achieve such an exhausting trek on her own? she wondered. Women might have equality in Russia but what about in the rest of Europe?

Since a man's protection was out of the question, then joining a troupe, a concert party with gypsies or a circus seemed to be the obvious answer. If they would let her travel to Europe with them, then her worries would be over.

Once more she turned to Vladimir and Boris for help. When they heard she intended to leave Petrograd their manner changed. She would no longer be a threat to them professionally. Although her acts and ability were those of an amateur there was an aura of femininity and a naïve quality about her that the audience seemed to like, especially when she sang in English.

With Vladimir's help she was introduced to the owner of the Katikav Circus. They were a little-known group of performing artists under the leadership of Ivan Katikav, a sleek-haired portly Russian Jew.

'Are you a member of the Communist Party?' was the first question he asked Fern.

'No, I'm Welsh,' she answered, smiling.

'If you are Welsh, as you say you are, then what are you doing here in Russia?' he asked before agreeing to see her perform.

When she explained that she had stowed away on the SS *Saturn* in order to be with Glanmor, his manner changed.

'You are resourceful, that is something I admire,' he told her approvingly. 'This Glanmor, where is he now? Are you no longer living together?'

In a subdued voice the told him about Glanmor's tragic death at sea but she made no mention of the baby she had lost.

Ivan Katikav made understanding noises then demanded that she sing and dance before he would consider whether or not she could come with them.

'You are quite talented, but you lack professional polish,' he told her. 'Hopefully, with practice, you will improve. Are you prepared to undertake the many other things that have to be done when we move from place to place?'

'Of course, if I can. Do you mean helping to put up the tents and feed the animals, things like that?' Fern asked anxiously.

'No, no, no!' He gave a dry laugh. 'Heavy jobs of that sort are men's work. In Russia they may treat women like men but here in the Katikav Circus we do not. We expect our women to help with domestic matters; the cooking, the washing and things that make life comfortable when we are on the road.'

'Of course I am prepared to help in that sort of way,' Fern agreed. She felt dazed; it was hard to believe that she was to be an exotic dancer; it was all so different from the life she'd known as a young girl living in the Welsh Valleys. She knew she could do it; she was determined to be a success, because her future depended on it.

'One other thing; we pool our money. You will receive bed and board but no set wages. At the end of each session, before we move on to the next town, we share out whatever money is left over after we have paid for all our expenses. Sometimes it is very good, at other times there is nothing at all. Are you agreed?'

Fern nodded. It would have been nice to know exactly how much she would be earning so that she could plan ahead. However, she knew only too well that she had no option but to accept his way of doing things and to consider herself fortunate that he was willing to let her join them.

She very much wanted to know details of their itinerary but some inner caution warned her not to ask too many questions. If he knew that she was merely using him as a means of getting back to Cardiff he might not let her join them. As it was, he seemed prepared to accept that she was tired of being in Russia and that she felt uncertain about what sort of future she could expect if she stayed there on her own without a man at her side.

'We have one caravan reserved for the young unattached women,' he told her. 'You will be in there. You will be sharing with four other girls. No drinking, no smoking and no taking men back at night. Is that understood?'

'Thank you. When can I join you?'

'We hit the road after our show tonight. I will now take you to your van and introduce you to your new companions.'

The van was small; two sets of bunk beds on either side took up most of the space. There was only a narrow gap between them, barely enough for one person to stand to get dressed, Fern thought critically. The only other furnishing was a table fitted into one side of the room with a small mirror over it. A ledge running right the way around the van was packed full of bags, cases, boots and shoes and all the personal belongings of the occupants.

'The costumes you will be wearing are stored in a separate van,' Ivan explained. 'This is merely where you sleep. You eat in the canteen which is a large separate van where all the cooking is done. No food or drink is to be brought in here, you understand.'

Fern nodded; she was already having second thoughts about whether to join the Katikav Circus or not, there were so many rules and restrictions.

'Come,' he broke into her thoughts, 'meet the girls who will be sharing with you. This is Helga,' he indicated a tall athletic-looking girl with short fair hair and bright blue eyes. 'Helga is making her way back to her home in Sweden. This is Anastasia and she is Russian, but she comes with us to escape the harsh regime that is now the backbone of Russia. She is sure that there is going to be another uprising quite soon,' he added with a dry laugh.

'Alina,' he went on, indicating a thin dark girl, 'is from Romania and she is not sure if she will leave us when we reach her country or not. Alina lost both her parents in the revolution.

'Finally,' he paused as his eyes rested on the fourth girl who had long blonde hair and huge grey eyes and was as plump as Alina was thin, 'this is Marlene, my special song bird from Germany.'

'Fern is coming with us, girls, so I want you to make her welcome and help her to understand our way of doing things. Although she is joining us as an exotic dancer she can also sing, so if you have one of your bad throats, Marlene, there is now someone who can stand in for you.'

He rubbed his hands together. 'Are you all happy with this arrangement?'

'There is no spare bunk. We are already crowded, so where is Fern going to sleep?' Helga asked.

'For the moment it will have to be on a mattress placed on the floor in between the bunks. If Alina leaves us, then Fern will be able to have her bunk.' He looked around at them all, smiling. 'Has anyone else any questions?'

The girls looked at each other and shrugged dismissively.

When no one answered he turned to Fern. 'In that case,' he murmured, 'why don't you go and fetch your belongings? Make sure you are back here in good time; we move off tonight as soon as the show is over.'

Fern found that although Ivan Katikav was a hard taskmaster his division of labour, when it came to running things, was scrupulously fair and he had no time for shirkers.

She also discovered that he was equally rigorous when it came to preparation for the shows he staged. She was not the only one to be put through their paces at least once each day.

No matter how tired they might be when the show closed at night or how far they had travelled when they were moving from one town to the next, the welfare of the animals was always the first thing that was ensured.

Those who had to attend rehearsals knew they must complete whatever duties had been allocated to them first of all. After that, no matter how exhausted they might be feeling, they were expected to put every ounce of enthusiasm they could muster into their practice session.

Fern noticed, however, that Marlene was

constantly being singled out for special attention. She had only to hold her hand to her throat and Ivan was immediately full of concern. He regarded her voice as something so precious that it had to be cherished.

At first Fern found the changing countryside as they moved out of Russia fascinating and arriving in a new town exciting. Gradually, however, the constant travelling and all it involved began to pall and she found herself caught up in the same grumbles as the rest of the troupe.

As they related tales of hardship about what had happened in their own families, Fern discovered it was the same the world over for the working class. The men went out to work and ruled the roost and the women, for the most part, were treated as skivvies. They had to rely on whatever their husband doled out to them as housekeeping money.

Apart from Anastasia, none of the others were Russian. Over a matter of weeks, Fern learned that they had all come to Russia from war-ravished Europe, after the Russian Revolution, expecting to find a freedom they'd dreamed about.

Gradually, they discovered that the new regime in Russia imposed rules that were even stricter than those they'd known in their own home countries. The equality the Russians boasted about that sounded so attractive meant you were expected to share everything.

As they moved further and further West, into Bulgaria and Romania, their company began to grow ever smaller. Sometimes members of the troupe openly announced that they were leaving; on other occasions nothing was said and they vanished quietly late at night.

By the time they'd reached Poland, their numbers were so depleted that Ivan Katikav announced that those who wanted to stay with the circus should tell him, because he was planning to sell out. He promised to negotiate with the buyers that those who wished to carry on working with the circus could do so.

Fern knew that this was the time when she needed to make a decision. The circus life didn't really appeal to her. When they asked Ivan why he wanted to sell, he said it was for personal reasons and refused to enlighten them any further. It had been an expedient way to get herself out of Russia and it had taught her a lot about the art of survival.

She had saved every penny she'd earned but she knew it wasn't enough to pay her train fare back to Cardiff. Nevertheless, she felt the time had come to leave the circus.

She didn't feel at all confident that she would be able to make her own way across Europe working as an entertainer, but under Ivan's rigorous training her singing had improved beyond measure and her improvised exotic dancing always won applause from the audience.

The thought of once more being back in the familiar surroundings of Loudon Square and the life she'd known in Tiger Bay would sustain her. Cardiff, Maria and memories of Glanmor were the last things in her mind every night when she settled down to sleep.

Chapter Twenty-eight

Fern felt uneasy about what Ivan was proposing to do; she didn't fancy being sold as part of the fixtures and fittings of the Katikav Circus. Furthermore, she was tired of being used to fill in between the more important acts, or as a warm-up artiste to keep the crowd entertained before the show started.

She was astute enough to know that she would never top the bill as a singer but she was also aware that her dancing skills were better than most and she was determined to exploit them to the full.

The circus had served its purpose as far as she was concerned; it had made it possible for her to get out of Russia and into Europe. She felt sure that from now on she could stand on her own two feet and make her way home.

Although she had only been a fill-in for the Katikav Circus, it had given her a taste for entertaining and she wondered if, before she went home, she could make a name for herself.

It was probably too much to hope that she would ever become so well known that she would arrive back in Cardiff as a famous celebrated dancer. The thought of how astounded Maria would be if that ever did happen brought a rare smile to her face.

There was no point in simply dreaming about it, she told herself. The thing to do was to set about achieving it. Now that Anastasia and Alina had left, there was only Marlene to compete with and Marlene was a singer not a dancer.

Perhaps she could persuade Ivan that it would be to his advantage to bill her as a dancer when he came to sell the circus, even though she had no intention of staying with them. She wished there was someone she could talk her ideas over with, but she wasn't too confident about confiding in Marlene.

She had noticed right from the first day she'd joined them that Ivan treated Marlene differently. Her name was always printed very prominently on all the posters and flyers; there was no doubt that she was his favourite.

It made Fern curious to find out what Marlene was going to do; was she going to let him sell her on, or would she be interested in teaming up with Fern so that they could strike out on their own?

She kept turning the idea over in her mind. Marlene was as blonde as Fern was dark, so they were the perfect foil for each other; they could be an ideal partnership in a singing and dancing act.

She kept her own counsel as she listened to all the rumours that went round about the sale of the circus. She noted all the comments from the other performers as they debated whether they were staying on or not, but she said nothing.

Several times she was on the point of asking Marlene what her plans for the future were but something always held her back. There was a secretiveness about Marlene, even about her comings and goings, that made Fern cautious. She didn't want Marlene telling Ivan of her plans; there was time enough for him to know when she was ready to put them into action.

Shortly after they arrived in Warsaw, Ivan announced that the sale of the circus had been accomplished and said they would all have to sign an agreement to work for the new owners. Since she had no intention of doing this, Fern felt she had no option but to make a clean breast of her own plans.

Summoning up her courage she went to see him. He listened in silence, his face impassive, his eyes hooded, as he leaned back in his chair with his hands together and his fingers making a pyramid over his rotund stomach.

'So you think that you can find enough work as a dancer to pay your way back to Cardiff, do you?' he said suddenly, sitting bolt upright as she finished telling him what she proposed to do. 'Within a couple of weeks, without an agent to represent you, or a man to support you, you will find it impossible; you will probably end up as a prostitute.'

'What nonsense,' Fern declared angrily. 'I'm not that sort of girl. Have you ever found me flirting with any of the men who work here or with any of the patrons?'

'No, but then, up until now, you have had no need to do so,' Ivan said quietly, his eyes narrowing. 'Since you are attractive, then why not sell your body? You will find you can earn far more money by doing that than by dancing.'

'Never!' Fern almost screamed the word at him, she felt so angry at his insinuation.

'I am only warning you of what the consequences could be if you set off on such a reckless adventure all on your own.' Ivan shrugged dismissively.

'You think I would do better to sign this piece of paper and become part of the property of the new circus owner, do you?' Fern said in a withering tone.

Ivan stood up and paced the floor. 'I have a suggestion. Marlene is not staying with the new owners. I am going to act as her agent and promote her as a singer and we will tour Europe. If you wish to accompany us, then I will put the idea to Marlene; a double act perhaps; Marlene singing and you dancing.'

Fern stared at him in astonishment. It was almost as if he'd read her thoughts. This was exactly what she'd had in mind. Not with him involved in any way, of course, but she was quick to realise that this could be to her advantage.

Fern didn't know what Ivan said to Marlene but she accepted the arrangement without question. Ivan told both of them to say nothing to any of those members who had elected to stay on when the circus was sold but to leave everything to him.

For the next couple of weeks things seemed to go on as usual, although there were rumours and speculations in plenty about what was to happen. Then came the big day when the new owners officially took possession and Ivan, Marlene and Fern quietly took their leave.

So that there was no infringement of the new owners' performing rights, Ivan told Marlene and Fern that they must move out of Poland and into Germany before they could announce or advertise their act.

Their lodgings in Berlin consisted of a very small two-bedroom apartment, but compared to what she'd once shared with Jacob and Dairvy, it was quite spacious.

Fern had assumed that she would be sharing a bedroom with Marlene but she was not altogether surprised when Marlene and Ivan moved into the larger bedroom together and she was given the room that ran alongside it. The single bed, a chest of drawers with a mirror over it and a chair almost completely filled it and left very little space to move around, but it was hers.

The important factor, as Ivan pointed out, was that they were now safely in Berlin which was renowned for its nightlife and as being a city of cabaret acts.

When she saw the new posters which Ivan

had designed Fern felt both hurt and annoyed that Marlene was billed first and in letters so large that they entirely overshadowed her own name and act.

As she feared, Fern found that their partnership was anything but smooth. The first week they were in Germany she and Marlene spent quite a lot of time together while Ivan was out arranging fixtures at various clubs and restaurants. Fern tried to find out from Marlene what Ivan's future plans were but her replies were so vague that in the end she gave up.

She wasn't sure if Marlene really had no idea or whether Ivan had told her not to say anything. When the three of them were together he talked constantly about the promotions he was doing for Marlene and how one day soon she would be even more popular than Marlene Dietrich, who at present was the top cabaret actress and singer in Germany.

'If only you were able to dance as well as you sing, Marlene,' Ivan would sigh.

'I can't be expected to do everything and, anyway, Fern is the dancer,' Marlene would say, pouting and fluttering her eyelashes.

'I know, I know, and Fern certainly can't sing,' Ivan would say quickly in an attempt to placate her.

Fern merely smiled at their exchanges but playing second fiddle to Marlene didn't suit her. If Ivan wasn't prepared to see that she had equal billing and publicity then she would split up with him and Marlene and make her own way, she resolved.

Berlin might be the city of cabarets, but there were other European cities equally as good. Her ultimate aim was to reach Paris and join the Folies Bergère.

Meanwhile, she consoled herself, she had a roof over her head and, with every show she took part in, she was improving her dancing skills.

Furthermore, although Marlene might top the bill and receive most of the accolades, Fern also had her admirers. One man in particular seemed to follow her from restaurant to night-club in order to watch her dance and without fail sent her either flowers or chocolates or both at the end of every performance.

Discreetly she tried to find out more about him and discovered that he was the head of a large chain of hotels in Germany and was extremely wealthy. When one night she found a slip of paper with a telephone number tucked into the flowers when they were handed to her, she felt both intrigued and jubilant.

Two days later she met up with Heinz Knox and listened carefully to his suggestion that she should work for him.

'I would give you star billing as a cabaret act at my hotels. You would travel throughout Germany, spending up to three nights at each hotel. Your act would be exclusive to my hotels for the next six months. After that we could talk some more,' he told her.

Fern promised to think about it.

'I need a decision promptly. If you do not wish to undertake such an assignment, then there are other artistes who are eager to audition,' he explained.

When Fern told Ivan what she intended to do he was furious. He immediately went to see Heinz Knox to suggest that Marlene should be included in the arrangement but Heinz was adamant that he wanted Fern on her own. He already had an established cabaret and all he needed was a dancer, and Fern was the one he wanted.

Fern ignored Ivan's warning that she was making a great mistake and decided to seize the opportunity to strike out on her own. Marlene expressed no view whatsoever when she told her what she was planning to do and Fern suspected that Marlene was quite pleased to see her go so that she had Ivan all to herself.

As Ivan had warned, working for Heinz Knox had its drawbacks. In return for giving her a star billing he expected favours; ones which she was not prepared to give.

Glanmor still figured exclusively in her heart and in her mind and she had no wish for a dalliance with any other man. It was a state of affairs which didn't please Heinz Knox and he repeatedly told her how much she owed him. When her six months contract expired he refused to renew it unless she conceded to his demands for sexual favours.

'There is no other man in your life, so why are you so frigid?' he asked contemptuously when she continued to reject his advances. When she tried to explain about her love for Glanmor he was cynical and disparaging.

'This Glanmor is dead, so it is time to forget about him. Move on. Soon you will lose your looks and your ability to dance and then what will you do?'

'I shall go home to Cardiff and find some other way of earning my living and it won't be sleeping with you or any other man,' Fern told him quietly.

'Perhaps then the time has come to pack your suitcase and start your journey,' he told her. 'There is no more work for you here and if I should be asked for recommendations I will not be giving them. You are finished in Germany.'

Fern didn't argue with him, she merely nodded in acceptance, which seemed to anger him all the more.

That night as she packed her few belongings she tried to make her mind up whether she ought to try and work her way through Holland and Belgium or whether she should spend more than half her savings on the train fare and go direct to Paris.

Deep down she longed to be back in Cardiff; she was missing Maria and she was worried because she hadn't heard from her or from Rhodri for a long time. She was so homesick that she wondered if, in fact, it might be better to spend every penny she had and head for Cardiff. The thought of arriving back there completely penniless and with only the few scrappy posters that Ivan had produced to prove how successful she'd been as a dancer, deterred her.

It would be wonderful to tell them that she had appeared at the Folies Bergère. It was one of her dreams and she resolved that now was the time to give herself the chance to do so.

If she failed the audition, she promised herself, then she would abandon the idea and head straight back to Cardiff. If she succeeded, then how long she stayed in Paris would depend on how successful she proved to be.

Chapter Twenty-nine

Fern was fortunate enough to find a window seat and as the train thundered across Western Germany, through Holland and Belgium and on into France, she either stared out at the passing countryside or closed her eyes and dozed.

As they neared their destination she tried to decide what her course of action should be when they arrived in Paris. How did she go about arranging an audition for herself at the Folies Bergère? she wondered. Should she book into the cheapest hotel she could find or go straight to 32 Rue Richer?

Mentally, she counted up how much money she had left after paying her train fare and wondered if it would be better to find out what her chances were of achieving an audition before spending it on accommodation.

Although becoming one of their dancers was her ultimate goal, if it looked as though it was going to be impossible, then perhaps the wisest course of action would be to go straight back to Cardiff. She was worried about Maria and longed to see her again. Even though she was sure that Rhodri was taking care of her as he had promised to do, it would be wonderful to see them both again.

Fern wasn't sure if Maria would have heard about what had happened to Glanmor.

As she alighted from the train and stood on the platform still debating with herself what to do for the best, a bustling porter picked up her bag which she had put down by her feet and loaded it on to his trolley.

Grabbing hold of it, she pulled it free, shaking her head when he began questioning her in voluble French before hurrying off in the opposite direction.

Deciding that it was no place to tarry she headed for the exit. Her mind was made up. She'd try her luck at the Folies Bergère.

Ignoring the main entrance she made her way down the passageway at the side to the stage door. It opened to her touch and, apprehensively, she made her way up the narrow wooden stairs, trying to work out in her mind what she would say when she met someone.

Before she reached the top a small wizened woman appeared, scowling fiercely.

Fern realised from the woman's tone that she was being scolded and that it was something to do with being late. Too breathless to explain she allowed herself to be taken by the arm and hurried down a carpeted passage and into a room at the far end.

'Madame Delcourt, the girl has arrived at last.'

The elegant woman wore a black woollen dress

and her dark hair was swept up into a smooth chignon. She was seated behind the desk sorting a pile of papers and didn't even glance up; she merely waved to the chair opposite her desk.

Fern sat down on the edge of the chair, clutching the handle of her suitcase, not sure what to say or do.

When Madame Delcourt finally looked up she spoke so fast that Fern had no idea what she was saying. Pointing to herself she murmured, 'English, not Française.'

The woman frowned and then, to Fern's relief, began speaking quite slowly, this time in English.

'You are very late,' she admonished. 'There was no need to bring your costume,' she said dismissively, indicating the suitcase at Fern's feet. 'If you are satisfactory, then you will wear something from our collection.' Standing up, she added impatiently, 'Leave your valise and come this way and show me what you can do.'

Fern opened her mouth to speak, to explain that there must be some mistake because she didn't have an appointment. Realising that this was an unexpected opportunity to have an audition, she slipped off her coat and followed Madame Delcourt.

Madame Delcourt led the way into a small ballroom; at one end was a stage with a piano in one corner. With a nod to Fern she sat down at the piano and began to play.

'Come, then; show me what you can do,' she said impatiently.

Fern hesitated; she couldn't believe she was actually auditioning for the Folies Bergère; it was nerve-wracking. To her consternation she was not familiar with the tune and she had no idea what was expected of her. It mattered so much that she made a good impression but all she could do was to improvise and simply let the music dictate what her feet must do.

In a dream, she danced for almost fifteen minutes. As Madame Delcourt stopped playing Fern felt as if she was coming out of a trance. Had it been real or was she imagining it was all taking place? she wondered.

Madam Delcourt's next words brought her down to earth.

'You are very talented. I am not sure you will fit into the chorus, but possibly you can still dance for us. Tell me something of your background. In English, if you must, but speak slowly.'

Haltingly, Fern explained that she had called there on the spur of the moment and that she was not the dancer that Madame Delcourt had obviously been expecting.

The other woman shrugged. 'She still has not come, so no matter. Perhaps it was meant to be this way,' she added with a smile that softened her features. 'Come, tell me about yourself and why you are here.'

Very concisely Fern explained about Glanmor being a sailor and how after he'd died at sea she had been working as a dancer in Russia. She said nothing about the baby she had lost.

'So you have become tired of Russia and the Bolsheviks' way of living?' Madame Delcourt questioned.

'I found that their ways were different to what I had been used to in Cardiff,' Fern murmured non-committaly.

'Very tactfully expressed,' Madame Delcourt commented dryly. 'Let us hope that you will find French ways are more pleasing. Now, where is it you are living?'

'I've not found anywhere, not yet. I only arrived in Paris a couple of hours ago and I came straight here from the railway station,' she explained.

'I see!' Madame Delcourt looked surprised. 'You were expecting to be auditioned without making any application?'

'No, no; most certainly not,' Fern said quickly. 'It has always been my ambition to dance with the Folies Bergère,' she sighed. 'I simply came to see where they were housed; to enjoy the atmosphere of such a famous theatre.'

Madame Delcourt shook her head as if in amusement. 'Yet you end up being hired as a dancer; all so breathless it seems untrue. Never mind; we have found each other. You will start dancing immediately; your first rehearsal and costume fitting will be in the morning. Are you agreeable to all that?'

'It sounds wonderful, I feel quite dazed by my good fortune,' Fern told her.

'That is good. Now I will find someone to

take care of you until then. I will arrange some lodgings for you. Our girls are housed quite nearby. It is a large house and they all have their own rooms but enjoy each other's company at mealtimes and whenever they are not working. There is a housekeeper who attends to their needs, arranges laundry and things like that.'

It took Fern several weeks to settle into her new life. The routine and rehearsals at the Folies Bergère were strict and arduous. She found living with so many girls was exhausting because it was so difficult for her to understand their constant chatter. She remembered with deep longing the cosy evenings spent with Maria and the close companionship she experienced when Rhodri joined them for a meal.

The highlight of her existence, however, was the fact that she danced a solo piece every night and the applause from the audience when she finished her dance was intoxicating and filled her with deep contentment.

The first time she saw her name listed on one of the Folies Bergère posters, she felt grateful that all her hard work had been worth it. She was no longer simply a dancer; she was a cabaret star and really had achieved her ultimate ambition.

Fern found that living in Paris was exciting, especially after the frugalities and regimentation she'd experienced in Petrograd. She spent a great deal of time window-shopping. The clothes on display were so wonderful that she wished she could buy them all, but she was equally content to simply view and dream. The elaborate costumes she appeared in each night – silks, satins and feathers – more than compensated her longing for glamorous outfits.

In many ways she had never been happier. At the back of her mind, however, there was always the feeling that she ought to return to Cardiff because she owed it to Maria to make sure that she was comfortable in her declining years. Maria had been like a mother to her. She missed Rhodri and his practical approach to life as well; they were her only remaining links with Glanmor.

She tried to tell herself that she had moved on and that that part of her life was now a closed book, but it didn't always work. When she was feeling tired she became homesick and then it seemed she could think of nothing else.

Yet, much as she wanted to return to Cardiff, she didn't want to give up the thrill of dancing to an appreciative audience every night and she knew quite well that there was nothing compatible with performing at the Folies Bergère. She even had a special admirer who came twice or sometimes three times a week to watch her dance. She always knew when he was in the audience because before the show started he would send round a single long-stemmed rose in an elaborate box.

She had no idea what he looked like, although she always tried to study the audience in the hope of picking him out.

The other girls laughed and teased her about him. Some said he was an artist who one day would want to paint her portrait; others said he was old and ugly and that was why he would never come to the stage door or arrange to meet her. Several told her that he was probably rich but married and had a wife who was so jealous that he dare not reveal who he was.

Many of the girls had admirers or patrons but they were usually short-term liaisons. Occasionally, one of them would receive a proposal and then the fortunate recipient would depart in a shower of good wishes for a life of luxury and never be heard of again.

It was many months before Fern discovered who her own admirer was and by then, she was curious to meet him face to face. When she did she found that she enjoyed his company.

Monsieur Laurain was a well-built man of medium height in his early fifties. His thinning dark hair was brushed back from a high forehead and his dark eyes were sharp and quite piercing. He was dressed in a flawless black tailcoat and dark trousers with a snow-white shirt and a dark grey bow tie.

Over a meal in an exclusive little restaurant in Rue Laffitte he told her to only ever call him Pierre. He explained that his need for discretion was because he was the head of a large financial organisation. He didn't name it and Fern thought it was wisest not to ask for details but resolved to find out in some other way.

He flattered her by saying how entranced he was by her and told her that he would like to set her up in her own apartment. It would be somewhere very discreet, he promised, a love-nest where he could visit her whenever he was free to do so.

Fern was hesitant. She realised what would be expected of her in such a liaison and she still wasn't at all sure that she was ready for such a relationship. Ever since Glanmor had died she had gone to great lengths to avoid becoming embroiled in any serious flirtations that might lead to romantic encounters because she was determined to remain true to his memory.

Even so, the thought of having her own apartment and being completely independent from the rest of the girls who danced at the Folies Bergère every night was tempting. Of late she had discovered that she much preferred to be on her own; working and living with the same girls day in day out was becoming claustrophobic. The only problem was whether he would be content with a platonic friendship or whether he would expect more.

He seemed to understand her hesitancy and emphasised that he didn't need an answer from her right away.

'I want you to take your time and think about it carefully but do not keep me waiting too long for your answer,' he told her. 'If you are agreeable to the idea, then I will go ahead and make all the necessary arrangements. I assure you that

I will seek your approval before choosing any apartment. I want it to be one that pleases you and is exactly to your taste.'

Fern found this reassuring; she thought that such consideration for her feelings showed how perceptive and kind he was. Even so, she didn't relish the idea of becoming his mistress, which she realised was what was involved.

It troubled her so much and she was in such a quandary about it, that she could think of nothing else. Finally, in desperation, she decided to confide in Madame Delcourt.

'*Ma cherie*, I fail to understand what your problem can be,' she said, frowning. 'Surely you are aware that Monsieur Laurain is being extremely magnanimous?'

'I know that, and I really do appreciate his generosity,' Fern told her.

'Then why are you so worried; why do you come to me to help you make a decision?'

'I am not sure that I want to be involved in a romantic liaison of that sort,' Fern explained hesitantly.

'Foolish girl,' Madame Delcourt scolded. 'Do you not see that he is doing you a great honour? You may be a dancer here at the Folies Bergère but, compared to him, you are an utter nobody. Monsieur Pierre Laurain is not only a highly respectable, very wealthy businessman, but he is also greatly admired and has tremendous influence throughout Paris.'

Chapter Thirty

Fern longed to accept the apartment that Monsieur Laurain had taken her to see in Rue Laffitte, which was only a stone's throw from the discreet restaurant where they had first met, but the thought of being under an obligation to him, and all that would eventually entail, deterred her from doing so.

She had been amazed at how very much in favour of her accepting Monsieur Laurain's offer Madame Delcourt had been, but far from convincing her that it was the right thing to do it had made her even more cautious.

Each day, as she endured the discomfort of sharing everything, from the bathroom to mealtimes with the horde of chattering girls from the chorus, she longed for the privacy of the apartment.

To a degree the girls were all friendly but several of them resented the fact that she was English and a complete newcomer and yet had a solo spot in the show, and they made no attempt to hide their jealousy.

The other thing that she found rather disconcerting was that they expected her to share with them what few possessions she had. They would borrow a dress, a hat, stockings, make-up, or anything else that took their fancy – even her hair brush and face flannel – without asking.

'You are welcome to any of our things,' they would retort with a cheeky smile or a nonchalant shrug, if she protested. 'It is ridiculous for all of us to buy a new dress, or anything else, for that matter, when we want to dress up for a special occasion, when it is so much more convenient to borrow from each other.'

Fern appreciated that this was perfectly true. She pointed out that she didn't mind lending her things, providing they asked permission first. She resented it when they helped themselves to possessions which were rightfully hers because it reminded her far too much of what life had been like in Petrograd.

There were many other ways in which she felt she didn't belong. In their leisure time most of the girls never wanted to go anywhere else in Paris but loiter around Montmartre. Although she loved to explore the quaint cobbled streets, unlike the other girls, the attraction for her was the atmosphere, not the hope of being spotted by an artist asking if he could paint her.

There were so many other beautiful places to visit in Paris that it was never at the top of her list. As a result, her excursions to take in all the other vistas Paris had to offer, from the Eiffel Tower, the Louvre and Notre Dame to the wonderful parks and gardens or walks along the banks of the Seine, were usually made on her own.

She knew this made her unpopular with the other girls and they regarded her as stand-offish. For this reason as much as any other she knew Madam Delcourt was perfectly right and that probably she would be far happier moving into the apartment she'd been offered. It was the commitment that Pierre Laurain was expecting her to make if she did so that worried her.

Her decision was taken suddenly. She was so incensed because one of the girls had borrowed her white fox fur stole without asking that she knew she couldn't stand communal living any longer. The fur was her most treasured possession because it was the very last present Glanmor had bought her.

'What a fuss to make about an old piece of rabbit skin,' the girl commented disdainfully as, with a cry of protest, Fern grabbed hold of the stole and pulled it from her shoulders.

The other girls regarded the scene in silence, some in disbelief, others in amusement, as, with tears trickling down her cheeks, Fern buried her face in the soft pile.

It was at that moment that she decided she couldn't go on sharing living quarters with them any longer. She knew she was taking a chance but if she couldn't have Glanmor she felt it no longer mattered. A week later she was installed in the apartment in Rue Laffitte and revelling in the spaciousness of her new home.

She padded around the three-roomed apartment in her bare feet, revelling in the feel of the deep-pile carpets. Every so often she would stop and pick up one of the velvet-covered cushions and hug it to her in delight and then flop down on the chaise-longue, or the sofa that was upholstered in gold brocade, completely overcome by all the luxury that surrounded her.

In the beautiful bedroom she was constantly running her hand down the smooth satin sheen of the luxurious heavy cream curtains that draped the windows. She stroked the rose-pink brocade bedspread that topped the soft satin sheets and the fur bedcover that was folded in three and draped across the foot of the bed.

Whenever she caught sight of her reflection in the cheval mirror or in the ornate gilded mirror suspended over the long narrow dressing table, she drew in a long, deep breath.

Then, remembering the frugal furnishings of the apartment in Petrograd which she'd shared with Jacob, Dairvy, little Egor and the two lodgers Boris and Vladimir, she felt a frisson of guilt that she was now living in such a spacious apartment.

She wished Maria could see it. Maria's home had been comfortable and cosy but this place, she reflected, was opulence greater than anything she had ever known in her life before.

Monsieur Laurain was most tactful. For the first few times that he escorted her home after the show he showed her to the door but made no attempt to come in with her. Gradually Fern's fears about what her move would entail faded into insignificance.

She had been living there several weeks when he asked, 'Are there any other items you require for the apartment? You may make any changes you wish, remember. I want you to think of it as your home and I want you to feel completely relaxed and comfortable living there.'

'There is nothing I need, it is very beautiful and I am most happy,' she told him.

'Then perhaps you would like to invite me in for a nightcap next time I bring you home,' he said quietly.

'You have the right to come in at any time,' she said quickly.

He shook his head. 'No, that is not so, *ma petite*. I would not dream of entering unless you invited me to do so. It is your home and I shall always respect that.'

Fern felt her colour rising as she realised that it had been slightly remiss of her not to ask him in before this. Her feeling of gratitude towards him increased because she realised that he had been extremely patient and courteous. He had allowed her time to settle in without imposing even the slightest demands.

'Please,' she laid her hand on his arm, 'you must always feel free to stay and have a nightcap, Pierre, and also to visit me whenever you wish to do so. If you don't, then I shall lead a very lonely life,' she added with a smile.

331

From then on there was a much more relaxed understanding between them. He never mentioned his family but she learned that he was chairman of several very important companies and had a great many friends in high places and in government circles.

'Perhaps, *ma petite*, you would like to meet some of them,' he suggested one evening as he sat sipping the glass of absinthe which she'd poured out for him, knowing that it was his favourite drink. 'I am sure they would be interested in meeting you,' he added with a twinkle in his dark eyes.

Fern smiled dismissively. 'It is very kind of you to suggest it but they must all be so clever and so learned that I wouldn't know what to say to them.'

'Nonsense! Anyway, you wouldn't have to talk to them if you didn't want to do so. They would enjoy watching you dance for them. I thought you could give them a private performance.'

Fern looked at him in silence. She was flattered but it seemed such an odd request that she didn't know what to say. If they wanted to see her dance then they could attend a performance at the theatre.

'Surely you are prepared to do that for me, Fern. It is the only request I have ever made of you,' he said sharply.

Fern felt her colour rising. She knew that was quite true and it was something that had puzzled her ever since she moved into the apartment.

Pierre Laurain had never made any attempt to touch her, other than to occasionally give her a chaste peck on the cheek.

'You are quite right,' she told him. 'Of course I will dance for your friends.'

Soon the other girls at the Folies Bergère discovered where Fern was living. When they found out that it was under the patronage of Monsieur Laurain, their comments reflected a mixture of envy and scorn.

'Imagine it! He is said to be one of the richest men in France,' Eloise sighed.

'I wouldn't fancy becoming an old man's darling,' Marguerite murmured, pulling a face and shuddering.

'No wonder she didn't want us borrowing any of her baubles, they're probably things he's bought her,' Dorita said scornfully, flicking her long tawny hair back from her shoulders disdainfully.

'I wonder what you have to do to earn such generous patronage?' one asked inquisitively.

'If you get lonely in that huge rambling apartment we'd always be willing to move in with you,' several of them told her.

'Or if Monsieur Laurain has a rich friend who wants to set another one of us up in such luxury you have only to tell him my name,' another giggled.

Fern tried to take their teasing in good part. Now and again a comment would hurt and she would wince inwardly, but she did her best to remain calm and apparently unfazed.

Madam Delcourt seemed to be delighted by her decision and even went as far as to wish her well. At the same time she cautioned, 'It may not last for ever, you know, so enjoy it while you can and don't be too heart-broken when it all ends.'

Fern knew this was sound advice. Since she no longer had to pay for her keep and Monsieur Laurain not only made sure that the larder was well stocked but also kept an excellent selection of wines and spirits, Fern prudently saved as much of her salary as she could.

She soon found that because she did not have to pay for anything other than her own personal beauty items she had money left over each week. It immediately became her ambition to save an adequate sum to live on for a few months if she lost her job. She also wanted to save enough to be able to return to Cardiff if ever anything went wrong or if she felt she couldn't stand living in Paris any longer.

As her savings grew so did her restlessness and, somehow, all the luxury and crowds of admirers had a hollow, unreal feel. She decided that as soon as she had saved up enough she would return to Cardiff and the life she missed so much, and take care of Maria in her old age.

For some reason, she found it very demeaning when she had to dance for Monsieur Laurain's friends, even though it was conducted in a very proper manner.

They came late in the evening, he was already

there and, after an exchange of pleasantries, he would pour out drinks for all of them and they would make themselves comfortable on the sofas or armchairs. Pierre would select a record and put it on to the gramophone and then signal to her that they were ready.

At the end of her dance session they would all applaud and say how much they'd enjoyed the evening. It was all conducted in such a friendly yet restrained manner that she couldn't understand why she always felt so uneasy and why, once she'd danced, she was so impatient for them all to depart.

Gradually it dawned on Fern that the reason for her feeling of discomfort was Monsieur Jacques Alfonse. He was a large dark-haired man of about fifty with florid cheeks, sharp green eyes and a goatee beard which he was continually stroking.

He was usually the first to arrive in the evening and always the very last to leave. Fern suspected that he was hoping one evening that he would find her on her own and the very thought filled her with unease.

When this did in fact happen, she was completely taken by surprise. It was a wet evening in early December and immediately after she had finished dancing Pierre Laurain had called for taxis to take all his friends and himself home.

Five taxis all arrived at once and in the flurry of their departure Monsieur Alfonse managed to retire to the bathroom and was still there on his own when everyone else had gone.

Fern tried to remain calm but her heart was thudding at an alarming rate as she suggested to Monsieur Alfonse that he should use the telephone to call another taxi.

She felt frightened as she moved between the sitting room and kitchen, clearing away the glasses and dishes they'd been using. She spent an inordinately long time stacking them by the sink in readiness for Marnie, the daily woman, to deal with the next morning – all the time hoping that when she returned to the sitting room he would be gone or at least getting ready to go.

To her dismay he was still there, reclining on one of the sofas and stroking his goatee beard thoughtfully as if he had all the time in the world.

'There will be a delay of half an hour before a taxi will be free,' he told her. 'Could I have another drink?'

'Of course.' She went over to the drinks cabinet, selected a glass and began pouring out a measure of absinthe. As she turned round to take it across to him she found he was behind her and once more she had a feeling of impending trouble.

Taking the glass from her hand he put it down on a small table then put one of his arms round her and, with his free hand, tilted her face so that he could kiss her.

As she felt his huge soft body pressed against her she struggled to free herself from his embrace but this only amused him and his grip tightened.

'I don't think Pierre would approve of you doing this, Monsieur Alfonse,' she gasped, placing both her hands on his chest and trying to push him away.

'Why not? He only keeps you as a plaything, so why would he mind sharing you?'

Fern realised that it was pointless trying to reason with him or explain that her relationship with Pierre Laurain was a purely platonic one. Jacques Alfonse had been drinking all evening and his breath was so overpowering that as his mouth hovered over hers it made her gag.

Before she could stop him he had picked her up in his arms and carried her through to the adjoining bedroom. Throwing her roughly down on the damask bedspread he held her there with one hand as he wriggled out of his coat and pulled the bow tie away from the front of his shirt front, then tossed it aside. In one swift movement he caught at the neck of her dress and there was a sickening sound as he ripped it from her body.

His immense bulk as he flopped down on top of her was so heavy that she was unable to move. He kept a hand over her mouth to stop her from crying out so all she could do was suffer in silence as he pleasured himself.

The sound of the taxi klaxon sounding outside seemed to bring Jacques Alfonse to his senses.

With an angry grunt he rolled off her, straightened his dishevelled clothing, picked up his tie and thrust it into his jacket pocket and left.

Tears of self-pity and revulsion trickled unchecked down Fern's cheeks as the door slammed behind him. She lay there sobbing and feeling sorry for herself. It was as if her world had collapsed and her life was in ruins.

Pierre Laurain had always acted towards her in such a gentlemanly fashion that she had convinced herself that there was nothing to fear or be ashamed about at being what the other girls termed a 'kept woman', but Jacques Alfonse had spoiled all that for her.

Her heart ached for Glanmor. Why did such a good and honourable man have to die while men like Jacques Alfonse went on living? she railed aloud.

Chapter Thirty-one

Fern couldn't sleep. She tossed and turned; one minute she was throwing back the covers because she was too hot and the next she was dragging them right up to her chin because she was shivering, not from the cold but from the memories of what she had endured earlier that evening at the hands of Jacques Alfonse.

She hated him so much that it hurt. She didn't know what to do for the best; whether to tell Pierre Laurain or to try and keep it all a secret. He was bound to notice the breakages and damage and she would have to account in some way for what had happened.

The trouble was that she didn't trust Monsieur Alfonse. He not only drank a great deal but he was also a gossip, so it was more than likely that he would boast to his friends about what had happened.

She enjoyed living in her apartment and was grateful to Pierre Laurain for providing her with so much luxury while expecting so little in return. If she said nothing then he might hear the rumours and, depending on how garbled the version was, he might even assume she had condoned Jacques Alfonse's behaviour.

If he questioned Jacques Alfonse directly, then he would probably say that she had led him on and put the blame on her for what had happened.

Added to which the news was bound to reach the ears of the other girls at the Folies Bergère and once that happened her life there would be unbearable.

Unable to remain in bed because she felt so stressed, Fern pulled on her peignoir and went into the kitchen and made a tisane in an attempt to calm her nerves.

Whichever way she looked at the problem it seemed as though her career at the Folies Bergère, as well as her days of comfortable living, were over. Madame Delcourt had been so much in favour of her accepting Pierre Laurain's patronage that she was bound to be angry about what had happened and if she felt it had brought disgrace on Pierre Laurain's name then she would sack her.

If that happened, she decided, she would return to Cardiff. She'd saved enough for her fare and, if she was very frugal, she could probably manage for a few weeks until she found a job. Rhodri Richards might even be prepared to let her help out on his stall; that was, if he still had one in the Hayes market.

She spent the rest of the day until it was time to go to the theatre trying to restore order in the apartment and sorting out her personal belongings.

Fern looked longingly at the pile of beautiful dresses, handbags, jewellery and perfume that Pierre had given her since she'd been living at Rue Laffitte. She would have loved to have kept everything but she felt that as she would most likely end up leaving Paris under a cloud it would be dishonest to do so.

Fern felt very subdued as she walked into the dressing room to change into her costume in readiness for the show. She was unsure if any of them knew about what had happened and she didn't know what to expect. Eloise was there but her casual shrug of greeting was no different to any other day.

Gradually, as Fern exchanged greetings with the other girls in the normal way some of the anxiety that had built up during the long dark hours of the night began to diminish.

As she changed into her glamorous costume and applied her make-up ready for her solo dance Fern decided that perhaps it was all in her imagination that there would be trouble; none of the others appeared to know anything about what had happened.

She resolved to do her best to forget about it, although she knew perfectly well that the horrendous attack that Jacques Alfonse had subjected her to would never be erased from her mind.

As her body responded to the music Fern found that, as usual, she was transported from all the turmoil of the world around her into a dream where the music never stopped and she floated as free as a bird.

Fern's momentary feeling of ecstasy vanished and she was filled with apprehension when later in the evening Pierre Laurain, accompanied by Madame Delcourt, entered the theatre and sat in the seats she kept reserved for special patrons.

Fern tried hard to concentrate on her dance, thankful that it was almost over. What should she do afterwards? she wondered. Her impulse was to go back to the dressing room, change out of her costume and then slip away quietly. She would probably have time to go back to the apartment, collect her valise, which she'd already packed, and be gone before Pierre Laurain missed her.

That was the action of a coward, she told herself. All her life she had always faced up to any problems that came her way so why should she behave in such a despicable manner now?

In the past she had had Glanmor to help her fight her battles, she reminded herself. Even when he was at sea he was there in her mind and heart, telling her what to do.

It made her pause and think; if she ran away, then she would be disgracing his memory as well as letting herself down. Why should she do so, anyway, she thought. The guilty one was Monsieur Alfonse, not her.

As she finished her routine, took her bow and retired from the stage, Fern's mind was made up. She would face up to Pierre Laurain and tell him the truth about what had happened whether he'd heard about the incident from anyone else or not.

Before she had finished changing he appeared at the dressing-room door. His manner was as cordial and polite as ever as he took her arm and escorted her out to the waiting cab.

They exchanged the normal pleasantries and Fern decided it would be better to wait until they reached the apartment before she began telling him about the incident.

As she handed him a glass of absinthe everything between them seemed to be so normal that, for a fleeting moment, she wondered whether it might be better to say nothing.

The moment passed. Sitting on the edge of a chair facing Pierre she related in a quietly controlled voice exactly what had taken place the previous evening.

He listened to her in silence, smoking his cigar and occasionally sipping from his glass. His face remained impassive as he glanced across the room at the damaged chiffonier.

When she'd finished speaking he held out his glass and indicated with a nod of his head towards the bottle of absinthe that he wanted her to refill it.

As she did his bidding the silence in the room was so oppressive that Fern could feel her heart thudding as she waited for him to speak.

He drained his glass before he spoke and

put it down with elaborate care on the side table.

'Why are you telling me all this?' he asked, raising one eyebrow speculatively.

'I felt you should know,' Fern said lamely. 'He not only damaged the apartment, he also violated me!'

'So what are you expecting, pistols at dawn? I hardly think it is worth risking my life in defence of your honour, do you?' he added with a supercilious smile.

Fern stared at him wide-eyed; she didn't know what to say. She had expected him to express some words of sympathy for what she'd been forced to endure, or even a show of anger, and his languid acceptance of what had happened infuriated her.

'In fact,' Pierre Laurain went on in a humourless voice, 'I had already received a detailed account of the incident from Monsieur Alfonse and I am more concerned about the chiffonier and the other breakages. Some of those pieces were very valuable,' he added, stifling a yawn and rising to his feet.

'You are leaving . . . so soon?'

'Why? Are you hoping for a repeat performance of last night?' he asked in a sardonic voice. 'I would have thought that by now you would know that I do not indulge in carnal relationships. Even so, I have no objections to my friends taking their pleasure whenever they wish, providing you permit them to do so.'

344

'I didn't permit it,' Fern exclaimed angrily. 'I've already told you, Jacques Alfonse ravished me against my will.'

'Really. You must have given him some encouragement.'

Fern felt incensed by the contempt in Pierre Laurain's voice. Positioning herself between him and the door she said angrily, 'You are not taking this seriously, are you? How can you stand there and say that you are more concerned over the damage to your possessions than you are about what happened to me?'

'Very easily, *ma cherie*. You are replaceable; some of those pieces are not.'

Before she could stop him he had brushed past her, slamming the door behind him.

Fern poured herself a drink of absinthe and gulped it down. She hated the taste but she felt she needed something to settle her nerves and stop her trembling.

She couldn't believe what had happened. The other girls were right with their sneers and innuendos. She was nothing more than a kept woman. They might be jealous of what she had managed to achieve but at this moment she envied them. She felt ashamed to be living in such luxurious surroundings when they were earning less than her and working even harder.

She didn't think she could bear to face any of them ever again. Monsieur Alfonse had been right when he'd described her as a plaything. Pierre Laurain had made it quite clear that this was what he regarded her as and that she mattered far less to him than any of his prized possessions.

Her head was spinning and she blamed the absinthe and wished she'd not been foolish enough to drink it. Foolish – that about summed her up, she thought bitterly. No girl with any sense of propriety or even plain self-respect would agree to become a 'kept woman', she thought bitterly.

This stage in her life was over, she told herself. She had no intention of returning to the Folies Bergère; she wasn't even going to give Madame Delcourt the satisfaction of knowing why she'd gone. The show would go on perfectly well without her; after all, it had done so before she'd appeared on the scene.

She'd had her moment of fame. She would give up the beautiful apartment and luxurious lifestyle she'd enjoyed so much and return to Cardiff and to the real world.

Even though it would probably mean she'd be living in one squalid room in Tiger Bay, her conscience would be clear and she would have her freedom and be able to look people squarely in the eye, knowing that she had retained her integrity.

Tired as she was she knew she couldn't stay a minute longer in the apartment. Putting on her outdoor clothes and picking up her valise she went out into the crisp, cold December night.

Tomorrow would be New Year's Eve, one of the busiest times of the year at the Folies Bergère; there would be a packed house and she was leaving without a word of explanation which would inconvenience Madame Delcourt because there would be a gap in the special programme she had arranged.

Fern knew that in some ways it was unforgivable but she calmed her conscience by reminding herself that it had been because Madame Delcourt had been so eager for her to accept the patronage of Monsieur Laurain that she was in this terrible situation.

She was on the point of hailing a taxicab to take her to the railway station when she decided it might be better not to do so. Pierre always used taxis when he left the apartment as well as when he brought her back from the theatre at night if the weather was inclement, so he was well known to most of the drivers. If he made enquiries as to her whereabouts then there was the risk that the driver might report to him that she'd left Paris by train.

As she trudged along the street, her luggage growing heavier by the minute, she knew it would probably have been more sensible to wait until the next morning. Though by then, she reasoned, she might have had second thoughts. The urge to get right away was too great; she wanted to put all that had happened in the last few hours behind her.

The journey by train and boat and then train

again seemed endless; it was almost as if she was leaving one world and entering another. Time and time again she wondered if she was doing the right thing and whether she would regret leaving Paris.

She was so tired that once she was on the train that would finally take her back to Cardiff she kept nodding off, sinking into a dark, tumultuous world peopled by laughing, jeering chorus girls and hideous lecherous men. Every time it happened she would waken with a start and stare round the compartment unseeingly for a moment as she tried to bring her thoughts back to reality. She was always so relieved to find she was still on the train that she endeavoured to stay awake until she reached her destination.

She finally arrived at Cardiff General around midday the following day. It was not only a Saturday, she reflected, but it was also the first day of 1927. Could this be an omen, she wondered, a new year and a brand new beginning for her?

Chapter Thirty-two

As she came out of the railway station in Wood Street and crossed over the road towards the Hayes, Fern was surprised by how quiet it seemed to be. Then she stopped in her tracks; the market was closed. For a moment she had forgotten that it was New Year's Day and there would be no trading.

It all seemed so strange that she felt disorientated. She recognised all the familiar roads and their names and yet, because there was none of the usual hustle and bustle of the market, she felt slightly dismayed.

She hesitated for a moment, wondering what to do for the best, and then she decided to go to Maria's and headed for the nearest tram stop.

As the tram lurched its way down Bute Street so many things looked different. She wondered if Rhodri still had a stall in the market and whether he and Maria would recognise her. It was almost five years since she'd left Cardiff; she'd been seventeen then; now she was nearly twenty-two, grown-up and a woman of the world.

As she knocked on the door of the flat, Fern found herself smiling as she imagined the look of surprise there would be on Maria's face when she opened it. She'd have so much to tell her, Fern reflected.

Her smile faded abruptly. It wasn't Maria but a stranger standing there. The woman was middle aged and frowning as though annoyed at the interruption. When Fern asked for Mrs Roberts the woman shook her head. 'You've got the wrong flat. No one of that name lives here, not now, anyway.'

'Do you know where Mrs Roberts has gone?'

The woman folded her arms across her print pinafore. 'I've already said she doesn't live here, isn't that enough?'

'Sorry to have disturbed you,' Fern retorted sharply. 'I'm an old friend of hers, see, but I've been away for several years . . .'

Fern stopped speaking as the door was shut in her face. Picking up her valise she made her way back down the three flights of stairs. She stood outside on the pavement wondering what to do next.

There was only one way to find out, she reasoned, and that was to go and see if Rhodri could tell her what had happened while she'd been away and where Maria was living now.

It had been so long ago that she had lived in Cardiff, and so much had happened since then, that Fern wasn't too sure which house it was in Loudon Place where Rhodri had a room or even if he'd still be living there.

She stood on the corner of the road feeling

completely lost and wondering what on earth she was going to do. For a moment she wished she was back in her warm, luxurious apartment, not standing in the middle of Tiger Bay, shivering with the cold and uncertain where to go or what to do next.

Perhaps, after all, she had been too hasty in leaving Paris so abruptly. Things might well have sorted themselves out if she had stayed and moved back in with the other girls and she would still have the job she loved as a dancer.

It was too late now for recriminations, she told herself. She was back in Cardiff where, in her heart, she had yearned to be for such a long time, so it was up to her to make the best of it. She'd see if she could get a room for the night in the Westgate Hotel which was only a short distance away. In the morning, after a good night's sleep, she'd be able to concentrate on what to do for the best.

As she stooped to pick up her heavy valise, a deep masculine voice which seemed familiar said, 'Would you like me to carry that? It looks far too heavy for you.'

Fern looked up, startled at the sight of the tall, good-looking man in front of her. 'Rhodri Richards!' she gasped.

'Fern?' He looked equally astonished. 'What a wonderful surprise!' he gasped. 'I was wondering what changes the New Year would bring but I never thought it would be seeing you again.'

The next moment they were hugging enthusiastically and wishing each other a Happy
New Year.

'So what are you doing here?' he asked as he
released her. 'With all that luggage, you must
be paying us a visit at long last,' he added with
a laugh.

'Not a visit. I've come back to Cardiff for
good. I have just been to Loudon Square, hoping
to see Maria, but it seems she's moved. A complete stranger answered the door to me and she
didn't even seem to know Maria. As a matter
of fact, I was on my way to ask you if you knew
where she had moved to, but I couldn't
remember where you lived in Loudon Place.'

'Then I'd better remind you where it is,' he
said, bending down and picking up her valise.
'Come on, it's too cold to stand around here
chatting, we can talk over a cuppa.'

'That would be more than welcome,' she
agreed. 'So where has Maria gone to live?'
she asked as she hurried to keep up with him.

'Let's wait until we are indoors, then we'll
talk when we've had that cup of tea,' he said
evasively.

The fire in his room had been banked down
and Rhodri stirred it to life before lighting the
gas ring and putting a tin kettle on it to boil.
While he was doing this Fern removed her coat,
scarf and hat. She eased off her heavy shoes
because her feet were aching so much and settled
down in an armchair.

The moment Rhodri brought in their cups of tea and sat down she again questioned him about Maria's whereabouts.

Instead of answering her question he shook his head and looked so despondent that Fern felt rather alarmed. 'Is it bad news?' she asked hesitantly.

He nodded. 'Maria's dead,' he said quietly.

Fern's face clouded and her hand shook so much that she had to put down her cup and saucer.

'When did it happen?'

'Four years ago, not very long after you left,' he told her.

'I should never have gone away when I knew she wasn't well,' Fern murmured. 'She was so good to me, it was selfish of me to leave her on her own.'

'She wasn't completely on her own. I did what I could for her,' Rhodri said quickly.

'Oh, I'm sure you did, I didn't mean it like that; you were always looking out for her, the same as you always did for me,' she added with a sad little smile.

'I did try to get in touch with you but I had no idea what ship you and Glanmor were on. The shipping office could only tell me the name of his last boat and that was the SS *Saturn* which didn't carry passengers only cargo, so I didn't think you'd be on that.'

'We were both on it; I stowed away the night it left port,' Fern explained.

353

'You did *what*?' Rhodri's eyes widened in surprise.

'We couldn't afford to pay for my passage so we thought that was the best thing to do.'

'Duw anwyl! So what happened when they discovered you were on board?'

'The captain wasn't too pleased. However, he allowed me to stay until we reached Russia.'

'So have you been in Russia ever since then?'

'No, not all the time.' Fern paused and picked up her cup and saucer and sipped her tea. 'It's too long a story to tell you all the details now, but I am back home again and it's where I want to stay.'

'What about Glanmor? Is he still at sea?'

Fern shook her head. 'In a way he is,' she said, putting her cup and saucer down again. 'Glanmor is dead.'

She saw Rhodri shudder as briefly she told him about Glanmor's terrible accident. The next moment he was at her side, his arm round her shoulders, giving her a comforting hug.

'So much bad news for both of us,' he muttered. 'Will you let me take you somewhere for a meal? There is quite a lot more I have to tell you but I feel we should have some food and a glass of wine first to welcome you back and to celebrate our reunion.'

'It sounds very tempting but think I ought to find somewhere to stay first,' Fern demurred. 'I was wondering if I might be able to get a room at the Westgate Hotel for tonight and then tomorrow look for something permanent.'

'You could always stay here for the night,' Rhodri suggested. 'I would be quite happy to sleep on the sofa,' he added quickly when she hesitated. He didn't want her to get the wrong idea. 'Anyway,' he went on, 'Let's go and eat first and then you can decide.'

'I'd be more than happy to stay here, if you don't mind,' Fern told him. 'I hesitated because I've been travelling for two days and I wondered if I could freshen up before we go out.'

Rhodri took her to a quiet little Italian restaurant tucked away down a side street off Bute Street. Since he seemed to be well known there Fern left him to order the food as well as the wine.

They had so much to tell each other that they were still sitting there long after all the other customers had left but no one seemed to mind.

'That was a lovely meal, Rhodri, and I feel so much better for it,' Fern said smiling.

'Good. There is one more piece of news I must tell you and I'd like to do it now while we are here. I thought perhaps it was better to wait until we had finished our meal because it concerns Maria. Before she died she gave me some money which she asked me to keep somewhere safe and give it to you when I next saw you.'

'Money?' Fern looked bewildered. 'What money, she didn't owe me anything.'

'No, it was her life savings,' he said quietly.

'I don't understand; I was under the impression that she was so hard up she couldn't afford to keep me on as an assistant,' Fern gasped in surprise.

'She said that because she knew how much you wanted to be with Glanmor,' Rhodri sighed. 'She wanted the two of you to be happy more than anything else in the world.'

Fern shook her head sadly. 'I wouldn't have left if I'd known how ill she was.'

'Once you'd gone she decided to sell her stall because she knew how desperately ill she was and that she was no longer fit enough to run it. As her health deteriorated still further she disposed of various other items she owned which she thought were valuable. Her final instructions to me were that after I'd paid off all her debts and her funeral expenses, the rest of the money was for you.'

Fern brushed away the tears that had come to her eyes. 'I don't know what to say. I'd give anything to have her back here with us; that matters far more than any money she's left me.'

'It's a tidy sum: nine hundred pounds, in fact. She hoped it would be enough to help you and Glanmor get a home and a future together,' Rhodri added.

'Nine hundred pounds!' Fern's eyes widened in shock. 'Nine hundred pounds,' she repeated in disbelief. 'That's a small fortune. I don't know what I ought to do, especially since Glanmor is no longer here to share it with me.'

'She would still want you to have it,' Rhodri said firmly. 'She thought a lot of you, Fern. She talked about you a great deal, you know. You were very special to her.'

Fern looked at him in astonishment. 'Even so, it is so unexpected that I really don't know what to think.'

They were interrupted from further discussion by the proprietor coming over to their table to ask if their meal had been to their satisfaction. Rhodri introduced him to Fern and he insisted on ordering another bottle of wine to celebrate her homecoming.

Fern said very little because she was so utterly astonished by what had happened that she could think of nothing else. So much money. What on earth was she going to do with it all? She didn't want to simply spend it, even though there were so many things that she needed.

She wanted to do something very special with it; something that would be a permanent memory to Maria.

Chapter Thirty-three

Fern had so much to ponder about that she didn't think that she would possibly be able to sleep but, to her surprise, she did – from the moment her head touched the pillow.

It was daylight when she opened her eyes and she had no idea what the time was or, for a moment, where she was. She stretched and then sat up in bed, smoothing her hair back from her face and looking around her.

The tumultuous events of the previous day came crowding back into her mind. She had met up with Rhodri the day before and because she'd had nowhere else to go she'd spent the night in his bed; most important of all, she was back in Cardiff.

She pushed aside the bedclothes; she couldn't lie there all day because she had to find somewhere to live and a job. Then she remembered that it was Sunday so there was no point in rushing, nothing would be open.

She went into the living room and wondered where Rhodri was. There was no sign of him and the blankets he'd used were folded neatly and piled up at one end of the sofa.

She lit the gas ring and put the kettle on. While

she was waiting for it to boil she washed her face at the sink and then went back into the bedroom to get dressed.

Before she was ready she heard him come in, whistling cheerfully. She smiled to herself, wondering whether he was whistling because he was feeling happy or as a way of signalling to her that he was back.

By the time she came out of the bedroom Rhodri had not only made the tea but also had a cup poured out and waiting for her.

'I thought perhaps you'd gone to work, even though it's Sunday,' she said smiling.

'No, I popped out to the corner shop to get some fresh milk,' he said. 'I thought you would prefer to have that in your tea, as I've only got tinned conny milk.'

'Did you sleep at all?' she questioned, nodding towards the blankets on the sofa.

'Like a log; how about you?'

'Yes, I slept very well.' She smiled. 'I didn't expect to do so because there was so much going round and round in my head after our long talk last night. Even though we talked for hours you didn't tell me very much about what you're doing these days. Have you still got the stall in the market?'

His smile vanished. 'I did have, up until two days ago. The lease ran out on the thirty-first of December and they doubled the rent they were asking for, so I didn't sign up to renew it.'

'Why ever not? You've been trading there for years,' Fern said in surprise.

'You've been away for years, so you probably don't know how things are these days. The miners went on strike last May and the next thing we knew it was a general strike and that affected the whole country, not just Cardiff.

'The docks here were being manned by soldiers and a lot of firms went bankrupt. In fact, things have been very bad ever since. People haven't any spare money to spend on things like records and musical instruments; some of them couldn't even afford a mouth organ even if they wanted one,' he added bitterly.

Fern shook her head in dismay. 'I had no idea; what are you going to do now?'

Rhodri didn't answer for several minutes. 'Believe it or not,' he told her when she pressed the question, 'I was thinking of coming to look for you and Glanmor. I worked it out that since you hadn't come back to Cardiff then life must be pretty good wherever you were. I know Russia is a big place, but I intended finding you, no matter how long it took.'

'Good heavens! Were you missing us both that much?' Fern said in surprise.

'Well, yes, but there was also another reason; I wanted to give you the money that Maria left for you. It was burning a hole in my pocket and I was afraid that if I became desperate then I might be tempted to use some of it.'

'If you were desperate enough for that

I wouldn't have minded and I'm sure Maria wouldn't,' Fern told him.

'Maybe not, but I wouldn't have liked doing it. The first thing I want to do after we've had some breakfast is hand it over to you.'

'There's no hurry,' Fern said quickly. 'Anyway,' she added with a smile, 'you can't do much about it today because it's Sunday and the bank won't be open.'

'It's not in a bank,' Rhodri told her. 'Maria didn't trust them, certainly not with all her life's savings. She kept it under the mattress and that's where I've put it.'

'Are you telling me that I was sleeping on all that money last night?' Fern gasped. 'I wouldn't have slept a wink if I'd known. Weren't you worried and afraid someone might find out and you'd be robbed?'

'Of course I was; I still am, which is why I can't wait to hand it over to you.'

'You can't do that,' Fern argued. 'I haven't even got anywhere to stay yet. The best thing is to leave it where it is until we decide what we're going to do with it.'

'We?' Rhodri looked puzzled. 'It's your money, Fern; it has nothing to do with me.'

'I still need you to advise me,' she told him. 'I've been racking my brains trying to think what to do with it. I feel it should be used as some form of tribute to Maria and I can't think what that should be.'

'I don't think she would want a big shiny

granite stone on her grave or a park bench with her name on it,' he told her quickly.

'I agree. It has to be something special that will help her to live on in our memory for ever.

'She'll always live in my memory,' Rhodri muttered. 'She was like a mother to me.'

'She was to me as well,' Fern admitted. 'It's because she meant so much to both of us that I think you should help me decide what to do with the money.'

'Since you haven't a job or anywhere to live then I think you should use it to get back on your feet,' Rhodri told her gruffly.

'No, I might use some of it to tide me over, but I want every penny of what Maria left to go into something more meaningful than that,' Fern said stubbornly.

They stared at each other in silence, absorbed in their own thoughts.

'Perhaps we should use some of it to pay the rent on your stall at the Hayes market and then you could start up again and perhaps I could help you?'

'Right fool I'd look, if I did that after more or less giving away all my stock,' Rhodri said bitterly.

'It needn't be a stall at the Hayes. It could be somewhere else; or perhaps even a small shop in one of the arcades. Trade may have been bad but things will get better again – they always do, and music is one of the things most people enjoy.'

'Did they enjoy music in Russia?'

'Yes, of course they did; not only in Russia but in the whole of Europe.'

'Not listening to music on records, though,' Rhodri said gloomily. 'From what you told me last night they preferred musical shows and the theatre and that sort of thing. Shows where there was something to look at as well as listen to.'

'If they enjoyed the show, then they probably went home and played the music,' Fern remonstrated. 'They either bought records to sit and listen to or instruments so that they could play the tunes they'd heard.'

'I suppose you're right in a way; you probably know more about that side of things than I do,' Rhodri conceded.

'People also love dancing to music. It's one of the greatest pick-me-ups in the world when people are feeling worried or depressed,' Fern went on thoughtfully as she sipped her tea.

'Perhaps we should go dancing, then, like we used to do on Saturday nights before you went to Russia,' Rhodri joked. 'It might help cheer us up and solve all our problems.'

'That's it!' Fern sprang up and went over to where he was sitting and flung her arms round his neck and hugged him. 'Why didn't I think of that?'

'Don't get all excited, it's only Sunday, so we have a whole week to wait,' Rhodri laughed.

'I didn't mean we should go dancing; well, not in that way,' Fern enthused. 'You've given me a brilliant idea, though; you're an absolute genius.'

'Give me your cup and I'll pour you some more tea. I don't really know what you are on about so perhaps you'd better tell me,' he added, looking bemused.

'Dancing, of course. You've been telling me that at the moment people are depressed – either because they are out of work or short of money or both. It won't last for long. Things will get better; they usually do, given time. It's a new year, so there's bound to be a feeling of hope in the air; there always is at the start of a new year. Well, we can cash in on that.'

'I really don't understand what you are talking about,' Rhodri said, shaking his head.

'We'll open a dance studio; somewhere where people can come to learn to dance. We'll use the money Maria left and as a tribute to her from both of us we'll call it Maria's Dance Studio.

'A dance studio?' Rhodri looked completely bemused. 'Are you completely crazy?'

'Of course I'm not,' Fern defended. 'We'll make it a joint effort and teach them to dance. You can be the manager and deal with all the bookings and the money side of things and I'll teach them to dance. You can also sell sheet music, instruments of every kind under the sun, as well as gramophone records.'

Rhodri looked at Fern in astonishment. 'You mean you intend risking the money Maria left you on starting up a dance studio and you want me to be part of it all?'

'There's no risk,' Fern enthused. 'I was a professional dancer at the Folies Bergère and when people hear that they will want to see me dance. We'll invite them to see me perform in our own studio and then get them to sign up for lessons.'

'How many people are there in Cardiff who will want to be professional dancers?' Rhodri laughed.

'We're not going to try and make them professionals, simply teach them how to dance.'

'Most people know already,' Rhodri argued.

'No, they don't. Look how many men won't get on the floor until they've had two or three drinks to give them courage. And when they do they simply shuffle around because they don't know the steps.'

'You'll never get men agreeing to come to a dance studio. Even if they would like to learn to dance they'd never openly admit that they needed to take lessons.'

'Don't be too sure about that; our grand opening will tempt them and they'll be eager to learn.'

'Yes? How do you make that out?'

'We will tempt them to come along by advertising that I will be doing some of the exotic dances that I did at the Folies Bergère.'

'Do I get a private preview so that I can judge whether you are any good or not?' Rhodri teased.

'The very mention of the Folies Bergère will tempt them,' Fern went on, ignoring his quip. 'They will want to see me dance and then we'll also give them a demonstration of ballroom dancing. If they bring their wives or girlfriends they will want to be able to dance like us.'

'Dance like us? You don't mean that you expect me to partner you in a performance, do you?'

'Of course. You always wanted to take me dancing. So this is your chance to do so.'

'Yes, but that was to Saturday night hops and you always turned me down. Anyway, neither of us knows how to teach.'

'I know how the instructors go about it; I should do, after training for the Folies Bergère,' Fern reminded him.

'Yes, but you were the one who was being taught, you weren't doing the teaching.'

'They won't know that and if anyone goes to the trouble to find out, by that time we'll be so good at it and so well established that people won't mind.'

'The way you are describing it all makes it sound a possibility but there are so many pitfalls,' Rhodri said dubiously. 'We would need to find the right sort of premises, for a start.'

'I agree; we certainly couldn't stage it in the middle of the Hayes market,' Fern admitted.

'Renting a property, especially if we had to put down three months' rent in advance, would eat up a lot of your money,' Rhodri pointed out.

'We'd probably have to decorate it as well and that would take both time and money.'

'We could probably save a great deal by doing that ourselves,' Fern told him.

'You are a real little optimist, aren't you?' Rhodri smiled. 'If enthusiasm has anything to do with success then we should be OK,' he added with a grin.

'So you will join forces with me? I know we'll make a success of it. We've always got on well, so we'll make perfect business partners,' Fern assured him.

'I don't like the idea that you'll be spending Maria's money to help me out,' Rhodri protested.

'I'm not! You needn't think that for one minute,' Fern told him quickly.

'That's not the way I see it,' he told her dryly.

'Well, I'm not,' Fern replied. 'I have to find work of some kind and I also need somewhere to live. I was even thinking that perhaps it might be possible to combine both.'

Rhodri looked puzzled. 'Sorry, but I don't understand what you mean by that.'

'Well, I thought that if we could find some shop premises with a flat up above them then I could live in the flat,' she pointed out. 'In fact,' she went on, 'if the flat was big enough, you might be able to live there as well.'

'If we rented a shop, surely we would have to put in a special floor, a polished parquet one, if people were going to dance on it?' Rhodri frowned.

'Yes . . .'

'And that would take a great deal of money,' he pointed out. 'I think', he went on, 'we ought to sit down with pencil and paper and list all the alterations we would have to carry out and try and work out what all this would cost before we start looking for a place.'

'If you say so; after all, you are the manager,' Fern told him with a cheeky smile. 'Look,' she laid a hand on his arm, 'I am well aware that planning everything is going to be a lot of hard work but I am positive it will turn out well in the end and that we'll make perfect partners.'

Chapter Thirty-four

Rhodri spent almost two hours writing down all the expenses they were likely to incur if they decided to go ahead with Fern's idea of a dance studio. Each time he thought the list was complete, either he or Fern remembered something else that needed to be included.

'I think we should stop before you run out of money,' he said at last.

'We're doing this together.' Fern frowned. 'Think of it as our money, not just mine.'

'Then in that case I'll go through the list again and see what we can cut back on.' Rhodri smiled.

The expenditure was quite formidable but the project wasn't completely impossible. So much depended on finding the right sort of premises, what rental they would have to pay and how much the landlord demanded in advance.

It was agreed that Fern should stay on in Loudon Place with Rhodri rather than waste any of their precious money renting a room of her own somewhere else.

'It's going to be a bit of a squash but I don't mind if you don't,' he told her cheerfully.

'If we have any luck in finding suitable

premises then it will only be for a short time,' Fern agreed optimistically.

'In that case, we'd better start looking right away,' Rhodri suggested.

'On a Sunday?'

'It won't hurt to look around. We haven't even decided whether we want to be in the centre of Cardiff or here in Tiger Bay. We could also look and see if there are any vacant premises in Grangetown or Canton.

'Come on, it's cold out but the sun is shining and if we go right away we might be able to decide the best place to look for a shop or perhaps even a hall.'

'I prefer the idea of a shop,' Fern insisted. 'Remember, we are hoping to live up over it,' she added as he helped her into her coat and she reached for her hat and scarf.

They took the tram to St Mary Street but by the time they reached it they'd both agreed that the properties close to the centre of Cardiff would be far too expensive to rent, even if they managed to find a suitable place that was empty.

'I suppose we really ought to think about the sort of people who will want to learn to dance,' Rhodri mused.

'Youngish, in their early twenties; men as well as girls,' Fern said thoughtfully.

'Most girls seem to know how to dance, so I suppose we should concentrate on youngish men,' Rhodri said.

'Yes, that's true,' Fern agreed. 'Girls certainly

want their boyfriends to be able to dance and not step on their toes all evening.'

'So we are aiming at youngish men who have just started taking girls out and want to impress them.'

'Yes, but remember, a lot of girls have only picked up dance steps from one another or from someone in their family. The majority of them are keen to be able to dance properly.'

'Let's walk down Wood Street and then along the Taff Embankment towards Grangetown and see what sort of properties are empty there,' she suggested.

As they passed street after street of newly built semi-detached houses that ran from the Embankment into Corporation Road it was obvious they were in the wrong area.

'If we are looking for a shop, then we should cut through into Corporation Road,' Rhodri suggested when they reached Aber Street.

'I don't think we'll find any there,' Fern murmured. 'We could catch a tram, though, as far as Clarence Road Bridge and start looking around there.'

'A tram?' Rhodri looked at her in surprise. 'Are your feet aching already?' he laughed.

'They are a bit,' Fern admitted. 'I was really thinking of saving time because all around here there are houses, not shops. If we could find a place near Clarence Road where it joins James Street, then we would probably attract people from both Tiger Bay and Grangetown.'

'I see what you mean,' Rhodri agreed. 'This is certainly a good working-class area but would people living here be interested in the idea of learning to dance?'

'I think they would, especially if we put on a show one night a week so that they can see how enjoyable dancing can be.'

'What sort of a show?'

'Like I said before, I could give a display of the sorts of dances I was doing at the Folies Bergère and then the two of us could demonstrate ballroom dancing. We'd do the more popular dances like the waltz, the foxtrot and the quickstep; the sorts of dances they would do if they went to a dance themselves.'

'You think they would pay to come to see something like that?'

'I'm sure they would once the word got round, especially if they knew that at the end of the display there would be an opportunity for them to get up and dance themselves. We'd probably have to do a couple of special free nights at first to get ourselves known.'

'We'd need to get some posters printed to advertise these shows and our studio,' Rhodri said thoughtfully. 'That's something we overlooked and haven't included in our list of expenses.'

By this time they had reached the tram terminal at Clarence Road Bridge and as they started walking Fern paused for a moment to look down into the River Taff. Flowing water always made her think of Glanmor and her heart ached with loneliness knowing she would never see him again.

'Well, here we are, St James Street, and there's an empty shop just a few doors down the road,' Rhodri pointed out.

They crossed to the other side of the road to get a better view of it. The building was three storeys high and sandwiched between a furniture shop and a hairdresser's. The other shops in the parade included a newsagent and tobacconist, a greengrocer and a general store as well as a pawnbroker.

'I wonder what sort of business went on here?' Fern mused as they peered into the empty window.

'It's very clean inside and there are a lot of shelves behind the counters so it might have been a chemist, or even a bookshop,' Rhodri observed.

They looked at each other hopefully. 'Perhaps we should come back first thing tomorrow morning and find out who owns it and at the same time what it used to be,' Rhodri stated.

'That doesn't matter as much as what the rent is and whether or not we can afford it,' Fern said, stepping back into the roadway and looking up at the rooms above.

'There's so much space up there that we could have the dance studio on the first floor and possibly live in the rooms up above,' she said.

'If we did that, then what would we do with

the shop itself? I suppose we could let it and that would help pay the rent.'

'I've got a better idea.' Fern smiled. 'We could use the shop to sell musical instruments, gramophone records and all the other things you used to sell on your stall. We could also stock special dancing shoes and things like that.'

'Hold it; you really are getting carried away.' Rhodri grinned. 'We don't even know for sure that it is vacant yet.'

'It's empty!'

'Yes, but it might already be taken. It's so clean inside that someone may already be getting it ready so that they can move their business in.'

As they made their way back to Loudon Place they could talk of nothing else.

'We would attract people from Grangetown and Tiger Bay if we took those premises,' Fern enthused.

'Yes, and because all the other shops are closed at night there wouldn't be anyone complaining about noise.'

'Not unless there are people living above the other shops on either side.'

While Fern prepared something for them to eat, Rhodri busied himself making more notes and working out the possibilities of what they could stock if they did retain the shop for their own use.

'We would probably only have enough money to be able to stock gramophone records at first

374

and that would hardly be profitable,' he said despondently.

'You had your stall for at least ten years so surely the people who supplied you would be willing to take a gamble and let you have some stock. Perhaps a selection of instruments on sale or return,' Fern suggested hopefully.

Rhodri frowned. 'I'm not sure; things are still pretty bad, you know, so they mightn't be prepared to take the risk.'

'If trade is slow, then that's all the more reason for them to take a chance and supply you with some stock. If you don't ask, you'll never know, and if they turn you down, then when the business is in full swing and they come along trying to sell you something, you can turn them down.'

'Whew! You are a hard-headed business-woman. Are you going to be equally tough with your dance customers?'

'No, I shall charm them with my dancing so much that they will be queueing up to come to my classes,' she said with a smile.

'Well, it's difficult for me to say what the chances are of that happening when I've never seen you dance,' Rhodri told her. 'Perhaps you should give me a demonstration so that I can judge whether you are any good or not.'

'I was a solo dancer at the Folies Bergère,' she reminded him, tossing her hair back in an affected, haughty manner.

'So you keep telling me! Then how about showing me what you can do?'

'I will after you've eaten this meal I've gone to the trouble of cooking,' she said, smiling.

Later, after she'd cleared away their dishes, she selected a record and put it on the gramophone then went through to the bedroom and unpacked one of her costumes and put it on.

Rhodri was sitting at the table still engrossed in the list he was making when Fern came back into the room. With a half smile on her lips she began to play the record. When he looked up she started to slowly twist and turn in time to the music and perform one of her favourite dances.

She was aware that he was watching her in astonishment but he said nothing until the record stopped playing.

'If that's one of the dances you intend to do then you are quite right when you say that we will have people queueing to get in the door,' he said, a look of admiration on his face. 'I never knew you could dance like that; it was incredible.'

'I'm so glad you approve.' She smiled, giving a sweeping curtsy. Then, moving across the room and selecting another record, she looked over her shoulder and asked, 'Would you like me to dance some more?'

Without waiting for a reply, as the music started, she began to dance once more. When the record ended she changed it and then held out a hand to him. 'Come on, this is a waltz, let's see how well you shape up as a partner.'

Rhodri hesitated then stood up and took her

in his arms and circled the floor with her. 'Will I do?' he asked when the music stopped.

'Very hard to tell because there isn't really enough room here for a proper performance,' she teased.

He didn't answer but pulled her back into his arms. 'There may not be enough room to dance but there is enough room for me to kiss you,' he told her as his lips sought hers.

The suddenness of his action took her breath away. For a brief moment she tried to resist his embrace then as his mouth came down hard on hers she found herself responding with such fervour that when he released her she felt overcome with embarrassment.

His lips on hers had brought back vivid memories of Glanmor; nothing that had happened since, not even her association with Pierre, had made any impression. Returning his chaste kisses had been purely perfunctory but Rhodri's kiss had stirred some response from deep within in her. So much so that it left her feeling quite unnerved.

As they broke apart she stood staring at him in bemused silence; a stare so intense that it made him uneasy.

'I'm sorry, Fern,' he muttered contritely. 'I shouldn't have done that but you looked so beautiful as you danced in that ... that very revealing dress, that I was completely bewitched and got carried away. Blame my hot blood,' he added with a rueful laugh.

She pulled away with an awkward little laugh. She wanted to refute what he was saying; to reach out and pull him towards her, entwine her arms round his neck and surrender her lips to his again, but some inner caution warned her that if they were going to work together then this wouldn't be wise.

Rhodri gave an imperceptible shrug of his shoulders. 'I hope you were not . . .' he paused as if seeking the right word before adding with a challenging lift of one eyebrow – 'that you were not offended.'

'Not at all.' There was so much more she wanted to add but once again an inner caution made her hold back. She knew he had always cared for her but at this moment she didn't want to complicate their relationship in any way; not when they were about to start up in business together.

Chapter Thirty-five

Cardiff had never looked so splendid, Fern reflected as they walked towards the city hall, all the relevant documents that were needed to register their dance studio and qualify for a licence safely packed into her large handbag. She never thought she'd get to this point and even now it seemed like a dream.

The Portland Stone edifice with its imposing clock tower gleamed like a welcoming beacon in the winter sunshine. To her mind, the winged dragon over the main entrance symbolised power; the power to achieve anything you set your heart on doing.

Rhodri had suggested that it might be better if he went on his own to deal with the officials on a man-to-man level but for once she had refused to let him assume responsibility.

'We're in this together,' she'd stated resolutely.

'I was only trying to be helpful,' he pointed out. 'I know it's your money and your idea, but you know what officials are like; they prefer to deal with men.'

'Then they are going to be disappointed, because I intend to be there and to have my say if necessary.'

'If you want to impress them that much perhaps you should wear one of your revealing costumes,' he laughed.

As it was she was dressed almost as soberly as he was. She'd chosen a plain navy skirt, pin-tucked white cotton blouse, a navy-blue coat and hat and sensible black shoes.

'You look more like a school marm than a dancer,' Rhodri teased when she made no reply.

'No, I look like a businesswoman,' she told him sharply.

When it came to the actual registering of the business, Rhodri admitted afterwards, he was glad she'd been there as well. Her responses to the sharp questioning about what was involved in their dance scheme were so much more concise and knowledgeable than his would have been. Once it became clear that she was the one who was going to answer his questions the official had treated her with the greatest respect possible.

When everything was signed and sealed the atmosphere between them was so friendly that he even asked her informal questions about the Folies Bergère and seemed to be very impressed when she told him that she'd been a solo dancer there.

Before they left, Fern invited him to come along to their opening evening as their guest. 'I will be giving a demonstration dance which I think you would enjoy watching,' she told him.

'In that case then I will most certainly be

there,' he told her gravely. 'Would it be in order for me to bring along a colleague?' he asked, his eyes twinkling.

'You certainly carried the day there,' Rhodri told her admiringly as they left the building. 'We really are in business at last so why don't we have lunch somewhere special to celebrate?'

Fern was on the point of refusing and reminding him of all the hundred-and-one jobs that still needed their attention before they opened. Then she remembered how hard Rhodri had worked over the last few weeks and accepted his suggestion.

He had been so practical as well as enthusiastic right from the very beginning that she knew she could never have achieved so much working alone. She was more than grateful to him for the way he had not only compiled all the work that would have to be carried out but also listed what it was all going to cost so that they didn't overspend.

He had kept within their very tight budget by carrying out almost all of the preparatory work himself. He had decorated their new premises from top to bottom and laid a new floor in the room they intended using as a dance studio. In between doing all that he'd also negotiated a deal with his former suppliers for stock so that they would be able to open the music shop at the same time as the studio.

Working together they had turned the attic rooms at the very top of the building into cosy living accommodation for them both. As well as sharing a good-size living room and adjoining kitchen they also each had their own bedroom.

They had agreed from the very start that everything to do with the dance studio and the shop must be contained downstairs. Behind the shop was a storeroom and behind the dance studio a cloakroom for patrons and a tiny slip of a room that was to be Fern's office. When they came up to their 'sanctuary' it was to relax.

A special lunch would be a wonderful way to celebrate the culmination of all their hard work. It would also give them the time to talk over any final last-minute changes they thought necessary in respect of the grand opening they were planning at the weekend. They also had to finalise a day for the professional signwriter to bring along the work they'd commissioned him to do. Fern was very much looking forward to seeing the name MARIA'S DANCE ACADEMY appear in gold lettering above the front of the premises.

'It's a bit early for lunch, even a special lunch,' she demurred looking up at the city hall clock. 'Why don't we take a stroll around Cathays Park first; that's if you don't mind being seen out with someone who dresses like a school marm?'

'I don't mind how you are dressed,' Rhodri told her, 'not as long as we're together.' He took her hand and squeezed it. 'I think we make a wonderful team, don't you?'

Fern let his question hang on the air and they

walked around the beautifully laid-out park. Some of the flower beds were already showing signs of spring; displays of golden daffodils and multicoloured polyanthus, crocus and early hyacinths made glorious patches of colour against the fresh, crisp green of the grass.

When they reached the Temple of Peace the gleaming white mausoleum-style building that had been built in memory of those brave soldiers and sailors who'd died between 1914 and 1918, they stood for a moment in silent contemplation.

Fern's thoughts were of Glanmor and she wondered what he would think of her latest enterprise. She recalled how jealous he'd once been of Rhodri.

Fleetingly, Fern wished that it was Glanmor who was walking by her side but since that could never be she owed it to his memory and to Maria's to make a success of her venture and with Rhodri at her side she knew she would. She would never forget how he had kept Maria's money safe and untouched even though there must have been times, when his own business was failing, when he must have been desperate to use it. Now they were partners and she owed him her loyalty in thought as well as action.

Fern enjoyed their celebratory meal. They toasted each other and raised their glasses to the success of their new venture before tucking in to the delicious spread that they had ordered.

'We really must get back to work, there's still

383

so much to do,' Fern sighed after Rhodri had paid the bill.

'Agreed!' As Rhodri pushed back his chair the waiter hurried over with their coats and helped Fern into hers.

On impulse she handed him an invitation to their opening the following Saturday night and was delighted by his enthusiasm when he read what it was all about.

'Well, we know that at least there will be two people in the audience now,' Rhodri said, grinning, as they left the restaurant.

'There will be a great many more than that once the posters go up,' Fern told him confidently.

The next few days were so hectic that they hardly had time to eat, let alone sleep.

'I think we should pack in now and have an early night,' Rhodri commented on the Friday night. 'If we carry on at this rate then you'll be too tired to dance at our opening tomorrow,' he added as they both yawned heavily. It was quite late in the evening and they had been selecting the gramophone records they intended playing on the opening night and stacking them up in readiness alongside the gramophone which was on a small raised platform at one end of the dance floor.

'Not a bit of it. I will be so excited and keyed up that the problem will be stopping me once I get started,' Fern told him.

'In that case there is still one more thing we have to check out and that's the demonstration dances we are going to do together tomorrow night.'

Fern looked at him in astonishment. 'Why ever do we need to do that? We won't have any problems; it's like breathing; it's natural for us to do things together.'

'Well, we haven't danced together for a very long time; the last time I took you to a proper dance was before you went away over five years ago.'

'We've danced together since then; the night I put my Folies Bergère costume on and gave you a demonstration.'

Rhodri didn't answer but went over to the gramophone and selected a record, placed it on the turntable, and lowered the needle on to it. As the strains of a Viennese waltz poured out into the room he turned and held out his arms to her.

As they circled the floor in time to the music Fern found that her tiredness seemed to ebb away leaving her in a pleasantly blissful state. She let her thoughts drift and rested her head against Rhodri's shoulder as they circled the floor.

When the music stopped Rhodri went on holding her in his arms and when she made no resistance his lips found hers. Her response seemed to inflame him and it took a supreme effort from both of them to draw apart.

'I think you were right, I probably should have an early night, tomorrow is our big day and I'm sure we'll find countless things that need our attention in the morning,' Fern said. Quickly she moved towards the door. Her heart was thudding crazily and she wasn't too sure what her response would be if she stayed there any longer and Rhodri tried to make love to her.

'This has to be a business partnership and nothing else. Unless we both concentrate all our efforts physically and mentally into making it a success we might very well fail. It's a new venture for both of us so we need our wits about us,' she told her reflection in the mirror when she reached her own room and had shut the door firmly behind her.

The opening evening was a tremendous success. Fern couldn't believe how well everything had gone and even Rhodri was impressed by the number of people who had turned up. There were so many more than they had expected that at least twenty were standing because there were no available seats.

Fern's opening solo, with her wearing one of the glamorous costumes that she'd worn at the Folies Bergère and brought back with her as a memento, never expecting to wear it again, was an overwhelming success and met with cheers as well as hearty hand clapping.

The demonstration dances they performed

together were carried out in perfect accord. Fern felt that she was under an incredible strain, though, because she was so aware of being in Rhodri's arms and pretty certain that he was feeling the same way.

Those attending had been given a glass of wine before the proceedings had started and Fern was sure this had done a great deal to help towards the goodwill and interest everybody showed. Proof came at the end of the evening when twelve of the people there immediately signed up to come to the first classes that they would be holding.

When the door closed behind the last of their audience they exchanged smiles of satisfaction. Rhodri led Fern back into the empty room and placed a record on the gramophone, knowing that they were far too keyed-up to sleep. As the strains of the waltz they'd been dancing to the night before drifted across the room he took her in his arms and once again she let her head rest on his shoulder.

This time, when the music stopped, she didn't pull away from him but stayed in his arms and gave a deep sigh of contentment.

'A tremendous success and a perfect evening,' he murmured, his lips against her hair.

'Yes, you were right, we really do make perfect partners,' she agreed, looking up at him and smiling.

'Does our partnership have to remain a strictly business arrangement?' he asked hopefully. 'You surely know how I feel about you; how I have always felt about you from the first day you came to help Maria.'

'I'm not sure; I think it might be detrimental to our business dealings if we let our personal feelings take over,' Fern murmured. Inwardly she was zinging with happiness because he'd told her he loved her and she knew that she felt the same way about him.

'On the contrary, I think our business might benefit,' he told her gravely. 'We could share so many more thoughts if we were married and together all of the time.'

'Mmm!' Playing for time she pretended to be giving his remark some deep thought. Tonight had been a revelation of how well they worked as a team and how her feelings towards him had changed from merely wanting him as a good friend and working partner to someone she loved deeply.

'Come on,' Rhodri coaxed, 'you know it's what you want as much as I do. You can't go on mourning for Glanmor for the rest of your life. I'm sure he wouldn't want you to do that and I know Maria would want us to be happy,' he added forcefully.

She knew that was true; Maria had tried hard to push her and Rhodri together and had always been telling her what a fine man he was and what a good husband he would make. If that was the case, she wondered why he had never married.

As if reading her thoughts Rhodri went on in a very serious tone, 'I've waited all these years for you, Fern; there's never been anyone else for me, not since the day Maria introduced us. I knew then that I didn't stand a chance because you'd already given your heart to Glanmor but I've never stopped hoping that perhaps one day you might change your mind. I've always thought of you as being my perfect partner.'

Fern smiled. 'Well, that's come true in a way. Tonight we've proved how very successful we can be working together. It's going to take time and a lot of hard work, but I'm sure that together we can build *Maria's* into something outstanding.'

'As long as we stay together,' he muttered. 'I'm not sure that I can tolerate our present situation; not any longer. If I have to go on seeing you and working so close to you day in and day out then I want us to become complete partners.'

Fern bit down on her lower lip; she knew quite well what Rhodri was leading up to but she didn't answer him because she couldn't trust her voice.

The very thought of not having him by her side filled her with alarm. In the past weeks she had come to rely on him so much that she knew that if he walked away then she wouldn't know what to do. She needed him; he meant so much more than a mere business partner.

'We are complete partners; I promise I will always consult you before making even the slightest change in our set-up,' she said with a bright smile.

'That's not what I am talking about and you know it,' he said abruptly. 'Fern,' he pulled her into his arms, 'I love you deeply and I know you have feelings for me. This is a new start for both of us and I want us to be married as soon as we can arrange it.'

Before she could answer his mouth was on hers, silencing any protests she might try to make; sealing their future with a deep, intense kiss. As she submitted to his embrace she knew it was time to let go of the past; Glanmor would always have a special place in her memories but now, she couldn't imagine life without Rhodri being part of it.

Epilogue

1927 was a difficult year bringing hardships to most people because of the continued after effects of the General Strike. Even so, due to Fern and Rhodri's hard work, determination and optimism *Maria's* thrived.

When baby Maria was born, she soon became one of the attractions. Tucked up cosily in her basinet in a safe corner of the dance floor, little Maria slept soundly as Fern danced or instructed. If she wakened there was always someone to talk to her until Fern was free to attend to her.

Later when she could sit up and watch what was going on around her, she would clap her hands in delight and chortle with excitement if either Fern or Rhodri swept her up in their arms and pirouetted around the floor with her.

Three years later, when baby Glanmor was born, the routine was much the same. He was a placid baby and loved nothing better than to watch his little sister dancing to the music or being swirled around in their parents' arms.

Fern was so happy that there were times when she wondered if it was all a sublime dream; then one of the children would demand attention and she was quickly brought back to reality as she combined her role as dancer with that of wife and mother. Life was good.

850